The Honey Gatherers

The Honey Gatherers

Theresa Murphy

HALE
CRIME

ROBERT HALE · LONDON

ISBN 0 7090 7601 0

Robert Hale Limited
Clerkenwell House
Clerkenwell Greent
London EC1R 0HT

2 4 6 8 10 9 7 5 3 1

Typeset in 10/13pt Palatino
Printed in Great Britain by St Edmundsbury Press
Bury St Edmunds, Suffolk.
Bound by Woolnough Bookbinding Ltd

one

The girl was a stunner. Her blonde hair was short, her breasts self-supporting, her red mouth a provocative pout. Eighteen, was Ed Bellamy's guess, but her eyes were older and bolder. Her face had a sensual quality, and her walk was a practised little parade that gave a tantalizing fillip to her hips. There was a heap of talent in a seaside town like Havensport in summer, but this blonde beat all he'd seen in his six weeks there. Was she a holidaymaker? That seemed likely. He would have noticed her had she been waitressing in a resort filled with café tables, but with never one to be had.

Maybe she was unavailable. She was only a kid, and a whole flock of immature guys with spotty faces were around her. But Ed was twenty-five, which probably meant that they had more chance with her than he had. In these fast-moving times, the generation gap had narrowed to around five years. Walking to the bar, he ordered a beer. He could use a spliff to give himself a much-needed lift. This was his first free evening in the six weeks he'd been in this south coast holiday town. But to light up here risked somebody getting a whiff of the weed and calling the pigs. This time tomorrow he would be back on duty as doorman at the sleazy Blue Angel club. A bouncer surrounded by crumpet but forced by his job to be as celibate as a Franciscan friar.

Lazily raising his glass, and his eyes flicked over its rim, he scanned the club for the blonde. She was easy to find. A girl like her was special, and the strobe lighting somehow picked her out and projected her. Her yellow dress was as close to her as body paint. She was a living doll that Bellamy would be happy to play with.

A young guy afflicted by one of those "Oh God, I'm going bald!' ultra-short haircuts sidled up to her and slipped an exploring arm about her waist. Annoyed, she knocked his groping hand away, laughing as she swayed to the music, clapping her hands to the beat. Unable to tear his gaze away, Ed saw her freeze, her raised hands stopping mid-beat as she caught sight of him.

Leaning against the bar, he knew that he'd got to her. Ed wouldn't describe himself as immodest, but he did know his strengths. With his black hair having a hint of a wave, and his brown, deep-set eyes, he had what it took to pull women. It had been like that since his school days. Now he worked out regularly and had a muscle-packed physique to complement his handsomeness. The switching of light and shadow across his face would accentuate his high cheekbones and bring out the strong planes of his jawline. What held her entranced would be the hint of something romantic, dangerous and threatening. He was a latter-day James Dean.

Her hesitation over, she was dancing with sinuous movements again, her head thrown back, eyes partly closed and mouth partly open. She moved animatedly, the thin-cotton yellow dress rippling over her lithe young body. Ed could tell that the blonde was putting on an act for him.

When the music stopped, he heard her say, too loudly, 'I'm bored. This is a dump, about as much fun as a ten-year-old's birthday party.'

Head bowed, he studied the froth on his beer like it was the most interesting thing in the world. She was trying to attract his attention, and he knew that it would benefit him to play hard to get. There was no competition in the place so he wasn't risking losing her. Ed didn't intend to buy her a drink. You didn't reward a performing animal until after it had done its trick.

The music started up again, pounding, and a weedy-looking young guy was hunched over the microphone on stage. His nasal voice whined the lyrics, his words rising in pitch until they sounded like a yodel. The blonde's hips were swaying again and the young baldy was convulsing around her like he was plugged into the electricity mains.

Sliding his still almost full glass away from him across the counter, Ed Bellamy walked through the dancers on his way to the door. He avoided meeting her searching eyes. Out in the cool of a moonless night, he strolled across the promenade to lean on the iron railings. The long stretch of silver sand was deserted. Little waves made a muted plopping sound as they lapped the shore. Close on his right was the pier, darkened at this late hour, while a quarter of a mile to his left was the black silhouette of a craggy mass of rocks.

Opening a gold-plated cigarette case, his fingers hesitatingly crossed the tightly packed row of cigarettes. He needed a boom to sharpen his senses, make everything crystal clear, to enjoy to the full what was to come. His timing could be wrong, but he doubted it. The blonde would have followed him out of the club. She would be here soon. Pushing the ordinary cigarette back in line, he selected a reefer by feel.

Elbows resting on the rail, he lit up, enjoying the familiar pop as the flame from his lighter ignited the bomber. After the first toke, with everything looking real good, he straightened up and slowly descended the flight of sand-covered steps leading down to the beach. His feet sank deep into loose sand that seeped uncomfortably into his shoes. He felt somehow exposed in the night, even though the subtle starlight was discreet. His eyes caught a flicker of movement between the pillars that supported the pier. Could it be her? Ed dismissed the idea. The blonde couldn't have made it to the beach ahead of him.

It was probably a peeping tom. Well, good luck to him. It had to be alfresco or nothing for Ed Bellamy tonight. Though he had a room in a boarding house so crummy that even the lowest summer visitors shunned it, there was a strict rule against boarders bringing anyone back.

A giggle from up on the promenade made him turn. He had been right: the blonde hadn't wasted any time in following him. The shaved-head punk was hovering around her, but she'd soon shake him off. Ed Bellamy was her target for tonight.

He paced slowly along the shore until the tiny waves were threatening his shoes. The sea had packed the sand tight and firm close to the waterline, making it easier to walk, but as he sucked the smoke of the reefer deep into his lungs his legs were rubbery and he felt as if he was doing a moonwalk. Holding the smoke for as long as possible, he let it filter out slowly through slightly parted lips. The lapping of tiny waves on the waterline took on a country and western rhythm, and he tried a haphazard line-dance. He tripped on a spur of stone, and then righted himself. But he was climbing high and fast and was worried that he would be clambering aboard cloud nine before the blonde caught up with him.

Every so often he turned, expecting to see the superb figure in a yellow dress trailing him along the beach. Switching his glance back to the pillars, he could just make out the solitary silhouette still lurking there. But there was no sign of the girl. She was playing a game with him now, keeping him waiting.

With time to spare, he clambered precariously over a ridge of rocks. Then he staggered through loose sand, managing to avoid the small waves that reached teasingly for him. Pulling himself up on to a large, flat-topped rock, he crossed his legs to sit and drag on the toke. Life seemed to be increasingly rosy.

Then she was coming his way, moving gracefully in a dance that included occasional little pirouettes. He waited for her to come nearer. But she stopped close to the sea, partly shadowed by the long stretch of pier. Kicking off her shoes, she raised both her arms. Ed hadn't grasped what was happening until the clinging dress dropped slitheringly to her ankles. Stepping out of the ring of yellow cloth into the starlight, she walked naked into the sea.

Inhaling the last drag from the reefer deeply, Ed Bellamy flicked the butt away. It produced an arc of faint sparks in the dark as he moved, intending to join the blonde in her late-night swim. The rock felt like foam rubber as he thrust himself off it. He thought he saw a figure leap from the darkness beneath the pier. But he couldn't be sure of that because the real and the unreal were spinning together in his head. Though muddled by the drug, a warm glow was stealing over him.

There were eight of them, four teenage girls and four boys. All of them in a state of drunkenness, laughing, shouting and singing as they skipped along the promenade. It was two o'clock in the morning, but there would be time enough for sleep when they got back home. Birmingham was Dullsville and they were having fun at the seaside. Ignoring the nearby steps down to the beach, they climbed over the railings like commandos and dropped to the sand below.

Linking arms, they made swaying progress towards the sea. They all flopped down before reaching the water, sitting in a circle like gypsies around a campfire. The boys passed round cans of drink, rings were pulled, alcohol breathed out hissingly, and they raised the cans, tilting their heads back.

A hi-fi stereo player was switched on, ear-splitting loud in the heavy silence of early morning. The young couples started to dance. The girls gyrated their heads, hair swinging as they slipped out of their shoes. Something primitive brought up by bare feet on the sand had them letting out high, undulating cries as their bodies twisted to the beat of the music.

A girl with dyed-red hair worn long, struggled from her partner's embrace. Fleeing to a cluster of rocks, she belched hollowly and then vomit erupted gushingly to splash on the rocks.

The others laughed. A girl called, 'Hey, Annie, if you can't hold it you shouldn't drink it!'

'Will she be OK?' another girl enquired.

'She will now,' one of the boys predicted philosophically.

But then they stood rigid, changed from an animated dancing group into a tableau as Annie let out a piercing scream. She followed it with another harrowing scream that went on and on.

The seven statues jerked back into life. They ran to Annie. Gathering round the screaming girl, they followed her gaze over the low wall of limpet-encrusted rock. There was a concerted gasp as they saw a girl staring up at them with bulging eyes. Her short blonde hair was tousled and her swollen tongue was caught between clenched teeth. Even in the poor light they could see the dribble of blood smeared across her chin. She was naked, her shapely body caked with sand.

Annie's screaming faded out, and the new silence disturbed her companions more than her shrieking had. In an instant they had all sobered up completely.

'Christ!' one of the boys exclaimed.

'Is she dead?'

'Yeah.'

'How do you know? You ever see a dead person, Jay?'

'No, but you can tell, can't you.'

'What do we do?'

'I'll go for the police,' Jay, a West Indian boy, volunteered.

'It's half past two in the morning,' the tall boy who had been embracing Annie pointed out, 'and you're black, Jay, which ain't a good thing in a town like this. You walk in the police station and the filth ain't going to let you walk out.'

'Then you go, Tony,' Jay suggested.

'Sod that.'

'Somebody's got to do it,' Jay complained. 'We just can't walk away from this poor girl.'

'I'm ready to run away. She's scared the crap out of me,' one of the other boys admitted.

A girl with a pretty face and an intelligent appearance took charge positively. 'Jay's right, we have to do something. We'll all go to the police together.'

Convinced by her authoritative manner, the others made various noises and gestures of assent. They quickly switched off the stereo, gathered up their belongings and hurried away, as silent as the dark night that had closed tightly and terrifyingly around them.

It had been a long day. It was really late now, but nobody seemed to mind. The band was still playing well; couples still wore smiles as they danced. Tired, eyes feeling scraped, Randy Logan took a sip that he didn't want from a drink that was of no interest to him. Rule number one of socialising was to know how to tactfully make your excuses and leave. But the wedding reception of Deputy Chief Constable Walden Griffiths was one occasion on which it wouldn't work.

The bride and groom would be in Athens now; doing whatever it is that a dreary deputy chief constable and his pompous Member of Parliament bride do on their wedding night. But the celebration here was going on and on, like some parody of a wake for the spirits of the bride and groom. Logan checked his watch. Five minutes past three. In a company of elite cliques, he stood alone. Most men of forty-two were either married, divorced or gay. He was none of those things. Logan was just *different*. Coming from the military police into the civil police set him apart. He had been a captain and was now a detective inspector. Logan often tried to define which was the superior rank, but there was no way of making a comparison between the two totally unalike disciplined bodies.

A loud voice beside him pulled Logan from his inner world. 'Randolph, old chap. Why the long face? As the jockey said to the horse.'

Chief Constable Kenneth Biles roared with laughter, clapping Logan on the shoulder. Of average height, obesity suggesting a tendency towards self-indulgence, Biles was normally distant and aloof. Of limited ability as a law officer, the chief constable owed everything to an uncanny flair for diplomacy. He ran with the hare when absolutely necessary, but spent most of his time keeping the hounds happy. Drink had eased his inhibitions. His face was red and glistened with sweat as he picked an ice cube out of his drink and popped it in his mouth. His wife was at his side. Melanie Biles was handsome in middle age, but her beauty was but a recollection, a shadow thrown behind that which has gone.

'You can do an old man a favour, Randolph. Mrs Biles wants to dance and I'm beat,' the chief constable appealed to Logan.

Aware that a refusal would offend, Logan politely but reluctantly escorted Melanie Biles to the floor. Luckily for him, as a limited dancer, a waltz was in progress and he was able to move into it effortlessly. She immediately complimented him.

'You are really light on your feet, Inspector.'

'At this hour,' he replied jokingly, brushing aside the compliment, 'I'd say dead on my feet would be more apt.'

'On the contrary,' she argued smilingly. 'Didn't Kenneth or someone tell me that you were a champion boxer?'

He gave a dismissive little shrug as they moved to the hypnotic rhythm of the music. 'That was a very long time ago, ma'am, a different Randolph Logan.'

'I suppose so,' she said with a little laugh. 'None of us stay the same. When I think back ten, twenty years, I don't recognize myself.'

'I wouldn't want to know myself how I was,' Logan said. 'I seem to have been incredibly foolish then.'

'Exactly how I feel,' she agreed. 'Perhaps we should just live in the present.'

'I'm not even doing too well at that,' Logan wryly remarked.

With a delightfully tinkling little laugh, she said, 'You are a fraud, Inspector Logan. You are thought of most highly in the force. I do detect a touch of levity behind your cynicism.'

Logan discovered that he was at last enjoying himself. Better late then never, he was thinking, when she spoke hesitantly, unsure of herself.

'I'm not sure that I should mention this, Inspector, but …'

'I was about to thank you, ma'am,' Logan filled in the gap as she faltered. He continued gallantly. 'I had wanted to forget that tonight ever happened, but now I'll treasure the memory of it.'

'That is sweet, and I thank you,' she said demurely. 'It is presumptuous of me to ask something of you, as we haven't had a chance to get to know each other.'

'I haven't been here very long, ma'am.'

'That is precisely why I wanted to ask for your help,' she replied. 'In an insular part of the country such as this it is difficult to know who one can trust.'

Her expression had far more meaning than her voice or her words. He asked, 'Is this a police matter, Mrs Biles?'

'I suppose that it is, or rather that it could be.'

'That puts me in an awkward position, ma'am,' Logan pointed out.

She understood the quietness of his tone and her face fell. 'I realize that, Inspector, and recognize that it is a big favour to ask, but I am terribly worried.'

'Couldn't the chief constable help you?'

'He could, of course,' she said, smiling up at him with tear-filled eyes. She turned her head to left and right, studying the other dancers. 'But it is an extremely delicate matter. I would be grateful if you would give me the opportunity to explain. I'm doing charity work at Barnfield tomorrow. I always have lunch in a delightful little inn named the Sailor's Return. Do you think that you could join me? It would have to appear to be an accidental meeting.'

For a moment Logan could find nothing to say. Later, perhaps, he would have ten reasons why he should turn her down, but right then he didn't know how to handle the situation. There was no doubting the foolishness of entering into some kind of intrigue with the wife of the chief constable. But whatever her problem was, the distress it was causing her was obvious.

He said, 'I'll do my best to be there, Mrs Biles, but no promises.'

'No promises,' she said in acceptance, looking relieved.

They remained silent then, both of them aware of a white-jacketed steward weaving through the dancers to approach them.

'I do beg your pardon, Mrs Biles,' the steward, an empty silver tray held on its side under one arm, began subserviently. Then he addressed Logan. 'Excuse me, Inspector Logan, but your presence is required at reception.'

Regretting the interruption, Logan took Melanie Biles back to her husband, who was in deep discussion with Maurice Rennett, the town mayor. As Logan was turning to leave, Melanie Biles mimed a one-word, silent question, 'Tomorrow?' Logan replied with an almost imperceptible nod.

As Logan made his way out of the ballroom he wondered whether the bride or the groom had attracted Havensport's top people. He assumed it was the former, as Walden Griffiths was mediocre both as a policeman and a person.

In reception a young woman leaned on the Formica desk, making small-talk with the porter. When Logan entered the porter said something to the girl and she came towards him. Her natural auburn hair was attractively careless rather than styled. Dressed in a flaring summer skirt and a white blouse tied round her waist, just under the moderate curve of her breasts, her manner was slightly cool.

'Detective Inspector Logan?'

'That's me,' Logan admitted.

She introduced herself. 'Detective Sergeant Shelagh Ruby.'

'How come I don't know you, Sergeant?' he frowned.

'I only arrived today. Transferred from the Met, sir.'

'Guv will do, Sergeant,' Logan told her.

'Sorry, guv.' She laughed, and he noticed how pretty she was. She had a delicate kind of loveliness that was serious in repose, registering intelligence. Between the attractive smile and the thoughtful expression was a great deal of character.

A grin twitched at the corners of his mouth. 'That's got the introductions over and done with. I've a feeling that I'm not going to like your answer, but why am I meeting a sergeant new to Havensport at –' he checked his wristwatch '– half-past three in the morning?'

'You're right, guv, you're not going to like the answer,' she cautioned. 'A dead girl's been discovered on the beach.'

'Bloody hell!' he exclaimed, then apologized. 'I'm sorry, Sergeant. It's just that I was hoping to get a couple of hours' sleep.'

'I'd probably have said something worse, guv,' she said with a smile that had an unexpected mischief.

'The body's been washed up?' Logan asked wearily, hopefully. All that would mean was a quick removal of the corpse to a mortuary slab for a pathologist and his forensic colleagues to prod, probe and dissect. Paperwork taking an hour maximum and Logan would be able to get some sleep.

'No, guv. From what I've learned, it's most likely murder.'

'What's happening, Inspector Logan?'

Chief Constable Biles had come into the foyer. The bewildered expression that most people wear in a crisis was on his round, red face.

'A body has been found on the beach, sir. A suspicious death, it would seem.'

'Right. You will be senior investigating officer, Inspector Logan,' Biles announced authoritatively, turning his head to look at the girl. 'I seem to know your face.'

'We met today –' Shelagh Ruby began, then adjusted the recently passed hours in her head and corrected herself. 'Yesterday afternoon, sir. Sergeant Ruby. I transferred in from the Met.'

'Of course, I remember. Rape was your speciality, eh?'

'No, fraud, sir.'

'That's it, my mistake, but it's academic right now, as you are seconded to Detective Inspector Logan in this enquiry, Sergeant.'

'I'll get down there,' Logan said. 'Will you arrange SOCO, sir?'

'I'll see to it now, Inspector,' replied Biles. 'In the absence of Walden Griffiths, I will oversee this operation.' The chief constable took on an aura of importance as he strode away.

'When do you think you'll get to bed, guv?' Shelagh Ruby asked archly as she walked to the door with Logan.

'Certainly not tonight. August in Havensport is a mad month, Sergeant, and we're just about to mix with a whole lot of lunatics,' Logan sighed, and they walked out of the building on to the esplanade together. The air was light and soft, advance notice that the coming day would be another unbearably hot one. In the unsmiling hours of early morning, what light there was showed Havensport as it really was.

He stood on the pavement for a little while, a benign coolness in the air refreshing him slightly. He glumly asked her, 'Have you ever been backstage at a holiday resort, Sergeant?'

'Can't say that I have, guv. Is it bad?'

Expectantly awaiting an answer, she suddenly realized that Logan had walked off to where his car was parked.

two

'**H**as she been in the water, Simon?' Logan asked the police surgeon.

Looking up from where he crouched beside the body of the girl, Simon Betts raised his eyebrows. Young and with a mop of unruly black hair, there was a twinkle in his eye as he replied. 'Swimming not drowning, as the lady poet put it.'

'Not waving but drowning,' Shelagh Ruby corrected. 'Stevie Smith.'

'That's her,' Betts said, nodding.

'Don't encourage him, Sergeant,' Logan cautioned. She looked very pale, and he asked, 'Are you all right, Shelagh? Is this your first time?'

'It is, guv. I've got a diploma in being a softy,' she said. Her shoulders slumped suddenly.

Logan reached to touch her hand. 'I'm glad. People who are not affected by this kind of thing worry me.'

'Is that a jibe intended for me?' the police surgeon enquired, his spectacles magnifying his disapproval.

'No, Simon. You put on an act to get by,' Logan said.

Simon Betts' small laugh died as an incipient noise: there was a dead person to be considered. Respect was due. They were inside a sealed-off section of the beach. The detective inspector and his sergeant were standing back so as not to contaminate possible evidence before a forensic team had examined the surroundings. The area had been cordoned off and a diverse route for approach had been established. This was marked by luminous tape. Though the sky was lightening, a greyish darkness shrouded the scene. The nervous minutes went by, the minutes of waiting.

'Cut to the chase, Simon, and spare me the Poet Laureate crap.' Logan, his face troubled, was looking at Betts and beyond him.

Rolling his eyes in mock exasperation for Shelagh's benefit, Betts stood from his task to admonish Logan. 'You're not in the army now, Randy, where everything is done by numbers. Here's all I can give you at the moment – female, fit and with a good physique. Age around twenty, blonde but not naturally so. Dead no more than two to three hours. I'd say she'd been skinny-dipping shortly before she died.'

'Cause of death?'

'Strangulation – throttling by hand.'

'Anything to suggest a sexual attack?' Logan enquired.

Betts shook his head of wild hair. 'No. But that's a guess at this stage, Randy.'

'Thanks, Simon,' Logan said. 'I'll let the forensic boys do their work, then I'll have the body removed.'

Packing his leather bag, Betts warned, 'I doubt SOCO will find anything useful, Randy. Yesterday there were hundreds of holidaymakers and their unruly brats here on the sands, and it was a gang having a beach party that discovered the body.'

'I realize that,' Logan agreed, spreading his hands in a what-can-I-do gesture to the understanding shadows around them.

The sun was coming up now. A red-tinged dawn oozed over the horizon. Close to them the sea lapped and glittered and there was the pungent smell of seaweed that was washed and dried twice a day, every day. The irregularity of the rocks behind Simon Betts was emphasised by the straight green mossy line that the high tides had painted in front of them.

There were already a few small sailing craft out on the water.

Their sails were quiet. A seagull swooped low, cried out in shrill complaint at what it saw, and then crossed high in the sky to tell the other birds wheeling there. A slowly rising sun allowed them to see the body clearly now. Hearing Shelagh Ruby's gasp of shock, Logan sensed that she had stepped back. The sergeant wouldn't have known what to expect, but she wouldn't have been prepared for the staring eyes and the grotesque expression on the purplish face.

Despondently, Logan waited a few minutes for Shelagh to fight down her sickness. Then he said to the surgeon, 'She had a good body, Simon. A gymnast, perhaps?'

'She certainly exercised regularly,' Simon Betts said with a non-committal shrug.

Logan asked, 'She wasn't a tom?'

Though the death of a prostitute was as tragic as any other killing, it wasn't so emotive. If this kid were a tom, then Logan would be spared pressure from the chief constable, the 'city fathers' and the press, both local and national.

'Not unless she'd just started on the game. There's none of the usual signs.'

'So, Sergeant,' Logan turned to his assistant, 'where do we begin?'

Shelagh, shuddering briefly but violently, admitted guiltily, 'I don't know, guv.'

Logan answered wryly. 'I haven't got the faintest idea myself.'

'Let the investigation begin, Randy,' Simon Betts said grimly, standing and looking down at the body. 'All but the deceased want to know what happened. When you're dead you're dead and I reckon it doesn't matter to her how she came to get that way.'

'Is that the way you see it, Simon?' Logan asked.

'To be perfectly frank, Randy,' the police surgeon replied flatly, 'I don't know how I see it.'

*

PC Leonard Cobbie parked the police car inside the entrance. He was glad that Sea View caravan park was small. There were the black silhouettes of just fifteen caravans parked uniformly on separate concrete bases. A lot of searching wouldn't be necessary to find the prowler that an anonymous caller using a mobile phone had reported. Getting out of the vehicle he closed the door quietly. Even non-violent criminals could turn nasty if you panicked them.

Cobbie decided to take a look around the dark spaces between the caravans, then radio for a dog handler if he didn't find whoever was reported to be creeping about.

Catching a movement from the corner of his eye, he swung his head to the caravan on his left. Seeing nothing unusual, he was about to move on, convinced that he had been mistaken. But then he saw it. A curtain in a window of the caravan had twitched. Someone was watching him. Cobbie walked over to the caravan door and rapped on it lightly.

'Police,' he called softly.

There was the sound of movement inside and a light was switched on. Then a woman opened the door ajar, asking, 'What is it?'

She looked to be in her mid-thirties, and had jeans and a sweater on. At ten minutes to four in the morning, the policeman would have expected the woman to be in a nightdress or dressing gown. Cobbie noticed that her eyes were swollen from crying.

'Did you telephone to report a prowler in the camp, madam?' Cobbie enquired.

'No, I didn't.'

A man of about her age came to stand behind the woman, a hand on each of her shoulders. His trousers sagged and there were heavy sweat stains in the armpits of his light-coloured shirt. Looking out at Cobbie, he announced with a disarming smile, 'That would be me, officer.'

'You telephoned the police, sir?'

'No,' the man replied with a short laugh. 'I would be your

prowler. I only got back a short while ago, and I crept into the park so as not to wake anyone.'

'Rather an odd time to return, sir, wouldn't you say?'

'It's a free country.'

'Even so,' the policeman countered with a shrug. 'Your name, sir?'

'Wright. Derek Wright.'

'May I come in for a minute or two, Mr Wright?'

'I'd rather you didn't,' the woman said swallowing hard. 'We have three kids fast asleep.'

'You are Mrs Wright?'

'Yes.'

'Mrs ...?'

'Mrs Alice Wright.'

Making notes in his book, Cobbie looked at Derek Wright. 'Could you explain why you returned so late, Mr Wright?'

'It's a bit embarrassing, really,' Wright began with a self-deprecating laugh. 'Me and the missus had a difference of opinion yesterday evening ...'

'We had a bloody great row,' his wife muttered, her snuffling making more noise than her voice.

Wright gave her a sharp look. 'Anyway, I went off in a bit of a temper.'

'You went into town?' the policeman checked.

'Into Havensport, if you can call that a town,' Wright said, grinning. 'I visited a couple of boozers, and fell in with these three guys. They came from Coventry, same as we do, and were Manchester United fans like myself. We got a takeaway and went back to where they were staying.'

'Until when?'

'Let's see? I've been back for about twenty minutes, so I was with them until I walked back from town, as you call it.'

'Where were they staying, Mr Wright?'

'I'm not sure. They were in a chalet at the rear of a pub just off the esplanade.'

'That sounds like the Coach and Horses.' Cobbie said.

Alice Wright turned her face away and broke into anguished sobbing. She jabbed an elbow into her husband's ribs. 'Go on then, report it like you said you would.'

'Not now. I'll do it in the morning, Alice, like I promised.'

'Report what?'

Derek Wright opened his mouth, and it stayed open. His wife answered. 'He only had his bloody wallet nicked, didn't he!'

'It wasn't nicked,' her husband protested. 'I took my jacket off in their place, and it must have slipped out of my pocket. I'll call on them first thing and pick it up. There's no problem.'

'Anything of value in the wallet?' Cobbie enquired.

'Only all of our bloody holiday money! One hundred and eighty quid.' Alice Wright tried unsuccessfully to conceal her agitation and anger. Burying her face in her hands she spoke tearfully through her fingers. 'There's three kids in there expecting to enjoy their holiday, and now we can't even buy the poor little buggers an ice cream. Our credit cards were in the wallet, too.'

A child began to cry inside the caravan, annoying Derek Wright who gave his wife a push with one hand. 'Now look what you've done.'

'What *I've* done?' she yelled indignantly. 'What *I've* done? I like that! It wasn't me who stayed out all bleeding night and lost our holiday money!'

Lights were coming on in a number of the caravans. Aware of this, Constable Cobbie wanted to speed proceedings along. 'I'll make enquiries about your wallet, sir, and come back to you.'

'There's no need,' Wright argued. 'I'll get it back myself in a couple of hours' time.'

'This is a police matter now, sir, so it's best that you leave it to us. Please call in at the station to make a statement at some time this morning.'

'And what are we supposed to do in the meantime, with not a penny to our name?' Alice Wright demanded. She smiled at the policeman. It was an unfriendly smile that Cobbie guessed wasn't intended for him. Alice Wright was aiming her malicious smile at a hostile world that had forever treated her badly.

A sympathetic Cobbie advised, 'All I can suggest, Mrs Wright, is that you see Social Services in the morning. You'll find them at the town hall in the High Street.'

'That's fine! That's just bloody fine!' an enraged Alice Wright wailed. 'We come down here as respectable holidaymakers and now you want us to become inadequates begging for charity.'

As PC Cobbie walked fast down the gravel path to his car, the Wrights were having a furiously noisy argument and the occupants of other caravans were opening their doors to look out.

'No one has been reported as not returning home last night, Randy.'

The speaker was an elderly sergeant who had been installed as office manager in the incident room that had been set up at the Havensport police station. With chubby cheeks, three or four chins and an honest face, he looked like the father Shelagh Ruby often wished she'd had.

Sitting among plain clothes and uniformed officers, Shelagh looked at Logan, expecting him to reprimand the sergeant for using his first name. But, standing facing them, Detective Inspector Logan accepted the familiarity without a murmur. Shelagh judged him to be around average height, but he might have been taller because his wide-shouldered build gave an impression of stockiness. He was said to be all cop, but most of the time his face was pleasant, almost bland. Yet Shelagh could feel the power of the personality that crackled out electrically. When they had been with the body on the beach he had been strangely detached. Logan seemed to underplay everything he did.

'I'm not surprised, Tom,' he answered the sergeant cynically. 'On an August night in Havensport the him or her who goes back to their own bed is the exception. With the population here inflated four or five times by visitors, identifying the dead girl is going to be difficult. All we've got is bleached blonde about twenty. Nice looking, a good figure that's more like that of an athlete rather than a model. It's possible that she came to Havensport alone.'

'Or with her killer, guv.' A detective constable with a newly smashed nose and a black eye folded his hands behind his head and grinned. He was a real toughie, young, strong and intelligent, with a reckless look that said he liked his job.

'A good point, Wallace,' Logan agreed. 'And he's not likely to report her missing.'

'Was she married?' a female detective constable named Ami Symes enquired.

The sergeant named Tom answered. 'She wore no rings and her fingers bore no marks of her ever having done so.'

Accepting this with a nod, Ami, who had seen too many things that a girl of her age shouldn't see, asked another question, 'Was she raped, guv?'

'I won't have the pathologist's report until later, but it wouldn't seem so,' Logan replied. He ran his fingers through his wavy fair hair. 'Before going any further, I'd welcome any input from you people. My neck is out so far on this one that it hurts, so any suggestions are welcome.'

'I think you ought to hear what Len Cobbie has to say, guv,' Tom said.

Standing by the wall at the back, the uniformed Constable Cobbie took a step forward and looked self-consciously to Logan for a response.

'Go for it, Constable,' Logan encouraged the young officer. 'This could put your foot on the bottom rung of the ladder to chief constable.'

'I doubt it, sir,' Cobbie replied, made less nervous by the

inspector's easy manner. 'Early this morning I had cause to speak to a married man who had been out all night. He said he had been with three male visitors to the town in a chalet at the rear of the Coach and Horses. The man's wife reported to me that he had lost his wallet, containing a considerable amount of money, during the night. He said he had probably left it at the chalet, so I called at the Coach and Horses on my way back to the station.'

'And …?'

'The landlord will only rent his chalets to families or couples, sir, because young men together are always trouble.'

'So there were no three men staying there. Your lost wallet man was lying.'

'Yes, sir.'

'You have his name, Constable?' Logan enquired.

'The name that he gave me was Derek Wright, sir. He said he was from Coventry, sir.'

Logan had no need to issue an order. Just turning his head to a policewoman had her fingers tapping the keys of the police national computer. She read loudly from the screen: 'Derek Norman Wright, sir. Born Coventry, 4 August 1960. Conviction for ABH 1982, indecent assault 1986. Three minor traffic offences since.'

The sergeant called Tom was the first to comment. 'That was a long time ago, Randy, but he's capable of violence.'

'I've asked him to come in to make a statement about his wallet this morning, sir,' Cobbie said.

'Good. He's all we've got right now.' Logan looked up at the wall clock. It was five minutes past eleven. 'Sergeant Ruby, you interview this Wright fellow with Constable Cobbie. If he's not here by noon, both of you go out and bring him in.'

'Right, guv,' Shelagh answered.

Logan addressed the sergeant. 'What I want you to do, Tom, is find out if anyone knows our blonde.'

'There's an awful lot of bleached blondes in Havensport at

this time of year, guv,' the detective named Wallace commented laconically.

'But only one dead one, as far as we know,' Logan countered.

In the noonday heat, Ed Bellamy hurried past small shops that were brilliant with highly coloured plastic seaside articles. Clutching a steak and kidney dinner, he turned into a narrow street. Upper storeys loomed darkly close together, shutting out the sunshine. Reaching the Mon Ami hotel, a dingy terraced boarding house, he went in fast through the lobby and ran up the stairs. Head down, he reached the landing and came to an abrupt halt when he found himself in close proximity to a coloured apron. His way was barred by the skin and skeleton figure of landlady Avis Fleming.

Her head was tilted to one side. Her hair was styled in the old-fashioned, rolled-under fashion of women he'd seen in Second World War movies. He caught the unmistakable dull smell of potato peelings from her reddened hands. On her own ground she was kind of regal, with an almost aggressive nobility.

'As you know, Mr Bellamy,' she began neutrally, her tone moving up a notch to become a whine, 'I am not one to bother my guests, but I really must have a word with you about your room.'

'Don't I always make sure that it is neat and tidy, Mrs Fleming?' he asked with just the right amount of puzzlement.

'I have had no reason to complain until now. I suppose it has something to do with what you got up to last night. I wouldn't know about it if Mr Fleming's trouble hadn't got him out of bed at four this morning, and he saw you come in.'

Bellamy nodded. 'That is correct, Mrs Fleming. It was my night off.'

'I think it amounts to something more than that, Mr Bellamy.'

'I'm sorry, I don't understand.'

'Sand.' She was suddenly frank and ruthless in her criticisms. 'There's sand everywhere in your room. Your shoes are full of it, and it's caked to those trousers that you left over a chair.'

He silently cursed himself. Though she didn't normally do his room until much later, he should have taken into account that she was occasionally early. A couple of tokes tended to make him absent-minded. He gave an embarrassed laugh. 'A few of us fooling about on the beach. I'll clean up the sand right away.'

'You had better. I've left a dustpan and brush in your room,' she said. 'But I warn you, if anything like this happens again, then –' She stopped speaking as the outside door opened downstairs. A policeman came into the lobby, his helmet under his arm. Avis Fleming looked baffled, irritated and apprehensive. Indicating the policeman with a nod of her head, the landlady said, 'I hope this has nothing to do with you.'

Not replying, Ed Bellamy squeezed past her and went quickly along the landing to his room.

The Sailor's Return was an ancient inn that belonged to a time when the thriving town of Barnfield had been a village. It was buried deep among trees down a country lane. Doing a lively business at lunchtime, its patrons in the main being the as yet unnamed successors of the yuppies. The low-ceilinged place had atmosphere; plenty of it. But the olde worlde charm had no effect on Logan when he walked in. Nostalgia was an illusion. Days gone by were no better than today.

His trained eye spotted Melanie Biles sitting alone at a small table in one corner, dressed in a light blue suit. Going to the bar, he turned, making a pretence of being surprised to see the chief constable's wife there. She played along with a remarkable show of acting.

'Inspector Logan, fancy meeting you here.' Her voice was as soft as a kitten's purr. 'Please, do sit down. I would welcome some company.'

Taking a seat, Logan warned, 'I won't be able to stay long, Mrs Biles.'

'I understand, Inspector. Kenneth told me about that poor girl. Isn't it awful, especially in the holiday season when everyone is so happy. Now, I'm sure that you have time for lunch, and it's my treat.'

The faces around Logan weren't those of his kind of people. They spoke urgently and their talk was of big money, big business. Aware of his hesitation, Melanie Biles smilingly rebuked him.

'Come now, Inspector Logan, a lunch paid for by the chief constable's wife could hardly be construed as a bribe.'

Logan was very tired. He was grumpy. His long night was resting heavily on him. 'Not a bribe, ma'am, but the wrong construction could be put on it.'

She smiled archly. She had a passionate, full-lipped mouth that was contradicted by a high-boned, haughty nose. Melanie Biles was a complex woman with too many contradictions for Logan to be at ease with. She playfully levelled a long and lovely finger at him. 'Is that a compliment to my attractiveness or an insult to my moral standards?'

'It was neither, Mrs Biles,' he assured her. 'I was simply making the point that small-town people have small minds.'

Reaching a hand across the table to him, she jerked it back quickly before it touched his. She took a moment to recover her composure. 'I understood what you meant, Inspector, and I was merely making fun of you, in the nicest possible way, of course.' She passed him the menu. A waitress hovered with an order pad. 'You order, Inspector. I'll have the ham salad.'

When the waitress left, Melanie Biles fixed Logan with a steady look. There was a little furrow on her forehead. Her usually cool blue eyes were no longer cool. He could see and feel her unhappiness. She had a trick of looking away suddenly. Then she was back with him. The little furrow had become a full-fledged frown.

'Do you mind if I tell you my problem while we await the meal?'

'Go ahead, Mrs Biles. That's why I'm here.'

Once again she did her looking away bit. 'I pray that you won't find this to be amusing, Inspector.'

'It's plainly troubling you greatly, ma'am, so I'm sure that I won't.'

'This will sound ridiculous, Inspector, coming from a middle-aged woman, but I am sure that I am being stalked.'

'Don't be offended, Mrs Biles, I have to ask,' Logan said diplomatically. 'Is it possible that you are imagining this?'

'Hysterical delusions? As a policeman, that is understandably your first reaction. I was once a lawyer, Inspector, and I'm too smart not to recognize when I'm being followed.'

Having anticipated a confession of an accumulation of embarrassing debts, Logan tightened his jaws to prevent himself from saying something from which he couldn't later retreat. What she had told him was both totally unexpected and mystifying.

It occurred to him now that Melanie Biles kept most of herself hidden. His dance with her at Walden Griffiths' wedding hadn't resulted from a whim of the chief constable. Using her womanly wiles, Melanie Biles had got her husband to arrange it without him realising what had happened. Logan was a part of some devious strategy of hers, and that made him wary.

'It would seem that I have unsettled you, Inspector Logan.'

'Not unsettled, Mrs Biles. It is more a case of you puzzling me,' he told her frankly. 'Surely the chief constable is your best answer?'

'No,' she answered with an emphatic shake of her head. 'I don't want my husband involved.'

Logan tried to reason with her. 'Every policeman makes enemies. Your husband could well be the target, Mrs Biles, and you the innocent victim, as it were.'

She smiled strangely. 'I am certain that it isn't like that, Inspector. This is personal, very personal. What I was hoping for, and have no right to ask, Inspector, is your expertise on an *ex officio* basis.'

'That would put me in a very difficult position, Mrs Biles,' Logan told her.

'I fully realize that, and I wouldn't ask if I wasn't desperate,' she said, her face brightening as the waitress arrived with their food. 'Ah, here we are. Let's eat, Inspector, and I'll do my very best to explain.'

Aware that he should stop her there and politely refuse to help, the usually self-possessed Logan found that the bewitching Melanie Biles had him behaving like some gauche teenager on his first date.

Concentrating on the knife and fork movements enabled her to speak freely. She candidly told Logan of a romantic liaison of ten years previously in Kent, when her husband had been an ambitious superintendent working long hours, and she a bored housewife with time on her hands.

'Was your lover in the job?' Logan enquired.

'Good heavens, no! Having an affair with a policeman would be too adventurous, even for me. I owned a little Metro at the time, a real old banger, and Brian, Brian Amhurst was his name, owned the one-man garage where I used to get it fixed.'

'And you believe it's this guy stalking you now?'

'I'm ninety-nine-point-nine per cent convinced. He was possessive. Probably obsessive is a better description. He took it badly when I finished with him.'

'But we are in the West Country, Mrs Biles,' Logan logically pointed out, 'and this man was in Kent. Stalkers don't normally commute.'

'Don't joke, please, Inspector. I am very frightened.'

Logan apologized. 'Forgive me. This man is plainly a threat to your marriage and your status in the county, but do you feel he might harm you physically?'

'I truly believe that Brian Amhurst could be violent,' she replied as they rose from the table. 'Will you help me, Inspector?'

'At this point, Mrs Biles, all I can say is that I'll give the matter consideration.'

'At this point, Inspector Logan,' she said with a faint smile, 'that is all I can ask for.'

three

Sergeant Shelagh Ruby had fallen quiet as Logan stopped the car outside the old brick building. Sensing her dread, he recognized a familiar uneasiness in himself. It was bone-freezing cold inside the morgue – not the bracing fresh-air cold of a winter's morning, but a sour cold filled with the stench of chemicals and death. It was eerily quiet, too. Simon Betts stood with his narrow back to them, holding up a test tube, tapping it with a finger as he studied the contents.

Becoming aware of their presence, the pathologist did a double take as he looked at Logan. 'I've seen better-looking corpses, Randy.'

'You're the expert, Simon,' Logan acknowledged. 'Lack of sleep is my excuse.'

'It couldn't be anything else.' Betts brushed his thick black hair back. The grey at his temples aged him instantly. He made a face at Shelagh. 'All work and no play have made Randolph a dull boy. Maybe having a beautiful sergeant will have him get his priorities right.'

'You're a worse matchmaker than you are a doctor, Simon,' Logan commented. He was keen to return to the station, where Derek Wright was being held for questioning. 'We're pushed for time.'

'You've come about Goldilocks,' Betts nodded.

'Is that her?' Logan enquired; pointing to the nearest slab on which a sheet-covered figure lay.

'I believe so.' The pathologist looked clownishly at Logan. 'There again, it could be one of the three bears – you know what they're like for fooling about with other people's property.'

Logan protested. 'I'm used to your sick sense of humour, Simon, but Sergeant Ruby is new to murder enquiries.'

'I am so sorry, Sergeant,' Simon Betts apologized. 'That was crass of me.'

'That's all right,' Shelagh assured him. Then she gave Logan a half smile. 'It's OK, guv. I'd rather laugh than cry.'

'I suppose that makes sense, Sergeant. Right, Simon, what's the score?'

Betts went to a row of steel filing cabinets and ran his finger along the drawers the way a child drags a stick along a wooden fence. Pulling a drawer out he removed a file and opened it. 'Death was due to manual strangulation, Randy. No evidence of recent sexual activity, and she definitely was not raped. The coroner will probably remove my nuts later for making assumptions, but I'd say she hadn't been messing with drugs.'

Logan pulled back the sheet and said, 'We need to establish her identity, Simon. Anything distinctive about the body?'

'Not a tattoo, scar, blemish, or even a wart,' Betts replied. 'There is one thing worth mentioning.'

'What's that?' Logan draped the sheet back over the corpse.

'I'd place her age at no more than twenty, and she wouldn't have been able to wear white without blushing had she married at any time after her fourteenth birthday.'

Logan shrugged. 'That might have been a useful lead back in the Fifties, Simon, but it's not remarkable in the twenty-first century.'

'Just trying to be helpful.'

'I know,' Logan said to ease the sensitive pathologist's hurt. 'Is there nothing else?'

'Take a look at her legs, Randy,' Betts suggested.

Going to the slab with the pathologist, Logan saw his sergeant wince as Betts folded the sheet back to display the dead girl's legs to the tops of her thighs. Lifting one leg by the ankle, Betts ran his fingers under the lower leg. 'At first glance, a nicely developed calf muscle. But a closer look reveals something of an over-development. It's the same with the muscles of her thigh.'

'Which supports the athlete theory,' Logan remarked as the pathologist pulled the sheet back into place.

Simon Betts pushed his lips out as he considered his reply. 'It would, Randy, but for the fact that her upper body is of normal development.'

'A runner?' Logan suggested.

'Her build is too heavy,' Betts said to cancel out the possibility.

'What does it mean, then, Simon?'

'You're the detective,' was the pathologist's unhelpful reply.

Ready to leave, Logan waited for his sergeant, who had moved to lift up a corner of the sheet. Looking down at the dead girl's face for a long moment, Shelagh's lips were pale. She let the sheet drop and walked to join the inspector, although she was somehow distant from him. When they were outside in the fresh air she turned to Logan with easy friendliness and they were in touch again.

'You had to force yourself to take a look at her, didn't you?' Logan said as they drove away station.

'Yes,' Shelagh replied with a nod.

'Then why did you?'

Aware that he wasn't prying, but assessing her as his superior officer, Shelagh answered honestly. 'If I'd left the mortuary without looking at her, I would have been running away. That would have meant things becoming more difficult for me later.'

'You're right,' he agreed. The interior of the car became oven-like in the white sunshine along the seafront. 'We all go through that sort of thing, Sergeant. When I started out – in the army, that was – I didn't sleep well when dealing with a murder or a suicide. I'd feel something touch my cheek in the night, waking me, and they would be there when I opened my eyes.'

With a shiver, Shelagh said, 'You put it pretty graphically, guv. How long did it take you to get used to it?'

'I haven't. Nothing's changed,' he said grimly.

'I wouldn't have thought ...' she began, but stopped speaking as his mobile phone buzzed.

Taking the phone from the inside pocket of his jacket, he passed it to her. 'You take care of that, Sergeant.'

Holding the instrument to her ear, Shelagh listened, then turned her head to speak to Logan. 'It's Sergeant Kane. A Mrs Harrington has rung in to report that her daughter, Norma, didn't come home last night. The daughter is aged nineteen, guv, and she's blonde.'

'Get the address, Sergeant.'

'The Clement Estate, guv,' Shelagh reported after checking on the phone. 'Mrs Harrington has heard about a girl being found dead, and she's very worried.'

'Tell Tom that we'll drive straight there,' Logan ordered. 'And also tell him to hold on to that Wright guy until we get back.'

When he'd put the car through a U-turn to the horn-blaring anger of other drivers, Shelagh passed his phone back, saying, '27 Stewart Road, guv.'

Ten minutes later they were turning into a large estate of grey-rendered houses with red-tiled roofs. Women stood at doors chatting. Shelagh envied them their normal lives, their ignorance of violent death. They were ordinary folk who didn't have to hold a weeping new widow or comfort a child who had been abruptly orphaned.

'This is it, guv, Stewart Road. She counted – 19 – 21 – 23 – that's the house on the left.'

A man in his late fifties, with Popeye-like forearms, opened the front door. He had a look of disorientation. When they'd shown him their police warrant cards he made a meaningless gesture with his hand and invited them in.

'The missus is pretty cut up,' he whispered before showing them into a front room.A woman sitting in an armchair turned a ravaged face anxiously to them. Starting to get up to greet them she couldn't make it. Falling sideways, she regained her balance and slumped back into the chair. She looked terrible. Even her hair didn't seem to fit.

'It's the police, Mother,' the man told her softly. 'They'll find Norma for us.'

'They've already found Norma,' she said numbly, absently.

'We don't know that, Mrs Harrington,' Logan said. 'I'm Detective Inspector Logan, and this is Detective Sergeant Ruby. Has your daughter ever stayed out all night before?'

The Harringtons exchanged wary glances. It was the father who answered. 'Only if she was staying over at a friend's house, and she always lets us know.'

'Where did your daughter say she was going when she left home last evening?'

'She was meeting Julie, wasn't she, Mother?' Harrington half stated, half asked. His wife nodded listlessly.

'Julie is a friend?' Shelagh asked in an effort to keep a dialogue going.

'Norma's best friend,' Harrington replied. 'The two of them have been close since school.'

'Any idea where they would be going, Mr Harrington?'

'One of the clubs in town, I suppose,' Harrington answered Shelagh glumly. 'I don't hold with such places, but what can you do?'

'Where does Norma work?'

'At the big supermarket in Sea Road. Both her and Julie are on the checkouts.'

'Does Julie live nearby?' Logan enquired.

'Just around the corner. Almer Road – number eight.'

Looking from one to the other of the Harringtons, Logan asked, 'Have either of you spoken to Julie today?'

'I went round there this morning,' Harrington said, 'but I was in such a state that I don't think I made much sense. I don't know what Julie thought of me, Inspector.'

'I'm sure that she understood how worried you are,' Shelagh consoled him. 'What is Julie's surname?'

'Bolt. She's Robin and Meg Bolt's daughter.'

'We'll have a word with Julie,' Logan said, then asked. 'Do you have a recent photograph of your daughter?'

Going to the mantelpiece, the man picked up a Polaroid photograph and passed it to Logan. 'That was taken last Christmas, Inspector.'

Shelagh moved close to Logan to study a family gathering round a food-laden table. There were two young people, a boy of about ten and a teenage girl with a tumbling mass of long blonde hair.

'It's her, isn't it,' the woman asked, her voice cracking. 'The girl that was found on the beach is Norma, isn't she?'

'I don't believe so, Mrs Harrington,' Logan replied. 'That girl had short blonde hair.'

Releasing a dismal howl, the woman covered her face with her hands. Shelagh went to her, asking solicitously, 'What is it, Mrs Harrington?'

'Three weeks ago,' the woman sobbed, 'our Norma had her hair cut short.'

Putting a hand on the man's arm, moving him across the room out of earshot, Logan asked, 'I appreciate this is most difficult for you, Mr Harrington. It's possible that we will have to ask you to come with us to ...'

'To identify the dead girl?' His teeth made harsh grating noises.

'Hopefully, to establish that she isn't your daughter.'

'But she could be?'

Having no answer, Logan looked across to where his sergeant had the weeping mother cuddled up under her arm. She asked the man, 'If it is necessary, is there someone who could stay with your wife, Mr Harrington?'

'I could fetch Mrs Barton from next door,' Harrington said decisively, his pale brown eyes changing. They looked cold and clouded.

'Good,' Logan said. 'We'll go to see Julie first, then we'll probably come back to you.'

Aged around eighteen, Julie Bolt was nice to look at. It wasn't just that the girl was pretty all over, but because there was something alive about everything she did. She seemed to be in touch with every part of her lithe young body.

After they had introduced themselves to the girl and her parents, she had asked Logan and his sergeant out into the kitchen. Propping herself against a worktop, she gestured for them to be seated, but they preferred to remain standing. Julie had on a light green summer dress, and she struck a tough kind of pose with her thumbs in the thin leather belt at her waist. The sun slanted through the window behind her, forming a cross-hatch pattern on the tile floor. She gave a little self-conscious laugh before speaking.

'I know it's silly, but I don't like talking about … you know … boys and things in front of my mum and dad.'

'Parents can be inhibiting,' Shelagh smiled. 'This is about your friend, Norma Harrington, Julie.'

'I guessed as much. Her dad came round earlier, but I couldn't really tell what he was on about.'

'But you do know that she didn't come home last night?' Logan asked.

Julie looked at his face for a second, then she nodded. 'Is that what this is about?'

'You didn't know?' Shelagh frowned. 'I thought you two were together last night.'

'We were, until around eleven o'clock. I met this London guy who's down on holiday, and me and Norma split up.'

'Was Norma with anyone?' Shelagh asked.

'Yes, he was my guy's mate, but I could tell Norma didn't

like him much.' Julie wrinkled her nose. 'She's only got time for one guy these days. Real gone on him, she is.'

'She's going regular with someone?'

Julie gave a delightful tinkling laugh. 'In her dreams. I don't reckon he even knows that she's around.'

'I don't know what it's called now,' Shelagh ventured, 'but it used to be known as having a crush on someone.'

'That's it.'

'Who is this man, boy, or whatever?' Logan asked.

'Man,' Julie replied. 'He's all man, Inspector. I have to admit that he's a hunk.'

'Is he local?'

'No. He came here to work for the summer.'

Shelagh quickly asked, 'Do you know where he works?'

'At the Blue Angel, ' Julie said, with a rueful smile.

'That's not the sort of club you girls go to, Julie,' Logan remarked.

'It isn't, Inspector, but Julie had me and her parading past the place, backwards and forwards, nearly every night. This guy she's crazy about is the doorman there, see.'

'Do you know his name?'

'No.'

'Could Norma have been with him last night?' Logan enquired.

'Not likely. They've never spoken. Like I said, I don't reckon he's ever noticed her,' Julie giggled.

'You don't appear to be at all concerned that your friend is missing.'

Julie's hands folded into tight little fists. She hunched her shoulders. 'I suppose she got lucky.'

'You mean that she probably spent the night with a boy?'

'Yeah. When that happens we always say that we stayed at Katie's place. Katie's a friend of ours and she always gives us an alibi. Her mother's a bit of a slapper, and she always backs us up.'

'But Norma didn't contact her parents.'

'Probably got carried away and forgot,' Julie said. 'Don't worry. Norma is probably round at Katie's house now. Once they've fixed up a believable story, Norma will come toddling home, you'll see.'

'Can you give us the name of the club you went to with Norma last night, Julie.'

Fiddling with some crockery beside her on the worktop, Julie stopped and watched Shelagh's face for a moment. There was a silence so thick it could be sliced with a knife.

'We did the rounds,' Julie answered at last. 'I reckon we visited every place in Havensport.'

Making movements that indicated he was ready to leave, Logan said, 'Thank you for your help, Julie. We may have to speak with you again.'

Reaching to take a biscuit from a tin, the girl placed it between white teeth as she slid off the worktop and gave Logan a look that was sexy right down to her sandals. Her voice was scarcely audible. 'Any time, Inspector.' Then she dropped her eyes quickly and turned her face away.

When they were back at his car and Logan was sliding in behind the wheel, Shelagh asked, 'What are you thinking, guv?'

'Apart from what happened to youthful innocence?'

'I long ago gave up wondering about that,' the sergeant laughed. 'What did you think of what she told us?'

Starting the car, Logan was caught up in an immense weariness. Eyes half closed, he spoke through his teeth. 'There are things that don't seem to make much sense, but just because right now we can't see what's holding them together doesn't mean that they're not there. Maybe we've just had a lucky break, Sergeant, and Julie Bolt gave us both the killer and the victim.'

'The Blue Angel bouncer and …' Shelagh paused, cleared her throat and continued. 'Norma Harrington. You think the dead girl is her, guv?'

'A possibility but not a certainty,' Logan answered as he swung the car head back towards the Harringtons' house. 'We'd better take Harrington for a ride to the morgue.'

'I can think of a better way of spending the next hour, guv.' Shelagh sighed unhappily.

'I can think of a better way of spending a lifetime, Sergeant.'

Dressed in his silver-trimmed uniform, an agitated Kenneth Biles waited inside the police station's double doors for Logan and his sergeant. With the chief constable was an equally agitated Councillor Harvey Reynolds. They both took a step forward as they saw Logan's car pull in.

'Well, Inspector Logan? Any developments?' Biles asked as Logan and Shelagh came in through the doors.

'Yes, sir.' Logan gave a little nod. 'Now we have a missing girl as well as a dead girl.'

'Surely one and the same,' Reynolds suggested hopefully. He was small, dark and greasy looking, with a built-in sneer that passed for intelligence.

Shaking his head tiredly, Logan said, 'I'm afraid not. We've just taken the father of the missing girl to the morgue. The dead girl is not his daughter.'

'God!' Biles exclaimed. 'This is becoming messy, Inspector. Damn it, we could have a serial killer roaming Havensport.'

'This will drive people out of town. There'll be nothing but donkeys on the beach,' moaned Harvey Reynolds, who was a hotelier in the town.

'We only have one corpse so far, sir,' Logan reminded Biles.

'Maybe that's only until we find the body of the second girl,' the chief constable observed miserably. 'I imagine that we can assume that the dead girl is not local. If she was, some relative or friend would have reported her missing by now.'

'I wouldn't like to make such an assumption, sir,' Logan said. 'With no clothes, no handbag, no jewellery, identification is a bummer.'

'The other girl went missing around the time the murdered girl died, sir,' Shelagh pointed out. 'And her family only reported her missing a short while ago.'

'You could be right, Sergeant. But I still feel that she is most likely a visitor to Havensport,' Biles said.

'I'm inclined to agree with the chief constable,' Reynolds announced. There was a snowstorm of dandruff on the shoulders of his dark jacket. He turned to Logan. 'This is bad for the town, and bad for the economy of the town, Detective Inspector. As chairman of the Police Authority, I would say, and I'm sure the chief constable will concur, that you have what might be termed as a free hand in this matter. No questions asked.'

Logan smiled at the councillor, but nothing was funny. It was the only way that he could arrange his mouth and be polite without letting Reynolds know how sick he made him feel. 'I won't divert from police procedure, Councillor.'

'That goes without saying, Detective Inspector,' Biles put in swiftly. 'I am sure that Councillor Reynolds was not suggesting otherwise.'

'My mistake,' Logan said laconically.

Reynolds stood there fidgeting, probably Logan reasoned, because the councillor didn't like him, mentally cursing arrogant detectives who didn't do their job the way he wanted them to.

'What of this missing girl, Inspector? Could it be another case of homicide?' Biles enquired, squinting, looking desperate.

'We have some lines of enquiry to follow, and then I will know more, sir,' Logan replied. 'At the moment, my feeling is that she will be found safe.'

'I pray you are right, Inspector. But we are no further ahead with the dead girl?'

'No, sir. It has been a difficult case from the start, and I don't envisage it getting any easier,' Logan reported.

'That's worrying, very worrying,' the chief constable said

unhappily. Then he brightened. 'I understand that you are holding a suspect here at the station, Inspector Logan.'

'I think that he may prove to be more of a prat than a suspect, sir,' Logan predicted.

'Perhaps, perhaps. Keep me informed, Inspector.'

'Will do, sir,' Logan promised, then looked past Biles and Reynolds to call to the custody sergeant who was shuffling papers on his desk. 'Fetch Wright and put him in Interview Room One, Sergeant.'

'Yes, sir.'

four

Once a fishing village, Havensport had grown haphazardly and was now too misshapen to be anything other than a yearly background for bucket-and-spade high jinks. It took Logan some time to drive along the esplanade in backed-up traffic caused by a desperate search for parking spaces. The sparkling blue bay was a mass of activity – with water scooters ploughing their white-waked way far out, and bathers bobbing shoulder to shoulder inshore. Shelagh Ruby looked out at meandering trippers with blank faces and disappointed, empty eyes, proof that all enjoyment is retrospective. They would get their pleasure when back home telling friends and relatives about their holiday. This was a different world to the one she had known in London. Here the people seemed close to you so that you became part of the crowd. In the city those around you are only movement and sound and the sign of life, they stayed withdrawn and far away even when near to you.

It was early evening and the mingled perfumes of suntan lotions, ice cream and perspiration clung in the air. Parents and children clutching rolled towels and beach balls stood embarrassed by foul language as drivers argued heatedly with drivers. Logan was completely detached. He had an oddly contemptuous look permanently on his handsome face. It was like an interesting scar or his own trademark. A man like Logan would leave the inanities of life to the inane. Detective

Constable Toby Walker had told her that Logan was a 'good cop', a specialist who 'keeps files in his head better than they're kept at the station'.

'I prefer the autumn and winter, when the air is brisk and people look as if they have somewhere to go,' Logan absently remarked.

This was the first time he had spoken since they'd left the police station. They had made no progress in the murder case. A yellow dress had been found floating among rocks, which Simon Betts was currently testing. They had gained nothing from the interview with the sly-looking Derek Wright, who had stuck to his story even when Logan had told him that no chalet at the Coach and Horses had been let to three men.

'Then it must have been a chalet behind some other pub,' Wright had countered arrogantly. 'Anyway, it wasn't me that said it was the Coach and Horses. It was that young copper.'

'There isn't another public house with chalets at the rear in Havensport,' Logan had pointed out.

Wright had been locked up in the station for the night, and Shelagh had arranged for Social Services to call on his wife and children at the caravan park.

At present the chief constable was making the right political noises in reply to questions from the media. But Kenneth Biles would pass the buck down to Logan if the dead girl wasn't identified soon – something the detective inspector wouldn't welcome.

'You have to watch journalists, Sergeant,' he had told her before they left the station. 'Like lawyers, they think themselves to be pretty clever.'

Now, motivated by the puzzle of how Wright had come to know about a chalet, they turned into the yard of the Coach and Horses and the car bumped over rough concrete. The whole place had a tumbledown look. The three 'chalets' that made up three sides of a quadrangle were just badly converted stone outhouses. The rotting woodwork was beyond rescue. A man's round, pale face stared suspiciously out through a small window in the rear wall of the pub. Logan stopped the car beside a chipped yellow OFFICE sign. An ageing rotary airer was motionless in the still air, dragged over to one side by two dripping swimsuits. The back door opened and the round, pale face came out. It belonged to a short man who was obese and careless about his clothes. He was balding, with a ring of grey hair that circled his head like wreath.

'You're in luck, folks,' the little fat man said. 'We've got one chalet left, owing to a last-minute cancellation.'

'Police,' Logan announced flatly as he and Shelagh produced their warrant cards. 'Detective Inspector Logan and Detective Sergeant Ruby.'

'What brings you folk here? We run a family establishment and don't have no trouble.'

The air was cooling, and Shelagh folded her arms, hugging herself. 'We're not here to give you any trouble, Mr … er …?'

'Barker. Sam Barker.'

'Are you the proprietor, Mr Barker?' Logan enquired.

'I am, for my sins.' Barker nodded and smiled.

Moving a pointing finger in an arc, Shelagh asked, 'Two of these chalets are occupied this week and one vacant, is that right?'

'That's it. Most unusual at this time of year,' Barker replied.

'Who do you have in the two occupied chalets?' Logan enquired.

'A father, mother and two young kiddies in that one,' Barker answered, inclining his head to indicate one chalet. 'And two young ladies, schoolteachers from Bristol, in the other. Real nice girls.'

'Who does the car belong to?' Shelagh pointed to a dull-red Vauxhall Cavalier.

'That's the teachers' car.'

Her interest quickening, Shelagh asked, 'Does that mean they are in the chalet at the moment?'

'S'far as I know.'

'Then we'll have a word with them,' Logan said.

Barker looked ill at ease. His eyes were like little black buttons. 'It ain't good for business to have the police around. Can I stay with you?'

Logan shrugged his big shoulders and said, 'You can knock on the door and introduce us, but then you leave, Mr Barker.'

There were sixteen of them sitting in dark oak captain chairs round the long table in the council chamber. Melanie Biles, one of only two women among fourteen men of various ages and appearance, was at the head of the table. It was a huge chamber, dark with old paintings and haunted by the ghosts of councils past. Melanie, a keen gardener, had introduced a feminine touch with a dozen roses in a vase. Now, the flowers were limp. A scattering of black-edged petals lay on the table. As chair-person of the Leisure and Resources Committee, she occupied the big chair and commanded the attention of the corporate heads that fronted for the modernized council. Above her head was a plaque bearing the names of the former mayors of Havensport. The name of Harvey Reynolds was there a record three times, and the name of his son, Gerald, once. Next year Melanie's name would be added to the list.

For a moment she watched a seagull stretch its wings and take off from the windowsill, riding the currents high above the blue bay. Melanie saw the bird hover outside the window, then suddenly dip away to the water and out of sight. For some odd reason her lunch with Randolph Logan came into her mind. There are men – and Logan was one of them – who have a kind of magic. Exciting things happen around them, and they seem to shape life with their strong hands. The detective was a strangely remote man, but his detached manner was compulsively attractive. Reluctantly, she turned back to the desk.

The controversial subject to be discussed was Moorfield, a

huge area of swampy land that stretched beside the coastal road running eastwards out of Havensport. Since the 1930s, consecutive councils had considered and rejected different plans for the level ground. But now a scheme put forward by a mammoth London organisation appeared to have real substance. It was for the creation of a twenty-first century cross between a theme park and a Butlin-style holiday camp.

Councillor Monica Shelby asked a question in her customary incisive manner. At forty-five, four years Melanie's senior, Monica was formidable, a stocky, severe-looking woman with opaque blue eyes hidden behind heavy glasses. 'Madam Chair. The considerable expense in the necessary draining of Moorfield has on all occasions been a stumbling block to any development. Will Compat Leisure, the people behind this new project, bear the cost of drainage, either in full or in part?'

Bowing her head to shuffle the papers in front of her, Melanie found the one she wanted and held it down with a forefinger. 'Alex Morton of Compat Leisure has assured me that Compat will carry the full cost of draining the land.'

'That sounds good enough for me,' said Larry Petersen, a laid-back youth elected to the council by Havensport's young people solely because he was the drummer in a local pop group.

Studying the young councillor for almost a minute, Melanie looked at each face round the table in turn, then seemed to take them all in at once. She was always alert to the possibility of Petersen's easy-going manner weakening her control. Both nationally and locally, politics had changed drastically in the past few years. Though recognising that modernism had its place in the order of things, she had no intention of sacrificing traditional standards to spin and sophistry.

'I think that we need to have something more concrete than a mere promise,' argued Gerald Reynolds, unconventionally dressed in a white short-sleeved shirt. Still as handsome at forty-seven as he had been when Melanie had first met him ten years ago. As he was unmarried, it was rumoured that he was homosexual. Melanie could testify to the contrary.

As an attractive woman with a husband older than her, Melanie was no stranger to advances from men. Maybe she flirted a little when socialising, but not enough to be taken seriously in the way Gerald Reynolds had.

'I agree with Councillor Reynolds,' Harvey Reynolds said, referring to his own son formally. The father's voice and choice of words had a classic courtroom aura. Facing him brought home to Melanie the enormity of her illicit undertaking. For a long moment there was fear in her throat, dry fear. Reynolds continued. 'I would remind Madam Chair that we are not considering an application from a small-time travelling showman who wants to operate a set of swinging boats on the sands. Compat Leisure can afford to employ legal experts capable of gaining an advantage that will cost our town dear.'

There was a general scuffling in the seats and a subdued buzz of disavowal. Tapping her pencil on the table while waiting for a soft murmuring to fade away, Melanie asked, 'What do you suggest, Councillor Reynolds?'

'I am not suggesting, Madam Chair, I am proposing.' Harvey Reynolds scraped back his chair and got to his feet. He had reached that point in life when ageing proceeds at a gallop. 'We are fortunate that in our county we have some gifted solicitors. I propose that we gather together a small band of the finest, and turn all the legal aspects of this project over to them.'

Reynolds' proposal would be disastrous for Compat Leisure. A group of lawyers would soon discover what the council members didn't know – that if planning permission could be legally granted for the leisure complex at Moorfield then it would involve anything up to ten years of argument and negotiation. Melanie had secretly agreed to help Compat Leisure by duping the council so that planning permission could be had without any delay.

Using humour as a weapon, she said, 'I am not in favour of

quangos or solicitors, Councillor Reynolds. You may be familiar with the old Yiddish tale about the two farmers who each claimed ownership of a particular cow. While one of the farmers was busy pulling at the head and the other was busy tugging on the tail, a lawyer milked the cow.'

This had the assembly laughing, and Larry Petersen laughed loudest. Gerald Reynolds' light brown eyes gazed steadily at Melanie as he mopped his brow. She could see the lines in his face, the ones in his forehead deeper than she remembered. Apart from that one time, Gerald had always behaved correctly towards her. But she sensed that under his thin patina of sophistication, Gerald Reynolds was a dangerous man.

Even so, neither he nor any other man was a threat to her marriage. She had first met Kenneth Biles in her Norfolk home-town. A clergyman's daughter, she had been Blanche Dubois in the local amateur dramatic society's production of Tennessee Williams' *A Streetcar Named Desire*. Kenneth had been in the audience. In retrospect, she was convinced that he had fallen in love with some kind of hybrid Blanche Dubois, and she had been mesmerised romantically by a blue uniform with silver trimmings. Though in the beginning their marriage had had the one-dimensional appearance of a union between a totally unsuited couple, it had gradually gained strength and substance. After her 'moment of madness', as the adulterers and perverts in Parliament referred to their sexual peccadilloes, she had been a faithful and loving wife.

She dragged her wandering mind back to the meeting. She appreciated Harvey Reynolds' concern, as he owned or had controlling shares in the majority of the holiday trade busi-nesses in the resort. Gerald Reynolds ran three of the resort's four nightclubs. The Reynolds publicly disclaimed any connec-tion with the infamous Blue Angel, but it was widely believed that the father and son had at least a vested interest in that sordid nightspot. Melanie's mission would break the hold the Reynolds' dynasty had on Havensport. When the monster-sized leisure complex opened at Moorfield it would rob Harvey Reynolds not only of business revenue, but also the power that meant so much to him.

He quickly returned to the subject. 'We owe it to the people of this town to examine the Compat Leisure project from every angle and in minute detail. We must consider the local businessmen who are here throughout the year, supporting the town through the long, dark winters. What contribution will Compat Leisure make to the economy of Havensport in the eight months of a year in which the sun doesn't shine brightly? I move that the council engage a body of private solicitors to negotiate with Compat Leisure's legal team.'

Gerald Reynolds seconded his father, but the motion was heavily defeated on a show of hands. The discussion was fast losing its momentum. Larry Petersen sat with his eyes closed, head wagging rhythmically to a tune playing inside his head. It was Monica Shelby who brought things back on course.

'I have every confidence in Madam Chair and the sterling work she has put in on this project to date. I believe that she should continue to deal directly with Compat Leisure. When Madam Chair presents this committee with her complete report we can prepare it for passing to the full council. I so move.'

'Yeah, man!' Larry Petersen whooped before beating out a drum roll on the table with the flats of his hands.

'Councillor Petersen,' Melanie said sharply, 'is that some private gig happening at the wrong location, or are you seconding Councillor Shelby's motion?'

'I second the motion,' Petersen answered with a face-dividing grin.

It was put to the vote and, to the immense relief of Melanie, the motion was carried. She could go back to Malcolm Braithwaite to report an initial success. An old friend of Kenneth and hers, the wealthy Braithwaite was the senior partner in a firm of London solicitors, and a director of Compat Leisure.

*

'Does this mean that I may have brought a murderer back here?'

Leanne Rodgers, standing in the chalet's kitchenette making coffee, glanced over her shoulder at Logan and Shelagh, fear on her plain face.

'Not at all,' Logan assured her.

'I bet anything he was married,' Leanne said in self-deprecation, carrying a tray bearing four cups.

'That's not important,' Shelagh said with a kind smile.

'It is to me. I'm always a loser when it comes to men.'

Logan glanced to where the other young woman, Noreen Tait, sat silently twining and untwining her fingers. She was portly, plain and dressed unattractively. Logan came back to Leanne. 'You were with Noreen when you met the man we are asking about, Leanne?'

'Yes,' Leanne replied. 'It was in a club on the seafront. I don't know the name of it.'

'The Ocean,' Noreen volunteered.

'That's it,' Leanne remembered.

'I'm sorry to ask personal questions,' Shelagh apologized, 'but did this become a double date?'

'No, my guy, figuratively speaking, was on his own,' Leanne answered. 'Noreen sort of got off with this other fellow, and we split up.'

'You and this man came back here?'

When Leanne nodded, Logan pressed on. 'What time would you say you arrived here at the chalet?'

'Not long after midnight. This makes me look pretty cheap, doesn't it?' Leanne finished her coffee, placed the cup in the saucer and began gyrating it in slow circles with a forefinger. 'He started coming on really strong when we got here, right from the start. Was I glad when Noreen arrived back.'

'I spoiled things for him,' Noreen said with a nervous smile.

'He said something about two being company and three a crowd, and went off.'

Leanne nodded. 'Thank goodness. He was horrible.'

A frown laddered Shelagh's forehead. 'What time was this?'

'That he left? I don't suppose he was here for half an hour before Noreen came back.'

'So he was gone from here before one o'clock?' Logan checked.

'Oh yes, definitely.'

'You are both certain of that?'

'I am,' Leanne said.

'So am I,' Noreen supported her.

'Please, both of you be absolutely certain,' Shelagh urged.

'We're certain,' the two young women said in unison.

'What about the guy you met, Noreen?' Logan asked, his voice softening.

A rueful Noreen made an admission. 'Even if I'd wanted to bring him back here I didn't get the chance. There was this blonde girl there, making an exhibition of herself.'

'He went off with her?' Shelagh tried to conceal her frantic interest.

'I suppose so. She went out of the club, and he went off after her.'

'Tell us about this blonde girl,' Logan urged.

Covertly watching Logan, Shelagh was impressed by the penetrating depth of a casual glance from his eyes. She recognized that it came from years of law enforcement and detection, of being on the raw-nerved edge of the hostile ground between the police and the rest of society. In the company of Detective Inspector Randolph Logan she felt herself to be an inadequate novice.

'There's not much to tell.' Noreen shrugged.

'Do you remember what she was wearing?' Shelagh prompted.

'Not really. Something clinging. It could have been a white dress – no, it was yellow.'

Surreptitiously exchanging glances with Logan, Shelagh took her cue from his nod. 'What can you tell us about this man you met, Noreen?'

'Nothing, really. He didn't spend enough time with me to even give me his name.'

'Was he on holiday?'

'Yes, he did say that he was, but he didn't say where he was from.'

'Any accent?'

Turning to reply to Logan's question, Noreen said, 'Probably London, but I'm not good at that sort of thing. He had one of those tight haircuts, you know, like the Mitchell brothers on *EastEnders*.'

Logan was at a loss, but Shelagh signalled to him that she understood. 'Did he come back into the club, Noreen?'

'Not while I was there, which wasn't long.'

Thanking the two teachers for their help, Logan and Shelagh went out of the chalet. Going to the car with the fast stride of a soldier, Logan unlocked the doors and they were getting in when he enquired. 'Would you say that we have just made progress, Sergeant?'

Chewing lightly on her lip, Shelagh answered dubiously, 'If establishing that one suspect is firmly in the frame and gaining another suspect is progress, then we've made progress, guv.'

'With the right training, Sergeant, you could become as cynical as I am,' Logan grinned at her. 'How tired are you, Shelagh?'

'Are you asking if I'm up to paying a visit to the Ocean club this evening?'

'I'm asking.'

'Then you've got yourself a date, guv.'

When the doors of the Blue Angel closed at midnight, Ed Bellamy had two more hours on duty inside the club. Though oblivious to the gyrations of lap-dancers with lusty figures, the tinny music did grate against his eardrums. He was as tired as a dog. Last night had been a practically sleepless one for him. Bothered by weird wide-awake dreams, he had been greatly troubled by what seemed to be a series of half-memories popping into his mind. He had seen the seashore on a moonless night. A beautiful naked girl walking towards the water. Perfect breasts rounded to perfection; long slender legs.

It had all gone out of his head by morning. But Mrs Fleming had brought it back by scaring him with her complaint about sand in his room. Hearing that a girl's body had been found on the beach, Ed had known he was somehow connected. But not seriously so. Though each successive spliff now had a drastic effect on his powers of recall, Ed knew that he wasn't capable of doing anything really bad.

Going to the bar, Ed gratefully accepted the double whiskey that Lofty the bartender, who was fifty but looked a couple of decades older, had ready for him. About to rest both elbows on the bar, Ed jerked upright. He was so pooped that he was likely to nod off.

Then he noticed a young guy standing at the bar to his right. His close haircut brought memories flooding back to Ed. This guy had been dancing with the lovely blonde girl. Jesus H. Christ! Ed exclaimed inside his head. The blonde girl was with the shaven-headed guy now.

Sensing Ed's eyes on her, the blonde turned her head to him. He released a mighty sigh of relief. It wasn't the same girl. This kid was unkempt and her crumpled clothes advertised that she had been sleeping rough. Putting a hand on the peeling plastic handbag on the counter in front of her, she smiled shyly at Ed. Becoming aware of the girl's interest, Shaved Head turned bodily to face Ed, and said, 'Hi. I saw you at the Ocean last night.' He held out his right hand and introduced himself. 'Rick Downton.'

'Ed Bellamy,' Ed said, shaking the proffered hand.

Putting an arm round the blonde, Downton moved her

nearer to Ed. She was watching him closely, her breath held so deeply in her chest that her modest-sized breasts threatened to burst through the soiled fabric of her dress. 'This is Norma.'

'Hi, Norma.'

'Hi, yourself.' She beamed a come-on smile at him. 'I've been wanting to meet you.' She made a humble and ashamed motion with her hands over the creased dress. 'I'm sorry that I look so untidy.'

Ed saw that she had the delicately boned kind of face that went with small boobs. Girls with large chests often have coarse faces. Nature loves to play games. She was holding a glass of orange juice, and for a moment Ed thought she was wearing a wedding band on her finger. Then he saw that it was a cheap amusement-arcade ring with a poorly executed fleur-de-lis design in some kind of blue paste.

'I'm really glad to meet you, Ed,' Rick Downton said fervently. He acted like their meeting was the start of something big. Narrowing his eyes, he shook his head. 'Last night was a right bummer. You must be as shit-scared as I am about being picked up by the police.'

'Why would I be?' Ed asked, mystified.

Downton gave a stiff-lipped grin. 'That little blonde raver. We both fancied her, but you were quicker off the mark than me.'

Everything, almost everything, became clear to Ed, and he was shaken. He could remember following the girl, remember seeing her step out of the yellow dress, remember getting down from the flat rock with the intention of joining her in the sea. But that was where his recall ended.

Downton studied Ed, shocked at the uncomfortable expression on his face. He said consolingly, 'Don't worry about it, Ed. Now we can back each other up. You saw that guy lurking under the pier, didn't you?'

'Very indistinctly. I just knew there was someone hanging around there.'

Pushing his unfinished drink away from him on the wet teakwood bar, Ed was aware of a man standing a short distance away. For a moment he thought that he was looking at the guy who managed the Ocean club down on the seafront. Glancing his way, Ed found his gaze met by a pair of reckless, challenging brown eyes. He was young, a tough-looking guy with a hollow face, thick black hair worn long, and the rangy nervousness of a wire-taut body. He had on an expensive silk shirt and jeans.

'I got a good look at him,' Rick Downton continued. 'I can give the filth a description of him if they try to pin anything on either of us. I'm sure I know him from somewhere.'

'He was probably some perv down here on holiday,' Ed said dismissively. The dark stranger was taking a real interest in them.

'I don't think so.' Norma pressed a clenched fist into her stomach and her breath seemed caught in her throat. She had spotted the long-haired man and seemed to recognize him. Then she cancelled the thought with a little shake of her head. 'From what Rick told me I think I know who it was. I was going to point him out to Rick tomorrow.'

A doll-like petite girl came up to them. A tall black boy was with her, his arm round her slender waist. She asked, 'Mistaken about what, Norma?'

'What I was telling you about earlier, Julie.'

Mystified, Julie enquired, 'What were you telling me earlier?'

'It doesn't matter now.'

'It couldn't have been important then,' Julie shrugged. 'Are you going home tonight, Norma? I think you should, you know. I feel really sorry for your mum and dad – frantic with worry about you. Pete's walking me home, and you can come with us if you like.'

Norma raised her arm to peer at a wristwatch that was as shoddy as her ring. She spoke hesitantly. 'I don't know what to do, Julie. It's nearly quarter to one. I don't want to spend another night in the park. I was really frightened on my own last night.'

'You must have been,' Downton sympathized, 'and you were taking a hell of a chance with a murderer on the loose.' He put a hand on Ed's shoulder. 'You couldn't help Norma out just for tonight, could you, my friend? She's left home because her parents are too strict. I can't help her because I stay with an aunt here. It's a free holiday, but the old dear cramps my style.'

'Sorry, I have a dragon of a landlady who won't allow visitors.'

'That's a pity,' Rick said. 'I'll walk you home, Norma. You'll just have to make your peace with your mum and dad.'

The blonde girl's lips protruded in a dubious expression. 'That ain't going to be easy, but I don't seem to have any other choice.' She turned to her friend. 'It's OK, Julie. Rick will walk me home. You go on.'

Kissing Norma on the cheek, the petite girl said, 'See ya,' took another sly look at Ed and then walked off with the tall boy.

There was the sound of glass shattering, and then voices were raised angrily. Ed excused himself to his two new friends. 'That's my cue. I've got to go.'

Delaying him for a moment with a hand on his arm, Downton said urgently, 'We should get together, Ed, as we're going to need each other. Can you call on me sometime – I'm staying at 33 Newent Road.'

'I'll try,' Ed said as he moved away towards where a group of men were now fighting.

Feeling the curl of his fingers, iron-hard against the palms of his hands, he smiled inwardly, not allowing the smile to show on his face. As he approached casually, the four men fighting each other became, as Ed knew from experience that they would, allies who regarded him as their enemy. The one nearest to Ed threw a clumsy right-hand punch at him. Grasping his assailant's wrist with both hands, Ed yanked hard on it, pulling the man forward, off balance. He was a young guy, body-soft from office work, and Ed saw his eyes go wide and scared for a brief instant. Then Ed bent his arm and drove his elbow hard into the other's face. It smashed the nose instantly wide and flat in a crimson splash. The man slumped, unconscious, but Ed grabbed him by the jacket to prevent him from hitting the ground.

Ed kicked the bars of the fire doors, and they flew open into a dark alleyway. Throwing the man out, Ed turned to find the other three men coming at him. Twisting sideways, he took some of the force from a blow to the jaw. He backhanded one of them so hard that he went out through the doors headlong, to collapse in a limp heap with his head cracking against the hard ground outside.

But the other two men pounced on him. Kneed in the groin, he doubled over and was caught hard by the heel of a hand up under his chin. Going down, he was in serious trouble. Both of his remaining attackers were putting the boot in when they were knocked sideways, away from him. Scrambling up onto one knee, Ed saw a blur of movement as his rescuer swiftly and completely dismantled a man with a series of hard blows, using his hands like dull cleavers.

With Ed now back on his feet, the man who had helped him stood back so that Ed could deal with his sole surviving assailant. Standing facing Ed, he was aged about thirty and in poor physical shape. He would be soft in the belly, Ed knew. His type always were. One blow to the guts and they were completely wrecked.

The man backed off a step. The artificial lighting glistened on a tear that rolled down his cheek. But an impassive Ed would show no mercy. These pretend-tough guys shouldn't start what they couldn't finish. Taking one quick step forward he screwed a hard punch deep into the man's midriff. The man screamed like a girl in his agony, and Ed bent over to catch him on his shoulder as he doubled up. Swinging round, Ed let the momentum propel the man out into the alley. He heard him being violently sick as he closed the fire doors and barred them.

Turning, he recognized his helper as the black-haired man who had been at the bar. Ed extended his right hand, saying, 'Thanks.'

Ed could feel the calloused ridge along the side of the hand that he held. It marked the man as a martial arts expert who exercised daily to keep the edges of his hands like steel. The Japanese had a name for the hard ridge – 'death-giver'.

'It was my pleasure.' The long-haired man shook Ed's hand, replying with a tight grin that gave his words a double meaning.

Undecided for a moment, Ed then said, 'I first want to check on a couple of friends at the bar, then I'll buy you a drink.'

'There's no need,' the black-haired man said. His smile didn't alter the hard set of his face or the coldness of his eyes.

Desperate for a toke, Ed lit up on his way back to the bar. The smoke from just one more spliff would go unnoticed in the heavy air of the Blue Angel. As he hungrily inhaled, a grey haze started to hem Ed in, stripping him of conscious thought. Then everything seemed to snap into place and his mind was crystal clear. Now he could remember the early hours of that morning in detail. From the girl doing her raunchy dance to her impromptu one-garment striptease on the beach. But still his memory refused to go past that point. His mind went kind of speckly and then completely blank, the way a videotape does when it runs out.

He scanned the bar area for Downton and Norma, but they had disappeared. Startled by this, Ed turned to look in the black-haired man's direction. He, too, had vanished.

five

I t was late in the evening when they went in through the pretentious mock-gilded double doors of the Ocean club. For Logan it was like landing on an alien planet. The building was a modern slab of polished concrete and blue-toned glass. It was crowded, the air was stuffy with perfume and body heat, and the loud music was close to intolerable. Couples writhed on a cramped dance floor. Together, but separated by modern dance, their movements were oddly convulsive, very sexual but at the same time impersonal. The assembly was happily homogenized in the close give-and-take of clubland. A few girls weren't dancing but stood as onlookers, minor attendant-goddesses.

Leaning close to Shelagh to compete with the thump-thump of music, Logan said, 'I've always preferred the behaviour of peasants to that of the aristocracy, Sergeant. Right now I'm not so sure.'

Laughing, Shelagh shouted back, 'Whose side will you be on when the revolution comes, guv?'

'My own,' he answered laconically.

Weaving through the dancers, they reached a small office that was partitioned from the rest of the club by glass. Gerald Reynolds was sitting behind a desk inside. He stood as Logan and Shelagh walked in.

Resplendent in a velvet tuxedo, a lace shirt and a drooping bow-tie, the club owner's face wore a suspicious expression as the two police officers walked softly across the carpeted, brightly lit room. Then Reynolds put square, brilliant-white teeth on show in a welcoming smile.

'I'm glad we found you here, sir,' Logan said.

'You couldn't miss me, Inspector.' Reynolds grinned. 'You know the old proverb – people in glass houses might just as well answer the door. I like to keep an eye on things. Drugs have become a matter of great concern in this game.'

'They would need to be on something to enjoy this abuse of music.' Logan pulled a face.

'It's an acquired taste, Inspector,' Reynolds said with a little chuckle. 'Sadly, the days of Dean Martin and Perry Como are long gone. Days that would mean nothing to your young assistant.' He looked at Shelagh, waiting.

'Sorry,' Logan apologized. 'This is Detective Sergeant Ruby, who has just transferred from the Met. Sergeant Ruby, this is Councillor Gerald Reynolds.'

'A charming addition to the local force,' Reynolds complimented Shelagh.

Logan waited for his sergeant to respond. She was a real looker with the kind of presence that actresses try to imitate and can't. Her teeth were big, big and white. They gave her full-lipped mouth an additional prominence. He had noticed how her smile brought out dimples that stayed buried most of the time. But she didn't smile now, and Logan was disappointed. A platitude is a great icebreaker, and has the best effect when spoken by an attractive woman. All she came back with was a neutral, 'Thank you, sir.'

An affable Reynolds asked, 'Now, permit me to get you both a drink. It has to be only television cops who never drink on duty.'

Going straight to a drinks cabinet, he poured a brandy for each of them. The bouquet filled the summer-heated air for a second. Reynolds went on, 'I assume your visit is not unconnected with the death of that unfortunate girl?'

'It is, Councillor Reynolds. It seems likely that she was here at your club last evening.'

'That's quite possible, Inspector.' Reynolds gave a slight shrug. 'But noticing a particular individual in a holiday business is a no-no.'

'This girl would be especially noticeable,' Shelagh put in.

'Blonde, good-looking, with a superb figure,' Logan added.

'I wouldn't have noticed.' Reynolds made this a half apology. 'But Terry, Terry Stevens who runs this place for me, may well have seen her. I'll get him.'

Reynolds was eager to divert the questioning to someone else. For all his charm and sophistication, there were occasional holes through which Logan glimpsed a man who was not so sure of himself as he appeared to be. At times a slight hesitation betrayed that something was wrong at the centre of the man.

Reynolds pressed a button on his desk. Though Logan heard no sound over the throbbing music, the man Reynolds had summoned arrived quickly. With dark hair worn long, he was of average height, a quiet man with a powerful musculature, and a lean, intelligent face.

Stevens had dark blue eyes that turned black as he looked at Logan when Reynolds introduced them. Yet despite this odd feature, Stevens had an unexpected easy friendliness and an easy tongue. Shelagh commenced the questioning.

'We have been told, Mr Stevens,' she began, 'that a blonde girl with striking good looks was here at the Ocean last night. She would have been prominent, and possibly wore a yellow dress.'

'I remember her.' Stevens gave an emphatic nod. He had not even glanced at Shelagh. 'She was a right little self-promoter.'

'You didn't know her?' Shelagh asked.

'Last night was the first time I'd ever laid eyes on her.'

Logan asked a question in his oblique style. 'Did you happen to see who she left with?'

'She went out of here alone, Inspector. But two blokes went

out after her, separately. The second one was a kid with what we used to call a crew cut. He's been coming in for close to a week and I'd put him down as a grockle, a holidaymaker.'

'You don't know his name?'

'Not really, but I think I've heard others call him Rick,' Stevens replied. 'He was taking a chance with the guy who went out right after the blonde left.'

'You know this other man?'

Stevens gave a shake of his head. 'Not know him as such. I do know that he's the bouncer up at the Blue Angel, a real hard nut.'

'Did the girl or either of the two men come back into the club afterwards?' Shelagh asked.

'I wouldn't know,' Stevens answered. 'I went off duty at that time. Rex Tablan, the under-manager, took over from me. I can let you have his home address if you'd like to speak to him.'

'I don't think he could tell us anything. Thank you, Mr Stevens, you've been very helpful,' Logan said.

'We wouldn't want anything to reflect badly on the Ocean or our other clubs,' Reynolds said. 'We'll co-operate with any enquiries.'

Logan shook Reynolds by the hand. 'Thank you, Councillor Reynolds, your assistance is very much appreciated.'

Shelagh gave the councillor no more than a curt nod in parting. They cut themselves a new route through the dancers and out into the sweet coolness of the breeze floating in from the bay. Shelagh had noticed that the dusk came in from the sea here; it did not descend from the sky as it did in London. The balmy languid softness of summer twilight gave them a false feeling of freshness. In contrast to the discordant blare of music they had just escaped from, the sounds of choir practice coming from a church across the road had a sedating effect. Even so, Shelagh was eager to make an observation.

'It struck me that Stevens must have a reason for remembering the girl so well, guv,' she suggested.

'Probably a sorority thing, Sergeant.'

'You mean he's ...?' Shelagh was taken aback. 'He looked a tough kind of guy to me, guv.'

Logan gave a half shrug. 'That doesn't mean a lot, Sergeant. They can either sing or fight. It's worth remembering, Sergeant, that the strong are sometimes dangerous, but the weak are invariably ruthless. Let's concentrate on identifying the girl, and then we'll take another look at Stevens, and pay a visit to this bouncer who keeps cropping up.'

It was night, with Havensport coming into its nether with the hint of menace darkness always brought to the countryside. A fox became trapped in the headlights of the Mercedes SL. Slowing the car, Melanie temporarily switched off the lights. Freed from the mesmerising beams, the red-furred animal raced across the road and vanished. Accelerating, Melanie glanced fearfully in the driving mirror. She shuddered on seeing the headlights behind her in the distance. The other car was still following, keeping well back. It was too much to be coincidence at midnight on a country road.

She had become aware of the headlights only minutes after leaving Radley Chase, the home of Malcolm and Madge Braithwaite. To Melanie it was a tragedy that the Braithwaites shared their lovely house separately and not as a couple. Their social status was all that kept them together. Was there a point in every marriage when the loving stopped and the hating began? Would it happen to her and Kenneth? Had it started to happen now?

She had sat beside Madge on the balcony sipping champagne from goblets that were expensively heavy and cumbersome. They had been serenaded by the delightfully tuneful splashing of a miniature stream tumbling into a pool encased in bamboo and stone in the Japanese garden below.

Malcolm had been delighted to hear about the preliminary moves Melanie had made at that evening's council meeting. He had the looks of a 1940s matinee idol. His sprightly white hair was close-cut; his brown face was lean with a straight high-boned nose, a square jaw and a stubborn chin. What could have been an intimidating ruggedness was diffused by a pair of somehow sad, compassionate green eyes. He was a closet womanizer, but had never bothered Melanie in that way. She knew now that he had other plans for her exploitation.

For the first time they had discussed face-to-face Melanie's abuse of her elected office. It had been uncomfortable. People found it easier to lie and cheat on the telephone, when their body language couldn't be observed.

An anxious Malcolm had voiced his worries. 'Most ideas look good on paper, Melanie. Once you put them into practice all the gremlins appear. Can we trust Wenzell Carmen to cut whatever corners it is necessary to cut, Melanie?'

'Of course. I'm absolutely certain that he can,' Melanie had replied, adding, 'We're dealing with the council's chief planning officer, Malcolm.'

Braithwaite had given a nod of agreement. 'I know that we have the top man on our side, Melanie, and this is reflected in the sum of money that Compat is paying him. How can we be sure that he won't come back again and again for more money?'

'He won't. Wenzell is a pretty straight guy with an extravagant wife. You are paying him enough to get him out of the debt she got him into. That's all he's looking for,' Melanie heard someone say, and was horrified to identify the voice as hers. It sounded like a clip from a television documentary on corruption, not the words of a woman of principle who had until recently cherished her honesty, particularly in service to the public.

Deceit, dishonour and distrust had begun to erode what had been her ideal life, eating away the armour of illusion that had always protected her. Braithwaite was blackmailing her, but Melanie kept telling herself that she was simply repaying an enormous debt that was long overdue. Probably Kenneth wouldn't see it that way, which was why she hadn't told him. She regarded that as being kind to her husband, not deceiving him. He needed shielding from unnecessary worry. Of late Kenneth had seemed curiously aged. His face was grey and his voice had an old tiredness.

Since that awful night three years ago, Kenneth and Melanie had owed Malcolm Braithwaite everything. Kenneth, who had been over the limit when leaving Malcolm Braithwaite's party to mark the end of his period as under-sheriff, had been driving when the late-night car crash occurred. Just a mile along from where she was now, the car had veered across the road to collide head-on with a vehicle coming the other way. Melanie and her husband had escaped with minor bruising, but a teenage boy and girl in the other car had been badly injured. The accident would have ended Kenneth's police career had it not been for Malcolm. He had taken care of everything, somehow securing the silence of the injured youngsters. Before daylight, both of the wrecked cars had been spirited secretly away and the truth of the accident had gone with them.

Driving slowly, Melanie tried to get a reassuring glimpse of the town, but the hills and irregular shorelines hid it from her. She felt terribly alone in the world as she passed a row of cottages that were in darkness. There were a number of rough farm roads off to the left, and round stones from one of them skidded under her wheels as she went over a rise. Being with the Braithwaites had put her on edge. She was out of her depth with them in every conceivable way. A line of dark shops snuggled beside a brightly lit pub that a litter of parked cars suckled round. Melanie felt better for that sign of life. Slowing before coming to what she knew was a rough surface, she concentrated as the road curved and dropped and rose again.

She could see her home up ahead now, a Victorian house with mullioned Gothic windows about a Renaissance doorway. There were no lights in the windows. With her husband away from home at a conference, Melanie had misgivings about going into the empty house that stood alone and lonely. The twin headlights were still following, unnerving her.

The car joggled and complained as she accelerated over the rough gravel of the drive. Guiding the vehicle in through a Tudor arch she entered the garage through automatic doors. Switching off the car's ignition, she sat in the new silence, waiting, momentarily unable to move. Then she scrambled from the car and hurried out into the night. She was just in time to see headlights switched off, fading into the darkness further down the cliff road.

It was still hot, but at least it was night and the air was breathable again. Despite the humidity, the house felt terribly cold when she went in. It was as if nobody had lived there for a long time, and the place had died while she'd been gone.

Locking the door behind her and resetting the alarms, she still felt uneasy.

Agreeing to perform what amounted to criminal acts for Malcolm Braithwaite had her feeling frighteningly insecure. She needed to talk to someone. Not to make a confession, but just to know that there was somebody strong on whom she could rely if everything went wrong.

Going into Kenneth's office, she flicked through his file of telephone numbers. She came to the one she wanted: 'DI R. Logan.' What was she doing? The Compat Leisure thing was unhinging her mind. She was deeply ashamed to realize her motive for ringing Logan. Aware that she was stupidly confusing love with desire, Melanie made a failed attempt at controlling her impetuosity. Frighteningly, events were beginning to overtake her. She thought illogically: Logan would be able to make everything in the world right for her.

Though an adept councillor, her emotions, not her intellect, would always be her mistress. Blind trust and dumb devotion to Kenneth was no longer enough. She hesitantly jabbed out the number with a forefinger. Only a few seconds passed before

Logan picked up the phone at his end and identified himself, his tone as frosty as Norway in January.

'I'm so sorry to trouble you at this late hour. It's Melanie Biles.' Her voice sounded oddly mechanical to her. It had the stiff self-consciousness of a telephone answering machine.

'Is there some kind of trouble, Mrs Biles?'

'No, not really,' she replied hesitantly. 'I've just driven home, and I was followed all the way.'

'Is the chief constable there?'

'No, he's away at the conference in Birmingham.'

'Is whoever followed you outside?' Logan asked, evidently wide awake now.

'No, the car stopped down near the bottom of the cliff road.'

'I can drive over if you're frightened.'

Melanie couldn't speak for a moment. Logan's innate diffidence, so alluring and so unusual in a modern man, came through in his tone. She was tempted, and was ashamed of it. She said quickly, too quickly, 'No, no, the house is secure. But thank you for offering.'

'I'll leave the offer open,' Logan said. 'If you are at all worried, just give me a ring.'

'That's very kind of you,' she told him gratefully. Then the collective disappointments of the past, the unfinished conversations and the lost opportunities in her life caught up with her, and she heard herself say, 'Maybe you'll have time to call out here in the morning just to check.'

What had made her say such a thing? It was so forward, so blatantly obvious. Her face felt hot and she had the ludicrous idea that Logan could see her blushing. There was silence on the line, and she began to fret. Though he wasn't a man who showed his feelings, Logan was no fool. The message she had given couldn't have been clearer. Then she caught an intake of breath at the other end of the line.

'I'll make the time to call,' Logan said in a flat tone. 'Goodnight, Mrs Biles.'

*

Winston Howard noticed that the wind had changed, from north-east round to south-west, the rain-bringer. But it didn't necessarily mean that there would be so much as a shower. By nine o'clock the wind would probably veer back as it often did. You got to learn this sort of thing when you are an early riser. As assistant caretaker at Havensport Comprehensive School, he began his first shift at five thirty. He liked the early morning when there were no other people around breathing the same air as he breathed.

The grey sky was still greasy with leftover night and the resort of Havensport was sleeping with all its bare bones showing. But he saw no ugliness in the town at this hour. Later, when the sky was brilliant blue and the streets and beach were packed with noisy invaders was when the place became an obscenity for Winston. He agreed with the slogans scrawled on walls and wooden hoardings in chalk and marker pen each summer – 'Don't worry. It will be all over by September.'

He passed along Stewart Road. Windows stared blank-eyed at him. Neat houses sat on their patches of lawn, and the lawns were bleached white as a winter snowfall. Maybe he was biased because he had lived there throughout the thirty-one years of his marriage, but the Clement Estate was the most pleasant and orderly part of town.

Planning the morning's work in his head, he was turning a corner when he noticed that something wasn't as it should be. It took him a little while to realize that the trimmed hedge bordering the garden of a house had been damaged. Several feet of stiff green leaves and branches had been crushed inwards. Vandals, Howard angrily decided as he stopped to take a look at the damage.

Then he stepped quickly back, saying something in a whisper but not using words. A girl in a tight summer dress of thin material was half lying in the gap of the hedge. Supported by the bushes, it appeared that she had collapsed against the hedge in a drunken state. But the girl wasn't drunk. Her head was turned so that she faced him, and she was peering at Howard with the half-lidded stare of a corpse.

Up on top of the cliff was a different soil, a different life, and a surprisingly invigorating air. Logan had purposefully left his car in a picnic area and was walking the short distance to where the chief constable's house stood loftily alone and lonely. Logan avoided closely examining his reason for walking so far. Maybe he wanted to delay, or even avoid, his arrival. Deep down he knew that accepting Melanie Biles' invitation to visit could be a mistake that would have grave consequences. He had long sensed that the Biles marriage was a myth woven of very flimsy fabric.

He took a shortcut to the house along a narrow path. On each side of him was a drunken, absurd confusion of tiny yellow flowers and small yellow butterflies. He could see Melanie in the garden. Back to him, she was sitting on her heels weeding a flowerbed. Unaware of his approach, she was whistling the opening bars of 'Anitra's Danse'. Without thinking, Logan answered, his soft whistle like an echo that gained resonance on the quiet air of morning.

She stood and turned to him, raising a hand to shield her eyes from the sun. 'My goodness,' she exclaimed, 'a cultured policeman, and one who appreciates Greig!'

'Not exactly a fan,' he warned.

Holding a bunch of weeds in one hand, she had on blue shorts and a brief halter to match. Working in the garden had not disturbed the perfection of her hair, and she had a recently picked red rose over her left ear. Bending, she put the handful of weeds on the ground, exposing above the waistband of her shorts the startling whiteness of untanned skin against that which had been sun-kissed. Disciplining himself, Logan looked away.

'It was good of you to come,' she said as she straightened up to face him.

'I wanted to be sure that you were safe.'

'There was no problem,' she said, smiling. 'It was a comfort to know that someone who would look after me was no more than a telephone call away.'

Logan's mouth tightened. She was cracking the hard veneer of his cool poise. 'That could well soon prove not to be near enough, Mrs Biles.'

'Melanie. What happened to Melanie?' she chided him.

An aircraft roared overhead, its white trail a ruler-drawn straight line across an expanse of blue. Logan delayed speaking until the noise of the plane faded.

'I can't give you anything like the necessary protection unless you make this official.'

'I've told you that is out of the question!' Melanie's eyes danced as she looked at him. 'My former lover is a violent man.'

'You have it wrong, Melanie,' Logan said.

'In what way?'

'I checked with the Kent police,' Logan explained. 'Brian Amhurst is in a hospice. He's been there for the past four months, so it isn't him who has been following you.'

'It couldn't be anyone else.' She was badly shaken, alarmed.

Taking a rake from where it was leaning against a rose bush, she lay it flat. 'Let's go into the house and I'll make us coffee.' Her eyes crinkled a little. 'You do have time, don't you?'

'I have the time,' he said solemnly, 'but I think it would be something that we'd both regret.'

They stood perfectly still and stared at each other. There was a silence between them, an unpleasant silence. It hardened, it congealed, it became an attitude. There was something primitive in it, almost hostile. Logan could sense that she was as puzzled by it as he was.

Melanie broke the menacing silence with the cutest little

laugh. 'I'm hopeless with quotes, Inspector, but someone once said that if life isn't lived dangerously it is not worth living.'

'Nevertheless ...' Logan began, stopping when the mobile phone buzzed in his pocket.

'Saved by the bell,' she muttered in a dull, flat tone. She caught her breath and raised her eyes to him. Her look was bleak and unhappy and seemed to say: 'I'm making a bloody fool of myself and I know it.'

It was Shelagh calling him. 'Norma Harrington has turned up, guv.'

'Dead?' he enquired, already knowing the answer.

'Yes, guv. She was found at the end of her road. It looks like a hit-and-run, but the traffic boys aren't happy for some reason.'

'I'll be right there,' Logan told his sergeant.

He was putting the telephone back into his pocket when Melanie kissed her finger, then touched the finger to his cheek. She gave what could have been an apologetic shrug. 'Don't think badly of me, Randy. I'd ask you to try to understand me, but that wouldn't be fair, because I don't understand myself.'

'Were you first on the scene, Constable?' Logan asked a young uniformed officer.

'Yes, sir, me'n Trevor, Constable Slattern, sir,' the officer replied, using a thumb to indicate a constable who was moving on some would-be sightseers.

'I understand that you don't think it was a hit-and-run,' Logan said as he saw Simon Betts' head come out through the flap of a small plastic tent that had been constructed against the hedge. The head twisted this way and that, spotted Logan and Shelagh, and then the rest of Betts crawled out like an animal from its lair.

'I'm not sure, sir. Several things don't add up. There are no tyre marks, not even on the kerb. To knock the girl into the hedge with such force the car would have needed to mount the pavement.'

Logan studied the pavement and gave a nod of agreement. 'How did you come to identify the dead girl so quickly?'

'The man who found her, a Mr Howard, was a neighbour who recognized her, sir.'

'I see.' Logan nodded as he awaited the approaching pathologist, who was holding a clipboard with a report sheet attached.

'Late nights and early mornings,' Betts complained, his eyes red and bleary behind the glasses. 'I took a hot shower and a cold shower but that didn't work.'

'Too much social life,' Logan told him.

Betts snorted. 'A doctor's social life, Randolph, is trying to enjoy a quiet drink while some silly bitch tells you about her hysterectomy.'

'Funny you should mention that …' a mock-serious Shelagh said.

'Don't ridicule me, Sergeant Ruby, please show compassion,' Betts pleaded exaggeratedly. 'I was a premature baby, and premature children are always nervous children. We start life at a disadvantage.'

'You've had plenty of time to grow out of it,' Logan remarked.

'We never quite get over it, never.'

'What have we got, Simon?' Logan asked to bring the pathologist back on track.

'Cause of death definitely a broken neck.'

'Could it have been a hit-and-run?'

With a slow shake of his head, Betts answered. 'That's a possibility, Randy, but a remote one. The way her neck is broken could only have been caused by the most freakish accident. Do you want to see her?'

'We'd better take a look,' Logan said gruffly.

Waiting to allow a lab technician in white overalls to come out of the tent, Logan bent over and went in with Shelagh close behind him. Though the shapely body dressed in a soiled dress and cardigan was that of a mature woman, the body looked almost schoolgirlish.

Noticing that Betts' head had come in through the flap of the tent behind them, Logan enquired, 'Do the stains on her dress mean anything, Simon?'

'Not really, Randy. They come from her having lived rough for a while. I'd say she hadn't been near soap and water or a toothbrush for twenty-four hours or more.'

'What about underclothing?' Shelagh asked.

'In place and intact,' Betts reported. 'Just a poor little kid, isn't she? This is what the worthies of the courtroom don't see – the judge, jury, witnesses, defending counsel. Maybe if they all came and took a look first hand, then we'd see less arguing on points of law and more justice.'

'I never had you down as a philosopher, Simon,' Logan remarked as all three of them went out of the tent to stand in the bright dazzling sun of a new day. Not many people were on the street now. 'Is there anything to connect her death with that of the girl on the beach?'

'Not on the face of it, my dear Randolph. One being naked and the other fully dressed means only that the first one had been skinny-dipping. Can I move her?'

'Yes,' Logan said, nodding.

They were silent for a while, and then Logan said, 'We'd better go and inform the parents, Sergeant.'

For one small moment Shelagh looked terribly unhappy. Most people could get through life by being both child and adult. That privilege was denied the police officer, who had at all times to wear all the accoutrements of worldliness. Logan was aware that his sergeant wasn't one of the shallow people he often envied – those who skimmed through life unfeeling, taking and not giving. Police work had to be hard for her.

She said limply, 'This is one bit of unfinished business I wish we could leave unfinished.'

'It helps if you put death into perspective, Sergeant,' Simon Betts advised, having noticed her distress. 'Most of us have got it wrong. People do nice things for the dead that they wouldn't do for the living. But in my job I see death as clean and anti-septic. It puts an end to all your troubles. Someone gathers up your belongings, the clergyman who never knew you lies about what a great person you were, and that's it.'

Shelagh made no reply. She was too choked up to do so.

SiX

I t was early in the morning and there were few customers in the supermarket. Carrying two bars of chocolate, her excuse for being there, Detective Sergeant Shelagh Ruby walked to where Julie Bolt sat vacant-eyed at a deserted checkout. Reaching for the chocolate bars robot-like, and sliding them along over a barcode reader, the pretty girl didn't raise her head.

'Ninety pence, please,' she said mechanically, looking up at Shelagh, listlessly at first and then becoming distressed as she recognized the policewoman. 'Is it true what I've heard?'

'About Norma Harrington? Yes, I'm afraid it is. I am very sorry, Julie.'

It was so quiet in the big store, so tense, that when a nearby cabinet fridge clicked on they both gave an involuntary little jump. When the hum of the motor reached them they relaxed a little.

For a moment Shelagh thought that the girl was going to burst into tears. That would be too much after seeing the bereaved mother collapse into hysteria, crying and screaming, sinking to the floor in a flabby, grey-topped huddle. Her head had dropped on to her drooping bosom like a branch snapped suddenly from a tree. The father had shown no reaction whatsoever, but had made a pot of tea for everyone as if it was an ordinary morning on which a couple of visitors had casually dropped in. Shelagh still hadn't decided which of the two behaviour extremes of the dead girl's parents had been the most traumatic to witness. Had the poised, capable DI Logan not been there to take control of things, Shelagh wouldn't have been able to handle the situation.

Pulling herself together with an obvious effort, Julie said, 'I was worried when she didn't come into work this morning. Norma told me that she was going home last night.'

'You saw her last night, Julie?'

'Yes, she was at the Blue Angel,' Julie answered.

'The two of you were together?' Shelagh asked.

'No.' Julie gave a small shake of her head. 'I was with a boy, and so was Norma.'

'Was she with this doorman you said she was after?'

'No. Her and the boy she was with were talking to him, but he was still working.'

'Do you know the boy Norma was with?'

'Yes, he's from London. He said that he was walking Norma home,' Julie replied, looking straight at Shelagh, who noticed that the girl couldn't quite focus her eyes. The effects of tragic news were many and varied. 'That's why I didn't worry for her. Now I wish that I'd stayed with her.'

'Do you know where this boy is staying, Julie?'

'Oh, yes. His name is Rick Downton, and he's staying with his auntie,' Julie said as a woman with a loaded shopping trolley came up behind Shelagh. 'His aunt, Mrs Wilmott, is a regular customer here. She lives in Newent Road. I don't know the number, but it's the last house on the left.'

'Thank you, Julie.'

As Shelagh walked away, her mind made a connection between the 'Rick' who had gone out of the Ocean club after the blonde girl found dead on the beach, and 'Rick Downton' who had last night been with the local girl found dead that morning.

Jason Fulton's mannerisms were camp, and he wore a brightly coloured silk cravat. Called to the station's front desk to see

him, Logan found Fulton puffing animatedly on a cigarette and
blowing a series of smoke rings along the corridor towards the
street door. The rings moved equidistant and in line, as if
controlled remotely by their creator.

Turning to give Logan a heavy-lidded, haughty look, Fulton
asked, 'Are you the senior officer here?'

'They don't come any more senior at the moment, sir.'

'Well, I haven't the time to wait until they do,' Fulton said petu-
lantly. He could have been anything between seventy-five and
ninety years of age, and had all the grooves and wrinkles to keep
you guessing. 'So I suppose that you'll have to do, Sergeant.'

'Detective Inspector,' Logan corrected him. 'Detective
Inspector Logan. How can I help you?'

Fulton drew on his cigarette, head back and eyes closed as if
he was ecstatically sucking on a teat. Blowing a column of
smoke at the ceiling, he said, 'This may sound like a line from
some trashy television programme, Detective Inspector, but it is
a case of what I can do for you.'

'I see. The duty sergeant gave me your name, Mr Fulton.
That's all that I know about you or why you are here,' Logan
said, ushering his visitor into an interview room. He pointed at
a chair for Fulton to take, but the older man stubbed his cigarette out in an ashtray and remained standing. As upright as a
soldier at attention, Fulton fixed his eyes on a high point on a
wall opposite, and began a recitation, his enunciation perfect:

> I know an old lady who swallowed a fly
> I don't know why she swallowed the fly
> Perhaps she'll die
>
> I know an old lady who swallowed a spider
> That wiggled and giggled and jiggled inside her
> She swallowed the spider to catch the fly
> I don't know why she swallowed the fly
> Perhaps she'll ...

Logan sat, embarrassed, momentarily incapable of taking control. Then he interrupted with, 'Mr Fulton, I assume that there was a serious purpose to you coming here.'

'Indeed there is, Detective Inspector.' Jason Fulton looked both hurt and indignant. 'Please try to understand that this is a new and rather disorientating experience for me. I am not accustomed to being in police stations, and that was my way of introducing myself with one of my monologues from the summer show at the Pavilion. I assumed that it would have you recognize me immediately. Don't say that you haven't caught the show this year, Mr Logan?'

Someone passed along the corridor outside, rubber soles squeaking on the polished floor, a sound of normality that Logan welcomed.

Not having caught the show that or any other year, Logan soothed his visitor's obviously fragile ego. 'I don't get a lot of spare time, but I should have recognized you, Mr Fulton.'

Fulton rolled his eyes. 'That was patronising though well meant, I am sure, Inspector. I only wish that it were true, my dear chap. I've been in the business all my life, even during the war years when I was with ENSA. I played to the troops with Charlie Chester in North Africa. I was in Burma with Vera Lynn. She sang "We'll Meet Again", but she and I never did. After the war, the others got all the breaks with radio shows – *Stand Easy*, *The Goon Show*, *Variety Bandbox*, and the like. Talent means very little in the business. One can spend years unrecognized on the stage, delighting audiences in Shakespearean roles, while a total buffoon on television gains fame and fortune with some inane catchphrase. I had to struggle along. I even spent one season travelling with a circus. That was a disaster. A bloody chimp, named Clive would you believe, bit off most of my little finger.'

Showing Logan a left hand that was half a digit short, Fulton gave his show a plug. 'We alternate two very different shows fortnightly to cater for the changeover of holidaymakers.'

'Very commendable,' Logan commented. 'Now, why did you come to see me?'

'Do you mind if I smoke, Detective Inspector? Filthy habit, but not as filthy as some. I once worked with an opera singer, a dear lady, but she had to have sex in the dressing room, haul the ashes, as they say, before performing. A messy business. But apparently it shoots adrenaline into the system and mellows the voice.'

'I've no objection to you smoking,' Logan said, 'but please warn me if you contemplate singing.'

Chuckling at Logan's wit, then lighting up, Fulton blew a smoke ring, poked a forefinger playfully through it and said, 'Right, Mr Logan, time to get the show on the road, so to speak. I believe that you have a dead girl who you are unable to identify, while I know of a girl who has gone missing.'

'You do?'

Bored and bewildered by Fulton up to that point, Logan sat upright in his chair, keenly interested.

'She's with the show, or rather was with the show. A beautiful girl, exquisite, gorgeous, divine, the whole bit, even if somewhat lax where morals are concerned. Still, the virginal qualities are not of great advantage in our business. She had a couple of singing spots in the show, but a rather insipid voice in my opinion. But I couldn't fault her as a dancer.'

A dancer! Excitement coursed through Logan. Simon Betts' emphasis on the muscular development of the dead girl's legs was uppermost in his mind. He enquired, 'Did the girl you are talking about have blonde hair, short blonde hair, Mr Fulton?'

'She did, Detective Inspector. It sounds to me like you have found Penny Silver, full-time exotic dancer, part-time whore, God rest her soul.'

Fulton was making sense now. Recognising that he wasn't mad, but just loquaciously eccentric, Logan was relieved. Mental contagion was as dangerous as the worst infectious disease. He said, 'There's something I would like to ask you to do, Mr Fulton. It's not pleasant, but ...'

Fulton raised a hand to stop Logan. 'Don't misjudge me, Mr Logan. A lot of people remember us as a bunch of poofs poncing around on the tailboard of a lorry. Far from it. Those Hollywood stars that entertained the GIs in Europe in '44 never heard a shot fired in anger, never met a frontline soldier. We were in the thick of it. A German shell killed eighteen boys and maimed God knows how many, right in front of my eyes. I helped to comfort some of the dying. It was simply awful. Oh, those poor lads ...'

Fulton's voice cracked and tears ran down his lined cheeks. 'I suppose it is to my credit that I didn't become hardened to death, Inspector Logan. It still disturbs me greatly to look upon a person asleep or a person dead. Both are weirdly subhuman, Detective Inspector – the first has no dignity and the second has no rights.'

For all his rambling the old entertainer was a keen observer of life and death, and he had an effective way with words. Fulton and Simon Betts could co-author a book that would knock Sigmund Freud out of the psychiatric bestsellers for all time. There was a knock on the door and Shelagh entered the room.

'Ah, Sergeant Ruby,' Logan greeted her. 'This is Mr Fulton. I think we're about to get an ID on our mystery girl.'

'I'm ready,' Jason Fulton announced dramatically, straightening his thin shoulders and fiddling with his cravat. 'Bring out your dead, Detective Inspector.'

It was yet another beautiful day, but for a bored Melanie Biles there was nothing more to be discovered about it right then. It consisted entirely of sky, a great expanse of cloudless blue, an empty, meaningless smile. Up on the links there was an occasional and tiny puff of wind to stir the little red flags. She didn't like playing golf, wasn't good at playing golf. But she did like golf dresses, and she knew that she looked great in them. Anyway, the ordeal was nearly over. Her husband and Harvey Reynolds were approaching the eighteenth hole. Soon they would be sitting on the long cool veranda at the clubhouse. She would be sipping a long cool drink and looking down through enormous rhododendron and dogwood trees at the other golfers.

'There's talk among us councillors about cancelling the town carnival because of these murders. It also worries me that we may be putting the wrong message across, Kenneth, a second girl dead and the chief constable playing a round of golf?' Harvey Reynolds remarked.

'Quite the opposite, actually, old chap,' Kenneth Biles answered, waiting for Reynolds to take his swing. He put his arm round his wife's shoulders and Melanie dutifully leaned against him. She caught the familiar aroma of his aftershave lotion, and was surprised to find that it sickened her a little. She kept her breathing so shallow that she came close to gagging. Biles continued. 'Not breaking the routine makes it clear that there is no panic and that I have every faith in my investigating officers.'

Looking idly round her, Melanie accepted that there was something nice about being out in the sun on one of the big smooth greens. It made a pleasant scene, and the topic of the discovery of another dead girl that had taken Logan away earlier that morning kept Reynolds from talking about the projected leisure centre. It was a subject she had come to dread.

'Do you, Kenneth?' Reynolds asked.

'Do I what?'

'Have faith in your officers,' Reynolds replied. 'Perhaps you are thinking of calling Walden Griffiths back from his honeymoon.'

This suggestion astonished the chief constable. 'Good heavens, no, Harvey. Randolph Logan is a most able detective.'

'I'd hesitate to question your judgment, Kenneth, but he's a loner, and there's no place in a disciplined force for a loner. Don't forget that I was a time-serving army man.'

'So was Logan,' Biles countered as he took his swing.

Unspeaking, they watched the white ball perform a high arc against a dark green background of pines, but Reynolds returned to the subject twenty minutes later when they were sitting in the shade enjoying a drink. 'My son tells me that Logan and that new woman sergeant questioned him and Terry Stevens at the Ocean club last night, Kenneth.'

Did Logan, a clever sleuth, suspect Gerald Reynolds? This possibility had Melanie thinking the unthinkable. It was said that no woman would complain about a man making a pass but would never forgive him for missing an opportunity. The pass Gerald had made at her was one she wanted never to have happened. Anger had raged in him when Melanie had limited the contact between them to his lips grazing her cheek at the rebuffing turn of her head. The newspapers said that the dead girl on the beach had been stunningly attractive, a fact that had Melanie pondering on just what Gerald Reynolds was capable of.

As a diversion she put her feet up on the railing and admired her long legs in the sun. She brought her legs quickly down when her husband gave her an admonishing look as he stuffed the bowl of his pipe with tobacco and lit it. Melanie found herself unaccountably irritated by her husband's unspoken rebuke. It wasn't his fault. She hated herself for abusing her position as a local councillor. In addition to the fear of being caught, Melanie had an increasing fear of the new her that was emerging.

'That would simply be a line of routine enquiry, Harvey,' the chief constable was explaining.

'Nevertheless, Kenneth,' Reynolds said with a slow shake of his head, 'Gerald wasn't impressed by Logan's attitude.'

'I cannot imagine DI Logan being anything other than professional, Harvey.'

With a slump of his shoulders, a kind of shrug in reverse, Reynolds said, 'Well, I don't intend to fall out with you over it,

Kenneth. Now, let's move on to more pleasant things. Can we depend on you to be guest speaker at the town hall on carnival night? You are always the star of the evening at the carnival ball.'

'That's pure flattery, Harvey,' Biles modestly protested. 'I think that locals and visitors alike have heard everything I have to say.'

'Nonsense. You have a creative mind, Kenneth, and we need your input.'

'We'll see,' Kenneth Biles said smugly

'The soliloquy from *Carousel*!' Simon Betts pointed a finger at Jason Fulton.

Fulton, who had solved the mystery of the dead blonde by confirming that she was Penny Silver, beamed a grateful smile at the pathologist. 'I do that in our number two show.'

'I know, Jason, I know,' said Betts, who had found an instant rapport with the entertainer. 'I've seen them both, twice, and the way you put that soliloquy across really got to me.'

To Shelagh's horror, Jason Fulton, standing in a laboratory where the body of Penny Silver lay on one table and that of Norma Harrington lay on another, began to sing in a rich baritone voice:

'*My boy Bill …*'

'We'll do without the cabaret, Mr Fulton,' Logan said sharply, stopping Fulton mid-lyric.

Relieved, Shelagh found that she was increasingly drawn to the strong detective inspector. The more time she spent in his company increased the frequency of a small tremor of excitement in her.

Shelagh had told Logan of the link between the death of the two girls and a holidaymaker named Rick Downton. Logan had phoned the station to have the custody sergeant release Derek

Wright on police bail, and to order DC Toby Wallace to bring Rick Downton in. He would be waiting for them when they got back.

'The soliloquy does go down very well, but my favourite is "Indian Love Call". When I sing that it means a lot to older people who remember that marvellous pair, Nelson Eddie and Jeanette McDonald,' Fulton was telling Betts in a preachery voice.

Logan interrupted Fulton once again. 'Your coming here and identifying the body is very much appreciated, Mr Fulton, but I need to speak with Dr Betts.'

'Then do, dear boy, please do.' Fulton gave Logan a quick, sliding look that glanced off.

'The cause of death of the Harrington girl, Simon,' Logan said. 'What can you tell me about it?'

Betts looked Logan over as if he was a scientific exhibit. 'That's difficult to answer, Randy. The neck was broken, but in a way that suggests either a lucky blow from the killer's point of view, or the work of someone skilled in the martial arts.'

'Which would you say?'

'A guess, maybe an educated guess, but still a guess, Randy, has me go for the latter. Something like a karate expert.'

Frowning, Logan commented, 'But that isn't so with the girl we now know as Penny Silver.'

'Definitely not. That was a crude, a very crude, case of strangulation.'

'So, are we looking for two different killers?' Logan questioned.

'Not necessarily,' Simon Betts replied with a shrug of his narrow shoulders. 'You know the old saying about horses for courses. It might well have been a matter of circumstances. In the case of the Harrington girl he may have wanted a quick, silent kill, whereas he may have started out simply trying to prevent the girl on the beach from screaming.'

'Which means the answer lies in discovering the motive for each of the two deaths,' Logan sombrely observed.

'Exactly, Randy, and you're the detective. I'm just the pathologist.'

'Which has me envy you at times,' Logan said.

'That's easily put right,' Betts said with a hard smile, picking up a long-bladed scalpel from a bench and proffering it to Logan. 'You examine the contents of Norma Harrington's stomach, and I'll go with the lovely Sergeant Ruby to ask a few questions.'

Betts' words about slicing the dead girl open caused a sweat to break out all over Shelagh, the perspiration going immediately icy cold on her skin. A large fly was unnecessarily loud as it tried to decide where to land. It kept buzzing and buzzing, and somehow there was an increase in the sickeningly sweet smell of the place. The skin on her face seemed to be pulled tight and her throat was dry. Being there with two young dead people suddenly had an especial kind of horror, too. Her sight became slightly blurred and there were violent flashes of pain through her head. She wanted to throw up. She was relieved when Logan ushered her and Jason Fulton out of the room.

Catherine Wilmott lifted her hands from the piano, clasping them, squeezing them, moulding them, as DC Toby Wallace entered the room behind her nephew. She made a fast move, the piano stool almost toppling over as she jumped to her feet. A portly little woman with vaguely porcine features, she was dressed discreetly and suitably in grey, as though she had just got home from church. Her hair was a courageous but unconvincing red. Her chin was raised defiantly, her mouth firm, challenging the detective's right to be there.

Wallace took a step towards the boy. Arms out at each side of her, Catherine Wilmott stood defensively between the white-faced Rick Downton and the detective, like a mother animal protecting her young.

'How do we know that you're really a policeman?' she objected. 'You look to me like someone who's been in a drunken brawl.'

'Wounded in the line of duty, Mrs Wilmott.' Wallace creased his damaged face with a patient smile. 'It has caused even my little daughter to wonder whether her daddy is a thug, but here is my warrant card.'

Wallace held out the document as if it were an olive branch, but Mrs Wilmott was not interested in peace between them. 'Yes, well, whatever, you can't possibly want my Roderick for anything.'

'Apart from the killer, your nephew may well be the last person to have seen the girl from the Clement Estate alive.'

'What total nonsense!' Catherine Wilmott exclaimed. 'My Roderick wouldn't even have known the girl.'

'Please, Auntie Cath.' Rick Downton made a tremulous plea.

The boy's eyes were funny. They had an unfocussed quality as if they were watching something totally alien. They watched the policeman and waited. To Toby Wallace the boy looked scared out of his wits. It was an odd but common reaction, this fear of imminent brutality from a police officer.

'Well, Roderick?' Wallace asked.

'Rick,' the boy corrected the policeman tonelessly.

'You did know this girl, Norma Harrington?'

'That is a preposterous suggestion!' Catherine Wilmott protested.

'Rick?' Wallace persisted, seeing the boy's whole body stiffen.

'I knew her.' The boy made vague, formless motions with his hands.

Catherine Wilmott gave a little gasp and her small body slumped. Her blue lips parted. She put a hand to her forehead.

'Were you with her last night, Rick?'

'Yes,' the boy admitted as his aunt sat down heavily on the piano stool. It was a sort of collapse. She touched the keys very lightly, nervously. Wallace heard a sequence of chords that, strangely, seemed to please the upset Mrs Wilmott. She played them again, elaborating.

'When did you last see her?' Wallace enquired.

'You don't have to answer that, Roderick,' Catherine Wilmott advised, coming up quickly off the stool.

'It would be in your best interest to answer, Rick,' Wallace counselled.

'What do I do, Auntie Cath?' Rick Downton asked desperately.

When the aunt's lips moved but couldn't form words, Wallace repeated his earlier question. 'When did you last see Norma Harrington?'

'I walked her home early this morning,' the boy miserably admitted.

'Don't say another word, Rick,' Wallace said quickly. 'I must ask you to come down to the police station with me.'

A spasm crossed the boy's face, and his hand came up and the back of it wiped hard across his mouth. His eyes were dulled by incomprehension. 'Am I under arrest?'

'No. Detective Inspector Logan simply wants to interview you.'

Catherine Wilmott touched the piano, this time so lightly that no sound came from it. 'I'm coming with you, Roderick,'

'Rick is not a minor, Mrs Wilmott,' Wallace cautioned. 'You will not be allowed in the interview room with him.'

'Nevertheless, I still intend to be there,' she declared, taking off her spotted pinafore.

With Shelagh driving, Logan twisted in the front passenger seat to ask Jason Fulton a question. 'Silver has an exotic ring to it, Mr Fulton. Was it a stage name the girl chose for herself?'

Fulton shrugged. 'That's a possibility, but something that I can't help you with, Mr Logan. You'll have to have a word with Walter Smythe at the Pavilion. He does the office work, insurance cards, PAYE, that sort of thing. If that isn't poor Penny's name, then he would know.'

'Thank you, I'll do that,' Logan said. 'What do you know about her?'

'No more than I do about the rest of the cast.'

'What age was she, Mr Fulton? Nineteen? Twenty?'

'Good heavens, no!' the entertainer exclaimed in his prissy way. 'She was sixteen, only just. I know that for a fact. There was some trouble with the school authorities when the show opened at the beginning of July. We learned that Penny had been naughty, leaving school before the end of term, before she was sixteen, in fact. It seemed that she would be made to go back home, but Walter, Mr Smythe that is, was able to settle the matter on the actual day of her birthday.

'Walter put on a little party for her after the show that night. Nothing spectacular, you understand, but we all had a nice little time.' Seemingly losing his train of thought, Fulton looked at Logan intently. 'Did you ever have the privilege of seeing the late great Max Miller on stage, Detective Inspector?'

'No.'

'That is something to be regretted, sir,' Fulton said with a sorrowful shake of his head. 'That man was brilliant; his timing was sheer perfection.'

Staying with the main subject, Logan asked, 'Did Penny Silver have any men friends, Mr Fulton?'

'My dear Mr Logan, a lovely young girl such as her acts as a magnet on men.'

'Do you know of anyone particularly close to her?'

'Though I wouldn't be so presumptuous to suggest the course your investigation should follow, Inspector Logan, and I shrink from speaking ill of the dead, but false sympathy for a young girl such as Penny can mislead the most clever of us,' Fulton cautioned.

'You're talking to an ignorant copper here, Jason,' Logan said, 'and your meaning escapes me.'

'I've said too much already, Detective Inspector.'

Logan spoke firmly. 'I have to insist that you explain your comments.'

'Very well,' Fulton sighed. 'Penny Silver was ... er ... I think the modern expression is streetwise. She was both promiscuous and cunning. Sex is the great emancipator, and emancipation always raises the servant above the master. Young girls with only a fraction of the good looks and charisma that Penny possessed have brought down some of the world's greatest governments.'

'You're not implying that she asked to be murdered?' a shocked Shelagh asked without taking her eyes from the road ahead.

'Heaven forbid that I should ever think such a thing!' Fulton exclaimed, stunned by Shelagh's suggestion. 'I was merely trying to help by pointing out that a man with a great deal to lose may well have had reason to fear Penny.'

'Are you saying that she was involved with local men?' Logan asked as Shelagh slowed the car and called a question back to Fulton:

'Is this it, Mr Fulton?'

Bending forward to peer out at a terraced row of dowdy boarding houses, Fulton said, 'Next on the left, Sergeant Ruby. Hardly Buck House, is it? But, alas, it has to be home for me over the next month or so. It was very kind of you to drive me back.'

'Not at all.' Logan, frustrated by his key question remaining unanswered, reached behind like a taxi driver to open the back door for the entertainer. 'We are most grateful to you for coming to the station.'

Out on the pavement, Fulton put both hands on the car door and bent to look in at Shelagh. Logan saw that his sergeant coloured a little, and that her hand went up to her hair, to smooth it back from her cheek. Fulton apologized. 'Forgive an old man for staring, my dear, but you evoke romantic memories in me of the beautiful women I shared a stage with in my younger days.'

'You are making me blush, Mr Fulton,' Shelagh said with a pleased little laugh. 'Thank you for the compliment.'

He wagged a finger in at her. 'You are wasted in the police, Sergeant. Look me up should you ever decide on a change of career. Instant stardom awaits you.'

'I could charge you with enticement,' Logan jokingly told Fulton. 'Thank you, once again, for your help.'

'It was my pleasure,' Fulton said with a practised smile. 'I am far from unmindful, Detective Inspector, of having left your question hanging in the air.' Breaking off, he fumbled in the inside pocket of his jacket. Bringing out two tickets, he passed them in through the window of the car to Logan. 'Here we are, a complimentary ticket for each of you. I look forward to seeing you and your most attractive sergeant in the best seats tonight.'

'It's a matter of time ...' Logan started to explain, but Fulton firmly stopped him.

'Far be it from me to tell you your job, Mr Logan,' Fulton said apologetically, 'but you'll learn more about Penny in an hour in the theatre than you would in months spent asking questions elsewhere.'

'I'm sure you're right, Mr Fulton,' Logan agreed.

Fulton stood at the kerb waving as Shelagh moved the car away. Logan looked back over his shoulder at the old man. 'Why does that old guy make the hair on the back of my neck stand up, Sergeant?'

'Maybe he's a ghost, guv.' Shelagh's remark was flippant but her face was serious as she concentrated on guiding the powerful car through heavy traffic.

'The ghost of summer shows past,' Logan said, smiling.

'I know that I have a lot to learn about the subtleties of police work, guv, but he struck me as not being quite right.'

'I thought he was crazy when I met him back at the station, Sergeant,' Logan agreed, 'but right now I honestly believe that Jason Fulton could be the only sane person I've met in a very long time.'

'That's one hell of an indictment on the rest of us, guv,'

chapter six

Shelagh commented, giving a little shudder as she gripped the steering wheel.

'Don't I know it,' Logan agreed soberly.

seven

Julie Bolt strolled aimlessly around the courthouse square that between autumn and spring was the centre of Havensport. It was her afternoon off and she was both unhappy and undecided. The heat of the day suggested the beach and a cooling dip in the sea, but she knew that the benefits of a swim didn't last long. Not only did you seem to get much hotter afterwards, but also uncomfortable because you couldn't dress properly under a towel on the beach. She needed something to occupy her mind, to stop her thinking of Norma. It worried her that she was just numbed by the death of her friend, not really grieving. In situations similar to hers in films and television dramas, some wise character always said, 'She'll be better once she is able to cry.' Julie didn't even remotely feel like crying.

An afternoon at the pictures was the only alternative to the beach. Walking on in the bright sun she stopped outside the small cinema to look up at the posters. It would be warm inside, but the darkness would make that preferable to the blazing heat outside.

'Whatever happened to the good movies they used to make?'

Head tilted back, studying the publicity for the film that was currently showing, Julie turned towards the voice that had spoken. The speaker was a man in his thirties with a thick mane of glossy black hair. Good-looking in a rugged kind of way, he had an aura of energy about him that gave the impression of movement even though he was standing still. His dress was summer-casual but smart.

Julie's intention to ignore him crumbled as he gave her a friendly smile, putting brilliant white teeth on show. It was plain that he was being sociable, not trying to score. Julie smiled back. 'I don't think they're too bad these days. What don't you like about them?'

He lifted his wide shoulders. 'All the fantasy rubbish they come up with, way out stuff about space, that sort of thing.'

'I enjoy them,' Julie confessed, using her thumbs to settle the straps of her top more comfortably. 'What are you into, the old horse operas?'

'The Westerns were good in their day,' he said with a self-conscious laugh. 'But I like something with a sensible story to it, a believable story. Anything with Harrison Ford, Richard Gere, Sharon Stone, stars like them in.' He looked at her quizzically, squinting his eyes against the sun. 'Did I see you somewhere last night?'

'Depends where you were,' an outwardly cool, inwardly thrilled Julie replied.

'I know where it was.' He levelled a forefinger at her. 'It was at the Blue Angel. You were with your boyfriend.'

'He was just someone I met. I don't have a boyfriend.'

'Oh.'

He seemed pleased about that, which in turn delighted Julie. Head down, she looked at him out of the corners of her eyes as she asked, 'Did you notice the girl I was talking to?'

Creasing his brow, he said, 'I don't think so.'

'Blonde and very pretty,' she said to jog his memory.

'Ah, I'm getting it.' He gave a nod. 'She was with a kid with a tight haircut, and you were all talking to the club bouncer.'

'That's right. That was Norma. Did you hear about that girl found murdered this morning?'

'Yes,' he said, seemingly dreading what Julie was going to say next.

'It was her, Norma.'

'No!' His face had whitened and he looked wide-eyed at Julie. 'My God, that's terrible. Your friend.'

There was a tremor in Julie's voice. 'My best friend since our schooldays. We lived close together, and worked at the same place.'

'That's awful,' he said consolingly. 'I don't know whether I could cope with something like that the way you seem to be.'

'It's all show.'

He dismissed that with a wave of his hand. 'No, you're very brave. You must have the police swarming round you.'

'No. A woman detective came into the shop where I work this morning, purposefully, I suspect. Otherwise they haven't bothered me.'

'Good,' he said. 'I suppose she wanted to know everything your friend had said to you in the past few days?'

'No, she didn't ask anything like that.'

His questions made Julie suspicious. It could be that their meeting hadn't been accidental and that he was a policeman. She was deciding to walk away when he gave her one of his radiant smiles and changed the subject.

'I didn't intend to pry. I was just interested because I know nothing about these things.' He surprised her by taking her right hand in his and shaking it as if they had just been formally introduced. 'I'm Matthew Colby, down here for a fortnight, all alone and very lonely. Maybe we could cheer each other up?'

'We could give it a try,' she said, really liking him. 'I'm Julie Bolt.'

'Well, Julie, you make a decision for both of us. Is it the movies or a stroll along the prom to see what that leads to? Perhaps we could try the funfair later.'

'I may not be good company, because of what happened to Norma,' Julie warned.

'We'll allow for that,' he assured her sympathetically.

An elderly down-and-out was shuffling around on the pavement near to them. In spite of the heat and the fact that he was wearing an ancient, frayed overcoat, the tramp was visibly shivering. He had a bundle under his arm and was looking around the square like a scared rabbit. Nobody paid any attention to him, except for Colby. Taking a two-pound coin from his pocket, he used a thumb to flick it towards the old man. Facing Julie, Colby had moved only his eyes, but the coin hit the pavement right between the tramp's broken-booted feet.

'You are a kind man, Matthew,' an impressed Julie said.

'Call me Matt,' he told her as they walked off together in the direction of the seafront.

'Let's just run through it again, Rick.' Shelagh rested her elbows on the interview room table. 'You walked Norma nearly all the way home, but left her at the end of her road because she was afraid of her parents and didn't want to be seen with a boy.'

'Yes,' Rick Downton mumbled.

He sat slumped in the chair, his body trembling. On arrival at the station he had been violently sick. His doting aunt had taken him into the Ladies, while Shelagh had stood as a sentinel in the corridor outside. Now she and Logan had him alone again in the interview room. Rick, or rather Catherine Wilmott, had refused Logan's offer of a solicitor.

Shelagh envied Logan his professionalism. He was deliberately emotionless, because emotion was likely to blur judgment, slacken reflexes, and cause that split-second hesitation that could ruin an interview. Yet there was no way in which she could bring herself to be as hard as Logan was with this boy.

She watched as Logan leaned across the table, bringing his face as close as possible to the boy. The detective inspector lowered his voice to what was almost a confidential whisper. 'That's where you tried it on, at the end of the road, wasn't it, Rick?'

'I don't know what you mean, sir.' Rick's eyes went glassier, and under his thin cotton shirt his young body started sucking inward.

'Don't play games with me, son,' Logan said menacingly, banging his clenched fist on the tabletop. The sudden loud noise caused the boy to jump up in his chair. 'You know what trying it on means. You are with this fit girl who is vulnerable because she has been living rough and has had a few drinks. It's what, gone one o'clock in the morning, and she wants to walk off and leave you. That's not what you had in mind when you offered to walk her home, was it?'

'All I wanted was to see that she got home safely,' the boy protested, useless tears shining in his eyes.

'Save yourself a lot of trouble, son, by telling it just like it was,' Logan urged. He advised caution. 'Closed circuit television could prove you to be lying. Eyes and ears are everywhere. The miracle of today. We know that you were also with that girl who was found dead on the beach, Rick. Two girlfriends in two days and both of them end up dead.'

'I wasn't with that girl on the beach.'

Logan said quietly, 'She left the Ocean club and you went out after her.'

'I didn't get anywhere near her. I was hoping to get off with her, I admit that. But the other guy beat me to it.'

'What other guy, Rick?' Shelagh asked.

'His name's Ed Bellamy. He's the doorman at the Blue Angel. You ask him.'

'We probably will,' Logan sighed, 'but right now we're asking you. Tell us what happened when you followed that girl out of the club.'

Nerves clearly strung tight, the boy spoke in a hoarse voice. 'When I got to the railings on the edge of the prom, she was walking across the sand towards the sea, and the other guy, Ed Bellamy, was walking behind her.'

It grew shadowed in the interview room as afternoon gave way to evening.

'How close was Bellamy to the girl?' Shelagh enquired.

'A long way back,' the boy replied, then blurted out defensively, 'I didn't even go down onto the beach, honestly!'

'There's no need to be afraid, Rick,' Shelagh said gently. 'We just need your help. You can go home with your auntie once you tell us what you know.'

'If it's the truth.' Logan qualified what his sergeant had said.

'I've been telling you the truth.'

'Nonsense!' Logan shouted, and the boy cowered in his chair. 'Let's go back to last night and Norma Harrington. I'll tell you the truth of what happened. She stopped at the end of her road and told you that she was off home. You grabbed her; she struggled, got away from you. That made you angry, didn't it, Rick?'

'No!' the terrified boy cried.

Logan stood up and walked away. He stood in the corner of the small room, facing the wall. Recognising a familiar questioning routine, Shelagh saw that Logan was achieving the effect he wanted in the boy. Rick Downton's wide-open eyes were staring in dread at the detective inspector's broad back. Delaying in silence for a full minute, that must have been hours long to the frightened boy, Logan then suddenly swung round and strode back to the table.

Remaining standing, he leaned across the table, using his closeness and muscular bulk to intimidate Downton. 'She walked away, not caring about you, after you had walked all that way with her. You weren't going to be slighted like that. So you ...' Logan raised his left hand, cupped, and punched his right fist hard into it.

The meaty smack was loud in the small room. Rick Downton's head fell back, his eyes rolling. Then he fell off his chair to the floor in a dead faint.

Expelling a slow breath, Shelagh dropped on to one knee beside the boy. He lay motionless, white-faced, and she looked worriedly up at Logan, asking, 'Should I fetch the FME, guv?'

'He doesn't need a doctor,' Logan disdainfully replied. Like all hard men he couldn't tolerate weakness in a male, even in a boy just edging out of his teens. Seeing Downton's eyelids flicker, he said, 'He's coming round, Sergeant. I'll lift him back up onto his chair, while you get him a glass of water. Bring the aunt in with you when you come back.'

When Shelagh re-entered the room with a plastic cup in her hand, Catherine Wilmott pushed past her, halting as she saw her nephew. Shelagh saw the aunt go pale and touch her heart as if she had been struck in the breast. 'Roderick, you look terrible.' She spun accusingly on Logan. 'What have you done to the boy, Inspector?'

'We haven't *done* anything other than ask him a few questions, Mrs Wilmott,' Logan answered absently.

'So, what happens now?' Catherine Wilmott questioned Shelagh.

Shelagh left it to Logan, who advised, 'The boy could use a good night's sleep, Mrs Wilmott. We will probably need to speak to him again, perhaps tomorrow. Sergeant Ruby will drive both of you home.'

'I've been over everything three times, Councillor Biles, and I'm satisfied that every angle is covered.'

Though they were alone in his office, Melanie noticed that Wenzell Carmen had spoken in a half whisper. Subterfuge came no easier to him than it did to her. What chance did a couple of amateurs like them have? They were both in their early forties. Childhood is pliable but age is rigid. Original thoughts, novel emotions and fresh reactions become rarer and rarer past the age of thirty. She and Wenzell were old dogs who were finding it difficult to learn new tricks.

'We'll be able to get it past the council, Harvey and Gerald Reynolds in particular?' Melanie asked.

'Neither the Reynolds' nor anyone else on the council know which way up a blueprint is, Councillor Biles,' Carmen answered with a tight little smile that owed little to mirth. He had a gangling six-foot-three string-bean frame and delicate facial features with a pallid, almost transparent complexion. 'What I've prepared will go through without a hitch providing that you keep the experts away. If Harvey Reynolds employs solicitors who bring in top surveyors to scrutinize the plans, then we'll be in real trouble.'

'Don't worry,' Melanie said. 'Harvey tried to go down that route, but I cut him off and the majority of the committee supported me.'

'Good.' Carmen's slender fingers were playing nervously with a pencil.

Melanie walked to the window and stood looking out. This side of the council offices fronted the esplanade. Below her the horde in bright clothing or swimming costumes milled about as if on important business. Farther out, the sea glittered like a jumble of broken jewellery. She compared the view with how she remembered it in winter. In those grey days there was always something mocking in the emptiness of a promenade and a beach that had known laughter and excited chatter and ice cream and gaiety. She was sensitive to that sort of thing.

Regarded as a member of the local 'aristocracy,' she gave much of herself to the community. She regularly visited a nearby prison, the hospital and homes for the mentally retarded, gave irrelevant lectures on the duties of a senior policeman's wife, and ran the Women's Institute ragged with her enthusiasm. All this had her highly respected, but it would count for nothing if she were to be found out.

Deep in thought, Melanie left Wenzell Carmen to work with his pens and protractors in silence. There was more than the Compat Leisure project on her mind. On parting with Kenneth at the golf clubhouse she had been convinced that she was being followed on the way into town. The stalking had been worrying but far less traumatic when she had believed that Brian Amhurst was responsible. Now it was alarmingly sinister. On arriving at the council office, Melanie had telephoned Randy Logan. It was easy for her to sense that the detective inspector was having a hectic day, but he had spared her time, sympathising but pointing out that there was nothing he could do because whoever had followed her from the links hadn't come close enough for Melanie to identify even the make or colour of the car.

'Be careful,' Logan had advised her. 'If you get a sight, even a glimpse, of anything that I can follow up, don't hesitate to ring me.'

That wouldn't happen. Melanie knew that the person watching her every move was cautious, showing nothing of themselves. Wenzell Carmen was saying something, and she turned to him from the window. He was putting folded papers into a large white envelope. Melanie understood what was happening. These were documents too incriminating to be left here in the Council Office. Carmen was frowning as he passed the envelope to her. Taking it, Melanie asked:

'Is there a problem that you haven't mentioned, Wenzell?'

'Possibly, but it's not in my domain,' the chief planning officer replied. He was sweating, but Melanie guessed that it wasn't from the sun that cooked the concrete walls of the office. 'It isn't a subject that I'm qualified to comment on, so I'd better leave it.'

Melanie shook her head slowly. 'If it's worrying you, it has to be a worry to me, too. Let's hear it.'

'It's draining Moorfield that's the problem,' Carmen said. 'In my opinion, the cost of doing so will have to be drastically revised. The final figure is likely to be phenomenal, Councillor Biles. As I said, this isn't my field, but I'd say the cost will be prohibitive.'

'You're saying ...?'

'I believe that when the true cost is known, Compat Leisure will regard the project as uneconomical.'

'You're suggesting that they'll pull out?' Melanie's insides felt hollow all of a sudden.

'Most probably threaten to, Councillor Biles, unless the council agrees to make a substantial contribution towards the drainage. That, of course, has been a sticking point right through past decades.'

Head down, Melanie considered what Carmen had said. Then she looked up at him. 'We'll keep the cost of drainage concealed for as long as possible, Wenzell, until the project is that far ahead that the council would find it difficult not to go on with it. Rather than upset the public by cancelling after things have gone so far, the council will pay up.'

'I suppose, Councillor Biles,' Carmen said sadly, 'that both you and me have good reason for getting involved in something underhand like this?'

'We have, Wenzell, and we need each other,' an equally melancholy Melanie answered.

'Are we going to see the end-of-the-pier show, guv?' a smiling Shelagh asked cheekily as she got in the car beside Logan.

It was late evening and the sea reflected the golden splendour of the setting sun. The heat of the day persisted, but a light breeze escaped as the last ray of sunlight was dragged over the horizon. The golden splendours had faded through orange, red, blue and violet into the dull indigo of night so fast that Shelagh was taken by surprise.

Starting the car, Logan grimaced. 'I don't think I could stand seaside landlady jokes and old dears in the audience dabbing at their eyes with handkerchiefs when the whole cast comes on stage at the end to sing "Now Is The Hour".'

Laughing, Shelagh said, 'If anyone ever accuses you of being a romantic, I'll act in your defence.'

'If anyone ever accuses me of being a romantic, you have my permission to shoot, Sergeant.'

'Them, guv?'

'No, me.' He turned his head to look at her intently. 'We'll get there when the show is over. That way we can speak to the cast without the ordeal of watching them on stage.'

'What are you going to do with the free tickets, guv?'

'Give them to someone I don't like.'

Shelagh laughed. 'Old Jason would be upset if he knew.'

'He won't know. We'll say that we were in the audience, and bluff our way through.' He kept his eyes straight ahead as he continued. 'I normally don't go in for making compliments or giving praise, Sergeant.'

'But ...' Shelagh questioned archly.

'But,' Logan permitted himself a hint of a smile. 'I wanted to say that I've really appreciated having you with me.'

'Thank you for saying that, guv.'

He glanced sideways at her anxiously. 'It's been a long day. Are you sure that you can carry on this evening?'

There was an easygoing candour between them that warmed Shelagh. In all modesty, she knew that he found her attractive, and she really valued a friendship with an older man who always met her on an equal footing.

'Wouldn't miss it for the world, guv.' She smiled at him.

'First we'll take a look at Ed the Bouncer,' he said, adding, 'but I reckon we could both use a drink.'

Shelagh guessed that Logan, being in the public firing line, needed a drink more than she did. The popular press was never so popular. Two beautiful young innocent girls were dead, and how many more would join them before the inept police did something about what was plainly a serial killer on the loose in Havensport? Under a huge-lettered heading of HORROR HOLIDAYS, the local evening paper had run the story:

There has been a series of serious incidents in Havensport in the wake of the brutal murders of two young girls. Shortly before midnight, a girl visitor to the town was returning to her boarding house when a man leapt out of bushes at her in

Petherick Lane. *The plucky victim was able to fight off her attacker, who left her unharmed but badly shaken.*

A little while later, in the Blackdown camping site, just 25 yards away from the earlier attack, a man who had crept into her tent molested a woman. Luckily, her screams alerted other campers and her assailant fled.

Councillor Harvey Reynolds told the Echo *that he was calling for all-out police action on these worrying incidents. "It is plain to all of us," Councillor Reynolds said, "that today's indecent exposure might well turn into tomorrow's serious assault, and that tonight's assault become tomorrow night's murder."*

As they drove slowly along a quay crowded with holiday-makers, Shelagh was angry at the newspaper for rabble-rousing. Neither of the two incidents described had been reported to the police.

To their right some fishermen were folding nets and carrying out other chores on lightly bobbing boats moored against the harbour wall. Their movements were slow and unhurried. Shelagh marvelled at the two different scenes that were separated by a century or more. The fishermen belonged to a long ago era when Havensport was a tiny community in which neither men nor women had a choice – from the age of puberty the boys and girls would have known whom they would have to marry. There was little variety in that life in comparison to that of the fun-loving, free-loving modern holiday crowd for whom marriage, if entered into at all, was not expected to be of long duration.

This was fuzzy thinking, and Shelagh sharpened her mind by asking Logan a question. 'The more I run the deaths of the two girls through my mind, the more complicated it all becomes, guv.'

'The murders aren't really complicated, Sergeant, it's only that we make them so. At some time, either sooner or later, we'll see that there was a natural series of events leading up to the killings. The facts are before us, waiting to be interpreted. What we have at the moment is no more than an artist's sketch on canvas. Do you follow me?'

'I do, guv. We have the outline and we have to begin by filling in the highlights.'

'Exactly,' Logan said as he stopped the car outside a quay-side pub named the Harbour Hotel. There was an unusual smell, slightly unpleasant, coming from the boats, like wet matting. But Shelagh found the strange but colourful boats fascinating.

The hustle and bustle around them had Logan complain, 'If this were a wet winter night it would be quiet and soothing, Sergeant. When it's wet the traffic is quieter and your feet walk softer. Even the dogs don't bark when it's raining.'

'I didn't know that, guv,' Shelagh said cautiously, uncertain whether he was teasing her.

'It's a fact,' he solemnly assured her. 'A rainy night can change everything, even rearrange time.'

Shelagh stayed quiet. Logan was a strange man, too deep for an obvious sense of humour, and until she knew him better she wasn't going to chance making a fool of herself.

The inside of the pub was a symphony of organized confusion. Space at the bar was at a premium. Shelagh kept close behind the broad back of Logan, using the space that he made as he pushed through the crowd and turned his head to her, his raised eyebrows silently asking a question.

'White wine, please,' Shelagh requested.

A table was vacated nearby, and Logan quickly moved her and himself into the plastic chairs. Shelagh lifted her glass and smiled at him, as if about to propose a toast. Logan held his drink briefly aloft, then sipped it. Though she got along well with Logan, Shelagh suddenly realized that she knew nothing about him. She asked, 'Is this your local, guv?'

'I don't have a local,' he replied, pointing a finger at her round his glass as he raised it. 'Your woman's curiosity is surfacing, Sergeant. That is the first question of many, I suspect.'

Feeling her face burning, Shelagh apologized. 'Sorry, guv. It's just odd that we've been together over the past couple of days but neither of us really knows anything at all about the other. But don't worry, I'll back off.'

'There's no need,' Logan surrendered. 'I suppose this should be where I ask you if you left London to get away from Mr Right who turned out to be Mr Wrong?'

'I never met Mr Right, guv.'

'But you've met some Mr Wrongs,' he suggested.

'Enough to last me a lifetime,' Shelagh laughed. 'What about you, guv? Or am I transgressing?'

His expression serious, Logan answered, 'Not at all, Sergeant. It was me who began the probing. Exercise your detective's mind by doing a psychological profile.'

Brushing aside a soft curtain of hair that had fallen over her cheek, Shelagh smiled at him a little dreamily. She had the look of someone who had just returned from some very pleasant place. 'On you, guv? That would be risking my career.'

'I give you a guarantee of amnesty in advance, Sergeant.' He lolled back in his chair, waiting.

Shelagh took a sip of her drink and began hesitantly. 'I start by cheating, because I know that you were a soldier. You strike me as being opposed to discipline, which is probably why you left the army for the police.'

'Which is also a disciplined service,' Logan reminded her.

'But rank in the police allows for more freedom than it does in the army,' Shelagh went on, speaking with an ease that showed her confidence. 'Yet I'm not certain that will be enough for you.'

Raising one eyebrow, Logan asked, 'You don't see me drawing my police pension?'

'You are of a restless nature, guv,' Shelagh went on. 'Yet as long as police work provides you with enough challenges, you could stay the course. Your work means everything to you, but you also hide behind it.'

'Hide from what?'

'Your feelings,' Shelagh answered. 'You're the rare kind of tough guy, guv, who wears his heart on his sleeve.'

'You've gone beyond psychology into fortune-telling, Sergeant,' Logan protested.

A smiling Shelagh gave a shake of her head. 'Not yet I haven't. Intuitions and hunches are either misunderstood or unappreciated. Guess wrong and it will be forgotten. Get it right and you're under suspicion. I'd say that you have been close to marriage at least twice.' She looked at him wide-eyed. 'Do you want to hear the rest of it?'

'No, enough!' Logan declared. 'You must be a witch. To let you go on could embarrass us both.'

'I'm not easily embarrassed, guv,' Shelagh countered.

'Maybe not, but I am.' Logan drained his glass. 'Come on, we've a date with a hard man.'

They stood to leave. Somehow, the enchantment Shelagh had been feeling had disappeared. But as they went out into the night together something else had moved in to take its place: the feeling that the two of them were now communicating closely without either of them saying a word.

Catherine Wilmott was dressed ready to go out, but she was at all times dressed to go out, even when she had not the slightest intention of doing so. This evening she definitely wouldn't be leaving the house. She was too worried about her nephew. Though Roderick knew all the fashionable catch-words of the day, and chased after girls, he was terribly immature. Not having gone out that evening, he sat huddled in a chair, making a pretence of reading a magazine. The room smelled slightly of chrysanthemums and was dark and gloomy. With the heat of the day abating, Catherine opened the curtains and a shaft of sunlight fell on his face that was as pale as that of a dead man.

She was over-tired, over-anxious, strained, and aware somehow that her nephew was withdrawn from her, inaccessible. Even the vitality of a middle-aged woman that allowed her to hide weariness for long stretches couldn't help her. She poured a glass of lemonade for each of them.

'Would you like me to go for some fish and chips, Roderick?'

He answered miserably, 'I'm not hungry, Auntie Cath.'

She knew that he was thinking about tomorrow when the bullying detective inspector questioned him once more. But tomorrow would come and they would get through it. Everyone gets through all their tomorrows in some way.

Catherine liked the woman detective sergeant, who had a face saintly enough to be that of a nun, but too beautiful to be turned away from the world.

'The girl was safe and well when you left her, Roderick,' she ventured, 'so you have nothing to worry about.'

By lightly touching on the subject of tomorrow, she had terrified the boy. She noticed with sudden misgivings how unnaturally bright his eyes were. He had a red blotch burning on both cheeks. But he was all right really, wasn't he? It was just the terrible situation he found himself in through no fault of his own.

'I'll have your best shirt clean for the morning, Roderick, and those nice beige trousers, I'll press them for you,' she promised. 'Appearances make all the difference.'

'Thank you, Auntie Cath.' His smile was brave but ghostly. 'But for the first time that I can remember, I just don't care how I look.'

The depressed boy had totally lost interest in life. Did that mean ...? No, Catherine Wilmott refused to even contemplate such a thing about her sister's dear boy. Roderick and violence just didn't fit together. But she collapsed into a chair, breathing heavily. Unable to deny herself any longer, she undid her shoes.

Head lolling back, eyes wandering to the ceiling, she tried to blot out the dire happenings of that frightful day.

She didn't succeed.

eight

Shelagh glanced up at the green canopy above the shabby entrance to the Blue Angel. She and Logan had discovered a special rapport in the pub on the quay, a magic that had been short-lived. Logan was his old distant self again, and there was a sordidness about this club that caused Shelagh to feel somehow intimidated. The foyer had a fake-marble floor. The lower four feet of each of the walls was sheathed in shimmering imitation maple. The club had all the expected cheapness and shining gaudy glitter. Two overhead fans turned the air round to fool you into thinking that you were cooler. Through the windows in double doors leading to the main part of the club, Shelagh saw figures moving vaguely around, fleetingly illuminated by strobe lighting.

Two girls sat at a glass-topped reception desk. They glanced up, ready to smile, but didn't. Standing behind them, a hand resting on the backs of each of their chairs, was a young man who Shelagh assumed was Ed Bellamy.

He was palpably attractive, beautifully attired in a suit of dark material, and though his welcoming smile was restrained it was far from daunting. He had a presence that Shelagh found to be unsettling. She was aware of a high-voltage dynamism; a macho male charm that exuded from him like sweat from a heavy-weight boxer in training. Bellamy epitomized Hollywood's representation of the mobsters in America's prohibition days.

She was acting like a schoolgirl, Shelagh thought. Like she was a teenager out for the evening, wondering if she'll meet the boy whom she would eventually marry. The effect Bellamy had was to rewind her mind several years. With an effort of will she fast-forwarded herself to the present.

'Are you Ed Bellamy?' Logan asked brusquely. There was a touch of contempt in the way he spoke. In the dramatic lighting of the club his features bore the hard physical traits of a professional soldier with overtones of a man used to command.

Bellamy's expression was a mixture of suspicion and aggression. 'I could be.'

'When you're sure, sonny,' Logan said sarcastically, 'we would like a word with you.'

Face flushing as the two girls at the desk stifled their sniggers, Bellamy said, 'You'll have to make it a quick word. I'm working.'

'So are we,' Logan responded as he and Shelagh produced their warrant cards.

'I'm sorry, I didn't know that you were the police.' Bellamy's voice grew faint.

'I'm Detective Inspector Logan, and this is Detective Sergeant Ruby. We want to speak to you about the night before last, when you followed a blonde girl out of the Ocean club.'

'This is difficult, really, Mr Regan.'

'Logan.'

'Sorry. Like I said, it's difficult.'

'Only if you have something to hide,' Shelagh pointed out. Her first impression of Bellamy, the impact made on her by his looks and dynamism, was fading fast. Crudely tattooed on the bouncer's fingers were the words LOVE and HATE – the Borstal brand. In Logan's presence he had become just another silly kid acting like some hero of film or television.

'It's not easy because I suffer from blackouts, periods of memory loss, and I only remember part of being on the beach that night,' Bellamy mumbled self-consciously.

'You're epileptic?' Logan enquired.

'No,' the bouncer protested, going on defensively, 'it's just that my time-sense is all confused.'

'You get your dreams and daydreams mixed up?' Logan suggested.

'No,' Bellamy protested animatedly. 'I smoke.'

'Reefers?' Shelagh asked.

Bellamy replied with a curt nod. 'That's the problem. I never touched that girl, never even got near her. I'm telling you about the dope because I'd rather have you pull me in because of it.'

'Your pathetic habits don't interest us,' an impatient Logan said. Shelagh heard his breath hiss in softly. Like a snake. His eyes were fastened on Bellamy's face so as not to lose sight of even the slightest expression as he went on, 'Just tell us about this girl.'

Becoming increasingly uncomfortable, Bellamy spoke nervously. 'I got down to the beach before her. I was sitting on some rocks, and when I saw her coming towards me I lit up a spliff. When she was a little way away she stripped right off and walked towards the sea. I took a deep drag and got down off the rock, and I don't remember anything after that.'

'That's convenient. What about the other guy who came out of the club after her?' Logan asked quickly, keeping up the pressure.

'Oh yeah,' the bouncer said. 'That was a kid called Rick. He stayed up on the prom, leaving the blonde to me. Not that it did any good.'

'Did you see anyone else other than the girl and this boy named Rick?' Shelagh asked.

'Nope.' Bellamy was adamant. Then he creased his brow in a frown. 'Apart from whoever it was lurking around under the pier.'

'There was someone under the pier?' Logan spoke sharply.

'I think so, but I wouldn't swear to it, though I believe that I did see a shadow moving. Rick said that there was a guy there, and he got a good look at him.'

'Did Rick know this man?' Shelagh questioned the bouncer.

'No, but he described him to that other girl, Norma, and she said that she ...' Breaking off mid-sentence, Bellamy's face took on a wary, apprehensive look. 'She's dead, too, isn't she? I'm talking myself into trouble here.'

'I'd say that you were talking yourself *out* of trouble, Ed,' Logan disagreed, no longer belligerent. 'You think Norma knew the identity of the man under the pier?'

'She thought she knew him from the description that Rick gave. Norma was going to point out the guy to Rick today.'

Listening to this, Shelagh could actually feel the tiny hairs rise on her forearms, and an icy-cold prickle ran down her spine. She was aware that what Bellamy had just said was of vital importance, but knew that she lacked the experience to successfully analyse it. Shelagh guessed that the astute Logan had picked up on it, but his facial expression gave nothing away.

'Norma didn't mention a name?' Logan asked.

'No, not that I heard.'

'We'll let you get on with your work, Ed. You've given us a lot of help, thank you,' Logan slapped the bouncer on the shoulder.

'Am I a suspect, Mr Logan?' a fraught Bellamy asked.

'Difficult to say,' Logan answered enigmatically.

That was something Shelagh took up with her boss as they drove away from the club. 'Did you believe Bellamy's account of his memory loss, guv?'

'I reckon it's kosher, Sergeant. He's on the skids. A year from now he'll be mainlining. In two years he'll either be dead or wishing that he was.'

'What a waste,' Shelagh heard herself say.

Chuckling softly, Logan remarked, 'Wasn't it you who said that I wore my heart on my sleeve, Sergeant? I wouldn't have thought Bellamy was your type.'

'He isn't, guv,' Shelagh said in hurried denial. 'Who has he modelled himself on? Clint Eastwood?'

'Possibly,' Logan laughed. 'All of us are plagiarists, Sergeant. Maybe there's a parallel universe in which we are real people. In this world we certainly aren't.'

'I admire you as a thinker, guv.'

'Thinking is a curse, Sergeant. I envy the Ed Bellamys and the football hooligans.'

'You won't get me to believe that, guv,' Shelagh said emphatically. 'Do you think that there was a man under the pier, guv?'

'I certainly hope so. He's our first link between the deaths of the girls, Sergeant. If he murdered Penny Silver, then he'd need to kill Norma Harrington to prevent her from identifying him through Rick Downton.'

'But how could he know that she could identify him, guv?'

'That's something we'll need to ask Downton.'

'Now?' Shelagh enquired.

His hard face illuminated dramatically by the faint lights from the dashboard, Logan smiled. 'Being a coward, Sergeant, I lack the guts to face Catherine Wilmott at this time of night. We'll go take a look at the seaside entertainers now, and speak to the lad again in the morning.'

Julie said, 'That's where I work.'

With Matthew Colby's arm around her waist, she slowed as they passed the brightly lit but totally deserted supermarket. The day had gone better than she'd dared hope. Matthew was great fun to be with. Although the tragedy of her friend was still uppermost in Julie's mind, it was bearable. They had gone to the second house of the summer show, where Julie had found herself enjoying the songs, and had even laughed at the comedian's simple jokes in spite of the easily anticipated punch lines.

'I'll do all my weekly shopping here in future,' Matthew said.

'You fool.' Julie jabbed an elbow lightly and playfully into his ribs. 'What do you do, Matthew? I bet it's something important.'

Steering her into a shadowy area he kissed her, and Julie responded. They moved on, their rhythmic walk almost a dance. He shrugged. 'There's nothing important about what I do, Julie.'

From where they were she could see the clock on St John's church and it was twenty to twelve. It wasn't late. She slowed their walk, not wanting the evening to end.

'You're fibbing. Let me guess. I'd say … yes, you're a film director.'

He laughed. 'I did own a Kodak Brownie when I was a kid.'

'You work for the government, then, the head of MI5 or MI6.'

'If I was clever enough for that,' he told her seriously, 'I'd forget my holiday and investigate the murder of your friend.'

Hearing Norma's death referred to didn't upset Julie as much as she would have expected. In a way she was glad that Matthew had mentioned it. They would soon be passing where Norma's body had been found, and that would be easier now that he had raised the subject. Julie asked, 'Why would you do that, Matthew?'

'Whoever killed that young girl shouldn't get away with it,' he answered softly.

'I agree, Matthew.'

'There has to be a reason, a motive.' He shook his head wonderingly. 'Did she seem frightened that something would happen to her?'

Julie was thoughtful. 'No, there was nothing like that. She was different in the Blue Angel last night. There was something worrying her about the boy she was with.'

'Did she say what it was, Julie?'

'I think so,' Julie said dubiously, 'but it didn't make sense.'

His voice was far away saying, 'Perhaps I could make something of it.'

They were nearing the corner of Stewart Road, and the depression in the hedge showed up in the street lighting as a chilling dark shadow. Julie begged, 'Can we stop talking about Norma, please?'

'Of course. I'm sorry, it was insensitive of me,' Matthew whispered.

Sitting at a dressing table in front of Logan, the phoney blonde stretched her chin forward. Her face was framed in the six lights encircling a vanity mirror. Shelagh saw Logan look quickly away as the girl peeled off false eyelashes. She guessed that, like her, he was already sickened by the perfumed smell of make-up that was layered on the heavy air. Backstage at the Pavilion Theatre was not a pleasant place.

The effervescent Jason Fulton was a charming host. He lit a cigar and had a comfortable halo of smoke above his head when he gestured with his head to the girl who was now removing her make-up. 'That's Debs. She shared digs with poor Penny.'

The communal dressing room was crowded with performers, all of them talking and nobody listening. There were no celebrities in the show. Shelagh picked out two or three retreads, performers from the 1960s recognisable only due to television repeats.

'More than a little sad, isn't it, Detective Sergeant?' Fulton commented. 'They and I have seen better days. In the way elephants head off into the jungle to die, people like us head for the seaside show.'

Shelagh gently chided him. 'That's a bit over-dramatic, Mr Fulton.'

'Not in the least,' Fulton objected. 'We were all music hall stars in our own right. What that meant and what we did is slipping out of knowledge.' He turned to Logan. 'Tell me, Detective Inspector, do you believe that the young people will listen to us before we leave?'

'Depends on what you've got to say.' Logan shrugged. 'But I doubt it.'

The brusque answer hurt. Jason Fulton was mildly rebuking. 'I could say much of importance, Detective Inspector. When I am on stage I'm truly in the presence of something divine which lies within as well as without, and fills me with awe. When I bow to the audience I stand quiet for a moment, with bowed head the way one stands silent and reverent before the altar in a church.'

Standing, the girl named Debs slipped out of a bright turquoise button-through dress. In her skimpy bra and panties she did a burlesque stage walk towards them. 'How can I help you nice officers?' she asked with a white-toothed smile as she sat on a stool.

'We understand that Penny Silver was your roommate,' Shelagh opened up the conversation.

'That's right.'

'We want you to tell us everything that you can,' Logan advised.

'There isn't a lot to tell. Penny was just a young girl who liked to have fun.'

'Having fun includes men friends?' Logan asked.

Debs raised plucked eyebrows. 'You can't have much fun without them, unless you're a lesbo, mate.'

'Detective Inspector Logan.'

'Sorreeeee!' the blonde girl said in exaggerated apology.

'Did she have any special boyfriend?' Shelagh enquired.

'They were all special to her,' Debs answered. 'But none of them seemed the slightest bit dodgy to me. Jason could tell you more than me. Penny got on with him better than I did.'

'Would you say that Penny was particularly intelligent?' Logan enquired.

'Too true,' Debs answered with an awed gasp. 'She was really sharp. Nobody got the better of her.'

'Her killer did,' Logan bluntly reminded the blonde. 'Can

you think of a reason why anyone would want Penny dead? Was she perhaps two-timing anyone?'

Debs gave a little laugh. 'She didn't know how to be faithful to any one guy.'

'Can you be sure of that?' Logan asked.

'Yeah, of course I can. All the guys knew where they stood with her.'

'Maybe one of them got the wrong message,' Shelagh suggested. 'What about any of the younger men in the show, the dancers or whatever? Was Penny involved with any of them?'

'Now you are really joking!' Debs laughed, swinging a hand to take in the other performers who were in various stages of dress or undress. 'Look at them, for God's sake! A bunch of screaming poofs.'

Suddenly changing her line of questioning, Shelagh caught the girl off-balance. 'Did Penny have a friend named Norma, Norma Harrington?'

'Not as far as …' Debs began but stopped speaking. Then she asked, 'That's the other girl who was murdered, isn't it?'

Shelagh gave an affirmative nod.

'Definitely not,' the girl said emphatically.

'You sound very sure,' Logan commented.

Debs' eyes tightened a moment and she watched Logan carefully. 'I am, because it occurred to me when the second girl was found dead. I explored every possibility, and came up with nothing.'

Logan probed further. 'Couldn't Penny have had anything to do with the other girl, Norma, without you being aware of it?'

'Definitely not.' Debs shook her head. 'Everyone in a show like this lives in each other's pockets.'

'Can you give us a list of the names of Penny's most regular boyfriends?'

Debs looked dumbfounded at Shelagh. 'They were just boys down on holiday. I don't even remember their first names.'

'All of them just boys?' Logan checked.

'Well ...' Debs gave a non-committal shrug. 'There was a guy rang Penny regularly from London. She reckoned it was her father, but I know for a fact her old man buggered off years ago, just like mine did.'

'This man, whoever he was, never came down here to visit Penny?'

'Never, Inspector,' the girl answered. 'Penny was boasting to me last week that she'd just hooked herself some toff here in Havensport.'

Shelagh said, 'Do you know his name?'

'No ...' Debs spoke dubiously, making a little moue. 'But he gave her a great bracelet a few days back. It was beautiful, real expensive-looking.'

'Penny's belongings have been examined, Debs,' Logan reminded the girl, 'and there was no sign of a bracelet.'

Debs pointed an accusing finger at Logan. 'You think I'm lying. Penny didn't like the bracelet, so she gave it to me. She asked me not to wear it until we left Havensport.'

Accepting this, Logan warned the girl, 'We'll have to take that bracelet off you, Debs. Hopefully just for a while.'

'That's OK,' the blonde said as Logan and Shelagh stood. 'Do you want to come home with me now to collect it?'

'No, tomorrow will do. I'll have a Detective Constable Wallace call to pick it up.'

'I'll have it ready for him,' Debs promised, giving them both an incredibly sweet smile.

Jason Fulton confronted them at the door, standing with an affectionate arm round the plump shoulders of a woman past middle age. Proudly introducing her, Fulton gave the name of a film actress of yesteryear that was still remembered. An attractiveness still lurked under her chubbiness. Shelagh couldn't equate this elderly woman with the image of a star of the silver screen that mention of her name had conjured up.

'We are the old guard,' Fulton informed them, giving his

companion a one-armed hug. 'In our profession we are the followers of noble causes, heroes and heroines who at times have risen to the heights of being demigods.'

'Only a real trouper could still be going at this time of night, Jason,' Logan praised the old actor.

'At the final sunset, Inspector Logan, I will be at the graveside reading my own eulogy,' Fulton called after them.

'I can believe that,' Shelagh laughed deep in her throat when they were in Logan's car.

They drove out of the theatre car park on to the seafront. A pulsing sheet of stained lights stretched along the promenade. The tourist traps. The air was uncomfortably sultry as midnight approached.

'I'm right in thinking that you're billeted in New Street?' Logan asked, slowing the car.

'Temporarily,' Shelagh replied. 'I've got a room with a Mrs Weaver. I'm her only boarder. I intend to get my own flat as soon as I can.'

They turned into New Street. The tall houses on each side of them were a reminder of London that made Shelagh slightly claustrophobic. Logan advised, 'Wait until the end of the season, Sergeant. You'll find it easier and cheaper to rent a place then.'

Without needing to ask the house number, he parked the car at the kerbside in the semi-lit road. Shelagh could sense arrival draining away the pleasure of the journey. Recent events rapidly began to creep up on her, especially being closely associated with death, the deaths of girls younger than she was. Logan had turned his head to study her solicitously.

When he spoke he used her name instead of her rank. 'It's been tough on you, Shelagh.'

'It catches up with you, doesn't it,' Shelagh said nodding.

'Every time. Does Molly Weaver operate a curfew – lock the door at midnight?'

'No. Why do you ask?'

'I was going to suggest that we go back to my place,' an unusually awkward Logan said. 'All that's on offer is a glass of Irish and some country music.'

'I'd like that. I don't think I could stand being on my own right now,' Shelagh said as Logan restarted the engine of the car.

Shelagh was surprised to be driven through the old section of Havensport. They passed an ancient cattle-market with eighteenth-century porticoes, and a corn merchants and saddlers shops that had resisted the passage of time. Woolworth's, although tiny by big town standards, was an anachronism balanced out by a black and white Tudor building that had been converted into a cinema – around the time of the Great War was Shelagh's guess. The area had an attractive urbane obedience that gave it an air of tranquillity.

Expecting an apartment, an impressed Shelagh discovered that Logan's home was a house that stood two storeys tall and offered good views of both the moonlit bay and the countryside.

'You have a beautiful house, guv,' she congratulated him.

Logan pulled a wry face. 'The one luxury I allow myself, Sergeant. I bought it with money from the army, but I expect the Police Authority has checked me out.'

'It's not a place they'd expect a detective inspector to live in,' Shelagh agreed as they went in.

The lounge was a surprisingly large square room with an oriental theme for its décor. Everything was aesthetically of the Orient – the carpet and wallpaper, even the light fixtures.

'Wow! This is marvellous, guv.' Shelagh enthused. 'Not a trace of anything ostentatious or vulgar. I envy both your skill and your taste.'

'I can't take the credit.' Logan raised both hands in a gesture of surrender. 'I had it designed. Make yourself comfortable.'

With a choice of either a settee or armchair, Shelagh chose the latter. Had she sat on the settee Logan may well have considered it a precocious move, an invite for him to sit beside her.

Shelagh still hadn't adjusted to Logan, a man who deliberately played down everything, keeping himself and all around him low key, having such a grand home as this.

Kris Kristofferson was singing 'Help Me Make It Through the Night' on the CD player. Eyes closed, Shelagh was wagging her head gently to the beat when Logan passed her a glass of whisky.

'Well, Shelagh?' he asked when he had settled comfortably on the settee.

'Well what, guv?'

'Will you be staying down here in the wilderness, or going back to the big city?'

Shelagh said thoughtfully, 'You're a man of the world. What would you advise?'

He shrugged. 'It's your life. I suppose it depends on whether you're ambitious or seeking the quiet life.'

'I don't really know what I'm looking for, guv.'

'I doubt that any of us do,' he said philosophically. 'We probably couldn't alter anything if we did know.'

'You think that our lives are predestined, guv, that we don't have any choice?'

'Maybe small choices,' Logan conceded. 'When I joined the army first I was hitchhiking home one morning and I met a tramp along the road. When I asked which way he was heading he said that it depended on the wind. If it were blowing in his face he would turn and walk the other way. Later I became a captain in the army and now I'm an inspector in the police, but I still envy that tramp his freedom.'

'If you're right, guv,' Shelagh said ruefully, 'I might as well stay down here in the West Country and let fate do what it will.'

'I'd like you to do so,' he said quietly, astonishing her.

She looked with sudden deep interest and something that was probably affection at Logan, whose stern features were contradicted not only by a glance that was sentimental and shy, but also by what seemed to be a warmth of feeling for her.

Made uneasy by her silent appraisal, he apologized. 'I'm sorry. That was selfish of me, Sergeant.'

'I'll take it as your professional opinion, guv,' she said with a lightness she didn't feel.

His eyes reached hers across the few feet that separated them. 'That would be a mistake.'

Logan had spoken meaningfully, and, stirred by his words, Shelagh was searching for a way to have him expand on what he had said, when the telephone rang.

'Excuse me.'

Resenting the interruption, Shelagh waited while he walked across the room to pick up the phone. Identifying himself, he first listened and then said, 'I'll be right there.'

Replacing the receiver, he turned apologetically to Shelagh. 'I'm wanted elsewhere.'

'Not another body?' Shelagh gasped apprehensively.

'No, thank God,' Logan replied. 'That was the chief constable's wife. She believes there is an intruder in the house.'

'I'll come with you, guv.' Shelagh stood, reaching for her handbag.

'No,' he said firmly. 'You need to rest, Sergeant. I'll drop you off at your digs along the way. This is probably a false alarm, anyway.'

Unable to argue, Shelagh followed him out of the house. She thought it strange that the chief constable's wife should call Logan instead of following normal routine by ringing the station. It posed a question that she didn't dare ask.

nine

Driving along the meandering road at the cliff top, Logan several times cut his headlights in high places when they were likely to be seen from the chief constable's house. If the intruder was still there he didn't want to scare him off. Whoever it was trailing Melanie Biles was both clever and endlessly patient. Reaching the picnic area where he had parked the car that morning, he let the vehicle coast silently in and stopped it. Closing the car door quietly, he ran through the night, his soft-soled shoes making no sound. Melanie had said on the telephone that she thought the intruder was in her study, which was on the ground floor. She had locked herself in her room, so Logan had no need to worry about her.

Reaching the house he leapt over a back wall, landing lightly and soundlessly. With his back against the wall of the house he edged towards what he knew to be the study window. Assuming that the intruder had gone in through the window, Logan estimated that he would come out the same way. Hearing a soft scraping noise, he ducked under the window to come up at the other side. With every muscle in his body relaxed to the point from where it could spring instantly into action, he waited.

Logan was caught out by a short but swift sequence of events. The sound of a door opening behind him, just a foot or so away, had him snap his head around to see a figure coming out fast. He glimpsed an agile man whose long dark hair flew about wildly as he rushed out into the night. Ready for him, Logan intended to use his right foot to trip the intruder, then fell him with a right-hand punch as he lost his balance. But he was distracted by the sound of an upper window being opened.

'Randy!'

It was Melanie calling down to him, her voice made squeaky by panic. Taking a glance up in her direction, Logan soon realized his mistake. The silhouette of the burglar was coming at him, wielding what looked like a stick but felt like an iron bar as it cracked against the side of Logan's head. The pain was momentary, but blackness quickly rushed in on him. Aware that he was dropping to the ground, he then knew no more.

The next he knew was Melanie reaching down to help him to his feet. She was talking fast, gabbling a mixture of explanation and apology. 'I'm so sorry. I remembered that I hadn't locked the back door after watering the flowers earlier. That must have been how he got in, and I wanted to warn you that he would come out through the door.'

Some of the darkness of unconsciousness was still there as Melanie pressed a folded handkerchief against his temple. Logan grinned at her in the night. 'Don't worry about it. No harm done.'

There was no point in pursuing an attacker who would be long gone. Though he had got only a fleeting glance of the man, there had been something familiar about him. Logan was sure that whatever it was would click into place once the pain in his head eased.

With a hand on his arm to guide him into the house, Melanie spoke guiltily. 'I'm sorry about your head, Randy.'

'My own fault for being taken unawares.'

'If I hadn't called out you wouldn't have been.'

'Who knows?' Logan shrugged philosophically.

In the study, the drawers of a kneehole desk had all been opened and the floor around them was littered with papers. It was the same with a couple of cupboards, the doors of which were open with documents spilling out.

Looking around her, Melanie commented, 'It's not so bad as I feared.'

'He wasn't your average burglar,' Logan said, gesturing with his head to an ornamental carriage clock and antique ornaments all left undisturbed on a shelf. 'What are all the documents, Melanie?'

'This is where I do my work,' she answered. 'All council stuff.'

He walked to check a small safe in one corner of the room. It was intact. Turning, he watched Melanie worriedly go to a steel filing cabinet, the top two drawers of which had been forced open. Dropping to sit on her heels with an anxious expression on her face, she unlocked the bottom drawer. Sliding it out silently on its metal runners, she reached into the drawer for a soft leather briefcase. Unzipping the case without taking it from the drawer, Melanie quickly examined the contents before zipping the case and closing and locking the drawer. Standing, she gave a heartfelt sigh of relief.

Logan watched her for a moment then enquired, 'Something particularly valuable?'

'Not really. Just family photographs and things. Sentimental value, as they say.'

'I see.' Logan nodded. 'Right, we'd better leave everything as it is and I'll get SOCO out here.'

'No!' Melanie said sharply. 'Look, Randy, as he came in through an unlocked door there are no signs of a break-in. I'd just like to tidy up and forget it. There is no need for anyone to know, not even Kenneth.'

Logan was certain that she was hiding something. Bewilderment creased his forehead, which boosted the pain in his head. Whatever it was would be no business of his had the burglary not made it so. He looked at her dubiously. 'You're asking a lot of a ranking police officer, Melanie.'

'I know that, and it is unfair of me,' she admitted. 'But I have no choice.'

'I never break the rules, Melanie.'

'Just this once, for me,' she pleaded.

He gave a tight-lipped shrug and then said, 'We'd better get this place cleared up before the chief constable gets home.'

'Thank you,' she said fervently. There was an odd note to her tone and her eyes were watching him carefully.

When they had the study back in order, she led the way into the lounge. She was plainly nervous and desperate for company and was planning to delay his departure. Standing at a drink cabinet clinking glasses and rattling ice, she invited him to sit down.

'Thank you, no,' Logan said. 'I had best be on my way.'

'At least let me show my gratitude by offering you a drink,' she said smilingly, coming towards him with a glass in each hand, held high.

Wanting to question her, needing to question her to find out whether her burglar was also her stalker, Logan found himself taking the drink and saying nothing other than, 'Thank you.'

He was very aware that there was no sign of either seam or hem of undergarment showing beneath the silken Pucci mini sheath that she wore. The exercise in tidying the study had warmed her body to bring out a womanly body-scent that drifted to him. Logan wondered what his face would show if he permitted it to be honest.

'The chief constable should be back soon,' he commented.

Glancing at a grandfather clock, Melanie turned her face back to him. She let out a low laugh and picked a cigarette up out of a silver box on the table and lit it. 'Almost two hours yet.' Her tone was calculated to perfection, not betraying whether there was any innuendo in what she had just said. Then her teeth glinted in a small grin and she raised her glass to him. 'What shall we drink to?'

'Absent friends?' Logan laconically suggested.

'Meaning my husband.' Melanie fiddled with her necklace.

'That's your interpretation,' Logan pointed out.

'The only possible interpretation you allowed me,' she complained, then questioned him anxiously. 'You can keep this break-in quiet, can't you? Does anyone else know that you came out here?'

'My sergeant, Shelagh Ruby.'

'Oh dear!'

'Don't worry, she'll say nothing,' Logan replied. Shelagh was the best sidekick he'd had either in the army or the police. Finishing his drink, he placed the glass down on a table. 'I must be on my way.'

She seemed to deliberately lean forward, and he jerked back away from her. Somehow able to contain his frustration, he was on the move when, with a fake pout, she took his fingers in a gentle handshake. 'You've been very kind to me, Randy Logan.'

Melanie walked across the hall to the door with him. The sound of her heels castanetting on the parquet flooring and the fragrance of her perfume were things alien to the life of all work and no play that he had been living.

Being with her made him really measure himself, and the fun was gone. The wild fun in the nightspots of Germany when he had been younger; the exquisite fun of the Orient; the fun of getting drunk, laughing, brawling with men like himself, hard men; the fun of women. He felt a sudden regret at time wasted.

Logan thought that his exit was graceful for a man who had just won a particularly violent battle with himself. He was halfway to his car before he could risk relaxing the superhuman resolve he had managed to muster when Melanie Biles had been standing close to him. She seemed to be in the car with him. Her odour was everywhere, her perfume in everything he touched, and it had even impregnated his hands. But he knew that it would fade faster than his memory of her.

Driving slowly back down into town, Logan flicked through his memories of the past hour. Melanie hadn't convinced him with her story about the briefcase containing family photo-graphs. From her relief on opening the case it was evident that its contents were what the intruder had been after but had failed to find. Thinking of the intruder had Logan's methodical mind come up with an answer to the question that had plagued him since seconds before he had been hit with the iron bar. The long dark hair had given the burglar away. It had been Terry Stevens, the man who managed the Ocean club for Gerald Reynolds.

At 9.30 in the morning, Chief Constable Kenneth Biles was still on a high from the press briefing he had just given. Wearing his high rank like a cape of royalty, he swept into the CID room. Of slightly less than average height and acutely conscious of it, he had an oddly-stretched-up walk as if he was constantly looking for something on a high shelf.

'Good morning.'

'Good morning, sir,' the assembly of detectives responded.

Walking to where Logan stood facing the others, Biles puck-ered his red face in puzzlement as he saw the dark blue swelling on Logan's brow. 'What happened to you, Detective Inspector?'

'Bumped into a door, sir,' Logan replied, waiting to learn if Biles knew anything of the break-in at his house.

With an annoyed grunt, Biles said, 'That is the kind of answer that detectives get not give. Is everyone here?'

'Everyone except for DC Wallace, sir,' Logan answered. 'I have him following up a lead.'

'Very well. I'll rely on you to bring Wallace up to date when he returns. Carry on, please, Detective Inspector.'

Using a marker pen, Logan wrote two names at the top of a large whiteboard affixed to the wall. He addressed the detec-tives: 'Edward Bellamy and Roderick Downton, our two principal suspects.' He added the names of the two dead girls below, and drew a line down from Bellamy to Penny Silver and a line from Bellamy to Norma Harrington. 'Bellamy followed Penny Silver out of the Ocean club and was on the beach around the time that she died. We also know that Bellamy was talking to Norma Harrington at the Blue Angel on the night that she died.'

'What of this Derek Wright fellow, the man staying at the caravan park?' Biles asked.

'Wright is an airhead who was cheating on his wife, sir. I've released him. He and his family have left for home,' Logan answered.

'As long as you are confident in the circumstances, Detective Inspector,' Biles said.

'I'm confident, sir.' Logan turned to a detective constable who sat on the edge of a table with legs dangling. 'Where was Derek Wright at the time the Silver girl died, Joe?'

'In Harper's Lane, guv, consorting with Hetty Hackett, one of Havensport's finest.'

'Not just an alibi, Inspector Logan?' the chief constable checked.

'DC Finnegan took a statement from the woman, sir,' Logan assured Biles. 'Years of professional whoredom tends to impart an unexpected honesty. The opposite would seem to apply to most other professions.'

'Including the police,' Biles said, annoyance crossing his red-purple face like a quick shadow.

Logan was aware that Biles detested his cynicism, his lack of respect for authority. 'I didn't say that, sir.'

Logan returned to the board to draw lines linking Downton to the two dead girls. 'Downton also left the Ocean club soon after Penny Silver, and the following night he walked Norma Harrington home, or rather, he left her in the area in which she was killed. We have two prime suspects, but that isn't enough.'

'Because neither of the suspects had a motive, sir,' a studious-looking detective constable spoke up.

'Exactly, Prior,' Logan concurred. 'We also have an X-factor that complicates things further. In fact, it's a Mr X.' Turning back to the board he wrote MR X. 'This is the man that both Bellamy and Downton say was lurking under the pier.' He added lines to link both Bellamy and Downton to MR X. Then he drew a line from Norma Harrington to MR X. 'We also believe that Downton described Mr X to Norma Harrington, and that she was confident that she knew him.'

The chief constable interrupted Logan. 'We need to bear in mind, Inspector Logan, that though we can't identify a motive for either of the two named suspects, neither have we a motive where the man under the pier is concerned.'

'I recognize that, sir. Consequently, I rate all three as equal suspects,' Logan answered, gesturing with his hand to where Shelagh Ruby sat. 'What do we know of Bellamy, DS Ruby?'

Shelagh's face was expressionless, but the tendons in her neck were taut against her skin as she answered. 'Born 1976, sir. Bermondsey, London. Served a three-year sentence for car theft at the Young Offenders Institute, Portland. He has worked as a doorman both in London and here at Havensport, but has no record of violence. Bellamy admits to following Penny Silver down to the beach. He recalls watching the girl strip naked and walk into the water, but remembers nothing after that. Bellamy uses drugs, sir, and suffers lapses of memory that apparently are attributable to his addiction.'

As Logan underlined the name Bellamy on the board DC Ami Symes raised a hand.

'What is it, Ami?'

'When I first left school I was employed at a factory. I worked with a woman who warned me that she suffered from black-outs. She told me: "Don't worry when it happens. I just fall down. Just let me lie still and I'll soon come round." That was what she *thought* happened, sir. In fact, when she had an attack she ran wildly around and had to be restrained to prevent her from causing damage and hurting herself.'

'The moral in your story, Ami?' Logan asked.

'It's possible that Bellamy wasn't as inactive when unconscious as he believes, sir.'

'A very good point, Ami,' Logan praised the detective constable and double underlined Bellamy's name on the board.

'I see what Ami says as a very real possibility, sir.' Shelagh scraped her chair back, her face thoughtful.

'But?'

'Bellamy was on the beach with the first victim, but he was definitely still in the Blue Angel when Norma Harrington was killed.'

'Which gives us two separate killers,' the detective named Prior suggested.

'Not necessarily, Ben.' Logan waved the suggestion away. 'Downton was in the immediate area when the Silver girl was killed, and there is no question that he was with the second girl shortly before her death. What do we know of Roderick Downton, DS Ruby?'

Shelagh shrugged, but that simple gesture implied an intense investigation. 'Born 1981, sir. Lives in Tottenham with his parents. Nothing known. Works as a sales assistant in a tailor's shop. I spoke on the telephone with his employer, who described Downton as a conscientious worker but immature and over-emotional.'

'Did the employer qualify his appraisal, Sergeant?'

'He did, sir,' Shelagh answered Logan. 'He claimed Downton was prone to what he described as tantrums when thwarted in even the slightest way.'

Underlining the name Downton three times on the board, Logan issued orders. 'Ami, you and Ben Prior ask around town about Downton. He's been here for something like a week, so ask the kids he's mixed with about his general behaviour. If he's thrown a wobbly of any kind since being in Havensport, then I want to know all the details.' He pointed at three young detective constables who were seated close together. 'You, Michelle, Joe and Edgar, do the rounds to gather everything you can about Norma Harrington – who her friends were, did she have a reputation, any long-term relationships that have gone wrong. You know the routine. Simon Betts' report says that she was *virgo entacta*. But a teaser is always in more danger from men than a raver.'

'And our mystery man, Inspector Logan?' Biles asked when Logan stopped talking.

'DS Ruby and I are going to interview the Downton boy again now, sir, and we'll get what description we can of the man under the pier.'

With the briefing at an end, Logan gathered up his papers from the desk and dropped them back in his case. Falling in beside Logan as they went out of the room, the chief constable had a curiously strange smile on his face. It wasn't a smile that had humour in it. He spoke confidentially, his voice low. 'I'd like your help on a personal matter, Randolph. I'm sure that Mrs Biles is not telling me something.'

'But ... well ... I don't think, sir, that ...' Logan felt ice in his stomach and a horrible dryness in his throat.

Biles' laughter cut off Logan's discomfort. 'Relax, Randolph. This isn't one of those I-have-this-friend-who-thinks-his-wife-is-playing-away pleas for advice. No, I think that there is something worrying her. Someone I put away may be back with an outsized grudge.'

'You think that's what could be happening, sir?'

'I'd say that's about the cut of it, Randolph.' Biles gave a nod of agreement. The blandness of his country face was more noticeable than usual and a garlicky smell hung over him from the previous night. 'Melanie is a loyal, loving wife who wouldn't want to worry me.'

'I can have Pat Flann increase the patrols in the area of your house, sir,' Logan offered.

'I'd appreciate that,' the chief constable said gratefully. 'I hesitate to ask more of you, Randolph, but I am so tied up with civic function at the moment that I'd appreciate it if you could take a personal interest in this. Possibly call on Mrs Biles occa-sionally, see if you can draw her out on what's worrying her.'

'I'll do my very best, sir.'

'I knew that I could depend on you,' Biles said, giving Logan's arm a grateful squeeze and walking off as DC Wallace came hurrying up. Wallace was a nice young detective who bubbled over with enthusiasm.

'Sorry I'm late, guv.' Wallace apologized. 'I picked up the bracelet from that chorus girl, or whatever she is?'

'I don't know what she is, Toby,' Logan said flatly. 'Go on.'

'Then I ended up in Twyverne, guv, but it was worth the sixty-mile round trip. I found the jeweller who sold the bracelet. It cost ... wait for it, guv, eight hundred and fifty quid.'

Logan gave a low whistle. 'Make my day, Toby, tell me it was paid for by cheque.'

'I wasn't that lucky, guv.' Wallace shook his head. 'But the jeweller remembered the customer. He said it was a youngish bloke with a hard face and long hair.'

Terry Stevens. The description fitted, and Logan was certain that it was Stevens who had attacked him in the dark. What did that mean? Logan doubted that Stevens could afford to buy an item of jewellery for a girl, and he was more likely to purchase cufflinks for a boyfriend. The bridge between the burglary and the purchase of the bracelet had to be Gerald Reynolds. Reynolds was a councillor and so was Melanie Biles. Where Penny Silver entered the equation was a question that had Logan stumped right then.

'I bought the wife a necklace while I was there. Cost me £4.99, guv,' Wallace said, asking cheekily, 'Can I claim it on expenses?'

'You can try, Toby,' Logan replied in a way that said he didn't recommend it.

The only other customers in the café that morning were a few workmen and a couple of housewives taking a break after shopping. Ed Bellamy sipped his coffee, hoping that caffeine might impart Dutch courage the way alcohol was said to. The visit from Logan and the woman detective sergeant had unnerved him. He was still panicking, but now it was a controlled panic. The decision to take action had eased things.

The girl behind the counter, her hair swept up like she was at some elegant ball and not serving in a greasy spoon, was trying to catch his eye. Ed wasn't interested. He had Rick Downton's address and he was building up the resolve to call on him.

If Downton was still free then the two of them could get things together, back each other. Ed had no faith in much-vaunted British justice. He had spent time with boys at Portland who had been banged up for offences they definitely hadn't committed.

Newent Road was just round the corner. Draining his cup, Bellamy left the café on reluctant legs. Turning the corner into Newent Road his two heels scraped, as though he was about to turn and go back the way he had come. Common sense told him to keep on walking, to arrange a cast-iron alibi with Rick Downton. He knew what the filth was capable of. They preferred to fit up the guy they had in the station rather than go to the trouble of stepping outside and catching the real culprit.

Finding the house, he pressed the doorbell. The only result was ringing somewhere deep inside the house. In a way he was relieved not to get a reply. He was considering using the bell again, when he heard a woman's voice behind him.

'Are you looking for Roderick?'

The question momentarily threw Bellamy. 'Rick Downton, yes.'

'Are you one of his friends?' she enquired, as she searched in her handbag for the door key.

'Yes.' Bellamy stretched the truth.

'Good. I'm glad you've come. Roderick needs cheering up.' Unlocking the door, the woman shoved her shoulder against it.

Sticking at first, the door opened with a rush. 'I expect he's still in bed.'

They were in a small lobby with a half-glass door in front of them. Bellamy kept himself away from the woman. Young girls were full of sugar and spice and smelled real nice, but older women had a staleness about them that got down into his stomach and caused him trouble.

'I'll soon have Roderick up and about,' she promised Bellamy as she turned the shiny-brass handle and pushed the door open.

He was planning his conversation when Catherine Wilmott spun round to face him. She looked very old and awfully silly with her eyes popping out of her head and her mouth hanging open. Then the old woman began opening and closing her mouth like a fish, making soundless screams. Rushing to get out of the house, she collided heavily with Bellamy, knocking her hat askew. Beginning to cry, little wild animal sounds, she pushed past him and ran out of the door.

Bewildered, Bellamy screwed up his eyes to peer through the shadows at the carpeted flight of stairs. There was no cheerful morning light to dispel the morbid grey gloom of the passage. Despite this being summer, there was a coldness in the house, a thin, watery coldness. He sensed something portentous and horrible, and when he looked to the right what he saw frosted his spine. Rick Downton was hanging from the banisters. His head appeared to have been half severed by a cord that was biting into his neck. His eyes and his swollen tongue protruded grotesquely.

As Logan swung the car into Newent Road, Shelagh gave a little gasp of astonishment at the sight of a large crowd milling around at the far end of the cul-de-sac. People jammed both the road and the pavement, forcing Logan to park some way back from the Wilmott house. As Logan and Shelagh got out of the car they exchanged puzzled glances.

The men, women and children who had crowded up backed away from them. Ed Bellamy was half collapsed and supported by the doorjamb of Catherine Wilmott's house. Catherine herself was sagging at the knees, held up by a big-built woman, her eyes staring into the distance, looking at something that no one else there could see.

'What's happened?' Logan asked no one in particular.

'There's someone dead in the house.' A man with a grubby towel over his shoulders and shaving soap covering one half of his face pointed towards the open front door. 'Blew his bloody brains out with a shotgun.'

A woman with her hair in curlers turned reproachfully on the speaker. 'There you go with your tales again, Vernon Kelver.' She looked at Logan. 'There was no shot, sir. Are you a policeman, sir?'

Not replying, Logan, with Shelagh at his side, went to where the white-faced Ed Bellamy was propped in the doorway. 'What's this all about, Bellamy? Get a grip, son.'

Bellamy's lips quivered like the sudden release of a static charge. Roughly gripping the doorman's arm with the intention of moving him into the house, Logan could feel the boy trembling. Struggling violently, Bellamy broke away from Logan and scrambled to stand, cowering several feet from the door.

'I guess it's up to us, Sergeant,' Logan said resignedly. As he used his foot to push the door of the house open, he added, 'Brace yourself, Shelagh. This is going to be nasty.'

ten

H avensport had been shocked into staring silence. It was something to talk about, but later on, perhaps in a few days after
the three funerals. This was too big for local and visitor alike,
too strange and incomprehensible: they could not understand
what had been in the mind of a young murderer, who had been
too much a complex character for their simple deductions. It
would have been more credible had he robbed or raped his two
victims. You often read about that sort of thing in the newspapers. But the matter of two motiveless murders they could not
fathom. And then killing himself? What could you make of it all?

Logan knew what to make of it immediately the first slanting
rays of the sun wakened him. They streaked across the rooftops
and were reflected from the rows of plate-glass windows of the
tall block of holiday apartments that stood at an angle between
his house and the bay. Folding his hands behind his head on the
pillow, he reflected. He was personally responsible for the
death of the boy. The legalized bullying of his interrogation had
caused Roderick Downton's suicide. His regret over the boy's
death was tempered by the reasoning that someone as delicately balanced as Rick Downton could never have enjoyed life.

Carefully worded statements from the chief constable had
guided the media. It had been arranged for Logan to appear on
television with a prepared script. He had been ushered into the
tatty local television studio to sit at a table with the programme

host, who had smiled continuously but coldly, a perfect example of what self-regard can do to a man. He had given a glossy version of the two murders and suicide, and had then turned to Logan.

'In the studio with me tonight is Detective Inspector Randolph Logan, the man of the hour. Solving this case so quickly must be a triumph for you, Inspector Logan.'

'I didn't solve it,' Logan had replied. 'If it has been solved, then the boy who killed himself solved it. There is nothing triumphant about a suicide.'

Carefully keeping off camera, the floor manager had approached to stretch out a leg to kick Logan on the ankle and hiss: 'This is a live interview, sweetie.'

Calming down, Logan had from then on stuck to what he had been told to say. That proved to be enough to placate the chief constable, who had afterwards made no mention of Logan's venture into free speech.

A show of public respect had been brief, and now the resort was once again programmed for pleasure. Posters advertising the coming carnival were appearing, and the murder of two young girls no longer figured largely in conversations. Logan was far from at ease with what others regarded as a successful end to the murder investigation. Sensing this, Kenneth Biles had stated unequivocally that the matter was finished.

There had been so much activity that Logan had not been to see Melanie Biles. It would have been painful had he done so, because he would have been acting a part, playing a game, hiding himself from her. Neither had the chief constable the chance to refer to the problems his wife had been having. This made life easier for Logan. Though uncertain as to what Melanie was mixed up in, Logan doubted that she was entirely innocent. Suspecting her duplicity in that mystery alerted him to how dangerous was her mildly seductive behaviour towards him.

It was another superb summer day. Apart from one hurrying

cloud, small and light as a puff of smoke, there was nothing ominous in the bright blue morning sky. Logan was mentally debating whether or not to make breakfast when the doorbell rang.

He found a nervously smiling Shelagh Ruby on the threshold. Embarrassed, her face was away from him as if watching something interesting out in the bay. When she turned back the early sunlight sharpened the colour of her complexion, giving her a fragile transparency. Her eyes focused sleepily and she smiled at Logan. Wearing a slender pale blue skirt and matching jacket, she was even more attractive than he had thought. Both of her hands were round a jar of instant coffee that she held up. 'This is like that coffee advertisement on the telly, guv. Am I intruding?'

'We're colleagues, Sergeant, so it wouldn't be possible for you to intrude,' Logan assured her.

Still hesitant, she said, 'You know what they say about every-thing in moderation. The happy medium, and all that.'

'I'd agree with that in most things, but not where you're concerned, Shelagh,' he told her gallantly.

She came in, the morning air still on her, carelessly using fingers to comb her hair back from her face, smiling at Logan. Following him into the kitchen, Shelagh put the jar of coffee on the table. 'There's my contribution, guv.'

'You don't have to sing for your supper, or breakfast, here, Shelagh,' he said as he took a jar of coffee from a cupboard. 'We'll drink mine and you can take yours home.'

She gave a little laugh and pure excitement glinted in her eyes. Extending her hands slowly like a magician about to perform a trick of levitation, she then clasped them together. 'I don't need the coffee, I have plenty in my room, guv. I bought it as a passport for a visit to the supermarket to have a word with Julie Bolt.'

'That case is closed, Shelagh.' Logan frowned, then raised an eyebrow questioningly, spoon poised over the sugar bowl.

'Two, please, guv.' She slipped smoothly out of her jacket. Her lacy sleeveless blouse was a quiet colour, a peaceful peach. 'How do you feel about Rick Downton taking the rap, as our American cousins say, guv?'

'Not happy,' he admitted. 'I regret pushing the kid that hard.'

'I didn't get a lot of sleep last night,' Shelagh said, almost to herself.

'It was a bitch of a night,' Logan agreed, 'but bad nights happen to everyone. There's only one cure.'

'Which is?' a dubious Shelagh enquired.

'You walk away from whatever is causing the problem.'

Taking her coffee from him, a surprised Shelagh remarked softly, 'I'd never have guessed that was your philosophy, but if you're prepared to walk away from the murder of those two girls, then you won't be interested in what I came here to tell you, guv.'

She was standing too close to him, causing them both to feel the jarring impact of new and sudden emotions. Things were moving too fast. Logan was alarmed by the easy relationship between his sergeant and himself. Ordinary conversation in the police was normally limited by the embarrassment of rank. After a pause he said, 'I'm always prepared to listen, Sergeant.'

'It's what Julie Bolt had to say, guv,' she said evenly. 'Norma Harrington told her who she thought the man under the pier was.'

Logan asked, 'Who was it?'

'That guy we met at the Ocean club, the manager, Terry Stevens.'

She took a sip from her cup while Logan shuffled recent memories around in his mind. He gave a nod of satisfaction. 'That figures. Good work, Sergeant.'

'Do you still want to walk away from it, guv?'

'Only in a tactical sense,' Logan replied.

She gave him a suspicious look that dissolved quickly. 'So we haven't quit for good?'

'I don't know about we, but I haven't, Sergeant,' Logan answered. He had an intuitive feeling about the murders. But he always mistrusted intuition because every hunch produced an opposite shadow. 'I don't want to drag you into something that you may well live to regret. The top brass are happy with the Downton thing. It's a one hundred per cent result that looks good on paper. I had a word with Simon Betts. He's of the opinion that it may have been possible for Downton to have killed Norma Harrington with a surprise lucky blow, but the boy lacked the physical strength to strangle a girl like Penny Silver.'

'That clinches it for me. I'm with you, guv.'

'Whether we are right or wrong, Shelagh,' Logan warned, 'we won't get any medals, we won't get any thanks, and we may even be thrown out of the job.'

'A clear conscience is more important to me than my career,' Shelagh replied firmly.

Pursing his lips thoughtfully, Logan replied, 'If you are sure. I want to lean on Terry Stevens, but not until Toby Wallace gets back with something for me. I also need another word with Ed Bellamy.'

'I assumed that he was out of the frame, guv.'

'He was never really in it, Shelagh. What I'm hoping is that he'll remember more about the guy under the pier.'

'Something that points to Terry Stevens?'

'That would make my day,' Logan acknowledged.

For the first twenty minutes of lunch with Terry Stevens, Gerald Reynolds adhered to small-talk. They were in a roadhouse on the outskirts of the resort. It was a kind of country club for local high fliers. Reynolds was able to get them a vacant table for two in the rear. They discussed the Havensport summer season, which to date was the most profitable one on record. They talked about the vagaries of the nightclub game, and the ever-growing problem of drugs among their young patrons.

A waiter brought them martinis. Though Stevens would have preferred beer or whisky and ginger ale, he was relaxed in the aura of sophistication that Gerald Reynolds created. A rough diamond that could act tough when required, Stevens could also be a gentleman with poise and impeccable manners.

The club owner decided right then that it was time to get down to brass tacks. He changed the conversation by saying, 'Carnival night will be the ideal time for you to try again, Terry.'

Having hoped that the subject of burgling the chief constable's house wouldn't arise, Stevens was rocked off balance. Reynolds flashed him a quick smile, but then turned it off rapidly. It was not until he had gurgled his ice-cold drink down to calm his nerves that Stevens broke the sticky silence. He said, 'I'm not really cut out for that sort of thing, Mr Reynolds. I am not a criminal.'

Though following Melanie Biles to log her movements and contacts had been time-consuming, it had not been dangerous. But he had not recovered from the night DI Logan had surprised him at the chief constable's house.

'What I'm asking of you hardly puts you up there among the Krays, Terry.' Gerald Reynolds' tone had a slightly mocking ring to it.

'Logan came close to catching me.' Stevens' fingers tightened on the glass, the whiteness under the nails showing the strain.

'Every policeman, including Logan, will be fully occupied on carnival night,' Reynolds said reassuringly. 'You'll have all the time in the world to find Melanie Biles' papers. This is for my father more than me.'

'Does Mr Harvey Reynolds know about all this?' Stevens croaked in surprise.

'Of course he doesn't,' Gerald Reynolds snapped irritably. 'My father is one of the old school, community-minded, Terry. This town is showing its gratitude by preparing to finish his business.'

'But Mr Harvey Reynolds isn't taking this lying down,' Stevens argued mildly.

'Oh no,' Reynolds agreed cynically. 'He'll make strong speeches in the chamber and try to stop Compat Leisure by a majority vote in council. But these people fight dirty, and I need you to help me, Terry.'

'I will, Mr Reynolds. Don't worry on that score.'

'You don't need to tell me that,' Reynolds said. 'You did a grand job reporting back to me on who Melanie Biles is dealing with.'

'It meant you having to put in a lot of time at the club, Mr Reynolds.'

'Even a very able person such as yourself can't be in two places at once, Terry,' Reynolds said smiling.

Still uncertain, Stevens hesitantly ventured, 'I'm scared, Mr Reynolds, real scared.'

'I see this as no more than a little favour, Terry, a chance for you to show your appreciation of what I have done for you.'

'I do appreciate everything, honest, Mr Reynolds,' Stevens said hurriedly.

Four years ago he had arrived in Havensport as a Social Security claimant with absolutely no prospects. A chance meeting with Gerald Reynolds had changed all that. He had become Reynolds' protégé, a flawed Jeeves for a ruthless Wooster. Instantly aware that Stevens was gay, the homophobic Reynolds had sternly warned him, 'Keep it apart from your work and away from me, kid, and I'll just about be able to tolerate it.'

'You've got your bread buttered on both sides,' Reynolds remarked now as his eyes studied Stevens over the top of his raised glass, 'and you'd be well advised to keep that in mind.'

'It's just that I worry a lot, Mr Reynolds. There's the business of that girl on the beach.'

A flat expression drifted across Reynolds' face. He played Stevens' question back to him. 'What about the girl?'

Stevens made a choking noise; 'They could connect you and me with her, Mr Reynolds.'

'That's all over.' Reynolds drew in a long breath. 'That grockle killed her, and the other girl, then topped himself, Terry.'

'That reporter from the *Gazette* came in the club this morning, Mr Reynolds. He was saying that DI Logan is still asking questions, so he isn't satisfied.'

'The case is closed. Take my word for it.'

'I hope so, Mr Reynolds.'

'I know so.'

'Yeah, but …'

'There's no buts, Stevens,' Reynolds hissed. Reaching across the table with his right hand, Reynolds gripped Stevens' forearm tightly. To Stevens it was as if he had been grabbed by the lapels of his jacket and jerked across the table. Reynolds said in a deceptively gentle voice, 'Now, Terry, we need to concentrate on your visit to the Biles' house.'

'Are you sure these papers are there, Mr Reynolds?'

'They are there,' Reynolds replied confidently. 'It's a crappy little office, Terry, not the Pentagon. Was there anywhere you didn't look?'

With an apologetic nod, Stevens confessed, 'I hadn't finished searching a filing cabinet when I heard Logan outside. There were two drawers to go, so they must be in one of them.'

'They may have been then, but they won't be now. Melanie, that godawful woman, is too cute for that. You'll need to allow yourself plenty of time to search, Terry.'

'I won't let you down, Mr Reynolds.'

'It's in your best interests not to,' Reynolds told him, bending his arm to study his wristwatch. 'We'd better make a move.'

As they stepped out of the lift into the lobby of the town hall, the only sound was the whirr of a floor polisher as a caretaker went about his job. With Harvey Reynolds at her side, Melanie went out through wide glass doors that were like polished air. The meeting of the full council had gone well, with the last-minute details of the carnival finalized. It had all become harrowing for Melanie when Harvey Reynolds had made his solemn speech.

'Next year,' the old councillor had grimly predicted, wagging a finger, 'Compat Leisure will be running the carnival, ostensibly for charity but largely for profit. Perhaps some of us here today might participate in some small way. We'll probably be permitted to walk beside the procession carrying collection tins if we have a mind to.'

That had had Melanie squirming with guilt in her seat. Now she felt contaminated by her involvement in local government corruption. As soon as she could politely take her leave of Harvey Reynolds she would do so. She had to cleanse her aura in a much-needed spell of solitude. To go home without detaching herself from those people she was betraying, by means of a short indulgence in what could probably be described as meditation, would be unbearable. Her favourite place for being alone was ten miles out of town high on the dark curving downland, the long slopes of which gave solitude a meaning that was almost oppressively mysterious.

The white sunshine of the seafront and the late afternoon heat made everything around Melanie proceed as if in slow motion. Reynolds placed a veined hand on her arm as he stopped her in the shade of one of the low-slanting palm trees.

Melanie stooped to take up a handful of sand. It was warm and silky, trickling through her relaxed fingers. Children ran screaming through the surf pursued by laughing children who splashed them with seawater. Couples lay side by side on spread towels, luxuriating in the still-intense sun. Old Reynolds looked contemplatively at the scene. He was in a shaky state after the long and emotional council meeting. The lines of discontent and bitterness on his face had become deeper and more distorting.

'What are we doing, Councillor Biles?' he asked unhappily. 'The folk of Havensport placed their trust in us, voted us into office to protect and further their interests. But we are about to betray them by trading the character and tradition of a family resort for the plastic and chromium monstrosity of the world of the fast buck.'

'But we must ask ourselves if they gave us a mandate to resist progress,' Melanie said hypocritically.

Reynolds looked very old, very tired. 'I've always been a man able to draw many conclusions when presented with a few facts, Councillor Biles, but the principles involved in this pleasure complex project defeat and distress me. I began by using borrowed money to open a small café on the beach in 1946, Melanie. This was a very different town then, and a very different world.'

'I can understand how you must feel, and I sympathise. Harvey,' Melanie said quickly, calling him by his first name though she had never before done so. 'You are, in a very real sense, Havensport, and as chairman of the committee I feel that I should make every effort to have the town remain as it is for you.'

Raising a wizened old hand, palm towards her, Reynolds objected. 'Indeed you must not, Councillor Biles. I am not important. The people elected you, so you must do nothing but listen to your inner voice and vote accordingly. You are your own person.'

If only, Melanie thought, turning away quickly so Harvey Reynolds could not see the tears brimming in her eyes as they moved off along the promenade. She was filled with a terrible sense of undefined loss.

'I recognize the group, but can't put a name to them,' Sherri Wallace said musingly as she studied the photograph Logan had placed on her dining-room table.

Her husband placed a fingertip on a long-haired man. 'I'd

say that he's important, not the group, Sherri. That's Terry Stevens, who manages the Ocean club for Gerald Reynolds.'

Logan sat rolling a brightly coloured ball to three-year-old Cait Wallace who, sitting on the floor, chuckled and hit the ball so that it returned to the detective inspector. Cait's long yellow hair was tied in braids framing a heart-shaped face. Wallace, a proud father, watched his daughter playing for a moment before asking, 'How come all four corners are torn off the print, guv?'

'I had to rip that picture off the wall in the Ocean club office without Gerald Reynolds or Stevens noticing,' Logan answered without looking up from the game he was playing with the child.

'That's theft, Mr Logan.' Sherri clicked her tongue in pretend disgust.

A small woman with a good figure, Sherri was a vivacious honey blonde, and her hair was a cap of small curls cut close to her head. Toby Wallace had once spoken openly to Logan of his feelings for his wife. 'I often can't believe that she's mine, guv. It isn't exactly a hallucination. Sherri's real – but at the same time she's not real. I sometimes don't believe she exists. I have this dread that when I turn around there'll be nothing but an empty space beside me in bed.' Unable to come up with any reply, Logan had envied Wallace the ecstasy of his love, but not the agony of it.

'I take it that I'm heading for Twyverne first thing tomorrow, guv,' Toby Wallace predicted, 'to show the jeweller this photo.'

'Exactly.' Logan nodded. Then he suggested, 'Take Sherri and Cait along for the ride.'

Sherri was looking at her husband with avid, beseeching eyes.

'Nah.' Wallace cancelled out the idea with a shake of his head. 'It wouldn't be fair. Sherri would expect me to treat her to lunch there, and I just can't afford that kind of luxury.'

Glancing sideways at him, Logan said, 'You push your luck to the limit, Toby. OK, but don't get it into your head that I'm a soft touch. Just this once you can put lunch for all three of you on expenses.'

Giving a delighted little squeal, Sherri Wallace jumped to her feet. 'That'll be nice. Thank you, Mr Logan. I could give you a hug, but maybe I'd better cuddle Toby.'

'That would be best,' Logan laconically advised her.

It hadn't been an easy decision for Julie Bolt. To enter Havensport's carnival queen competition so soon after her best friend's death hadn't seemed right. Mr Ludlum, her boss at the supermarket, had asked her to be a contestant. Pushed by the area manager, who saw a win for Julie as great publicity for the store, James Ludlum had offered her all kinds of inducement. But Julie had delayed her answer, first asking her parents what they thought about it.

'Like you, we both grieve for Norma,' her father had told her solemnly. 'But you are young and should be enjoying yourself. I personally don't think that anyone, especially Norma, would see the sense in you going into some kind of semi-retreat from life in memory of her.'

This eased Julie's main reservation, and she felt a thrill at the prospect of winning the competition. She had asked, 'Then you both think that I should go in for it, Dad?'

'We do, Julie, but I'd advise that you first speak to Norma's mum and dad. This is a very hard time for them, and seeing you doing the things that their daughter may have been doing could cause them even more distress.'

It hadn't been so bad with Norma's father, who seemed to be holding things together, but the dead girl's mother had aged twenty years. When she did manage to speak she was barely coherent. So Julie had relied on the father, who had given her his blessing to enter the competition. When he had shown Julie out of the door he had embraced her briefly. There had been tears in his eyes, and Julie had wept in the knowledge that in his mind he had been holding his daughter in his arms.

Now she was on stage at a special performance of the summer show. One of three finalists dressed in swimsuits, Julie was being interviewed by the compere, an elderly member of the show. Sitting at a table at the side were Councillors Melanie Biles, Gerald Reynolds and Larry Petersen, the three judges.

'Should you win the title, Julie, what would you spend the one thousand pound prize money on?' the compere asked into a microphone before holding it out for her answer.

'I think ...' Julie began, but then dried up completely.

Covertly smothering the microphone with a gnarled hand, the old man who Julie had heard called Jason, whispered to her out of a corner of his mouth. 'You'd take your mother on the holiday to the Algarve that she's always wanted.'

'She's never wanted to go there,' the honest Julie whispered back.

'She does now, you silly girl,' Jason Fulton hissed at her urgently.

This would be cheating, but Julie desperately wanted to win the contest. Anyway, she wanted to do it for Matthew Colby, who was out there somewhere in the collective anonymity of the darkened audience. Whatever it was between them had developed past a holiday romance.

'I'd like to take my mother for a holiday on the Algarve,' Julie announced confidently. 'That is somewhere she has always wanted to go.'

'With a thousand pounds you'll be able to go along as her chaperone, Julie,' Fulton joked, and as the audience laughed he whispered more instructions to Julie, who listened intently then repeated his words loudly.

'I'd rather that my dad went with her. They both deserve a good holiday.'

'You'd give up your prize money?' Fulton asked in feigned amazement. 'And we hear so much about how selfish young people are today.' Fulton looked out at the audience to ask, 'What do you think of that, folks?'

There was a roar of approval and applause from the audience, and Fulton played it up. 'Are your parents here tonight, Julie?'

'Yes.'

At a signal from Fulton a spotlight slowly searched the audience and Julie saw it stop, picking out her parents as her mother raised a hand. Fulton called to them. 'Welcome, Mr and Mrs ...'

'Bolt,' Julie whispered.

'Mr and Mrs Bolt, you must be very proud indeed of Julie. Stand up and take a bow.'

Julie saw her mother and father get to their feet, terribly embarrassed. Then the spotlight swung away. Jason Fulton was gesturing for her to move to the side of the stage, and was beckoning the second finalist towards him.

The elderly entertainer brought out the best in the other two girls with his patter, but Julie was sure that he didn't prompt them the way he had her. She wondered why, as her two rivals came to stand near to her while Jason Fulton stood centre stage and addressed the audience.

'Three lovely girls, ladies and gentlemen. I'm really thankful that I don't have to choose a winner. That is the unenviable task of our three distinguished judges.' He indicated the three councillors with a sweep of his arm. 'Please show your appreciation, ladies and gentlemen.'

When the burst of applause for the judges faded, Fulton announced: 'While the important decision is being made, the delightful Miss Deborah Welling will lead the entire company in that grand oldie, 'Beautiful Dreamer'. An apt title for our three aspiring contestants tonight, but, ladies and gentlemen, I would ask you to indulge an old trouper and all those with me in the summer show. We would like this to be a tribute to Miss Penny Silver, a dear friend of ours who sadly and tragically met her end here in Havensport just a few days ago. Penny was indeed a beautiful dreamer.'

There was total hush in the theatre as, head down, Jason

Fulton walked off and a blonde girl moved forward singing the moving song in a remarkably sweet voice. The whole company came behind her, softly humming the melody.

Caught up in the atmosphere of sadness, Julie, who had never known Penny Silver, thought of Norma Harrington and had to fight back tears. Suddenly the beauty competition seemed frivolous and totally inconsequential. Julie didn't care if she won or lost.

eleven

The elderly sergeant walking away down the corridor turned on his heel and waited for Logan and Shelagh as they came in the door of the police station. He said, 'Good timing, Randy. You have a visitor.'

'Who is it, Tom?' Logan asked cautiously, fearing it was the chief constable come to share his worries over his wife.

Logan had been anticipating a spare hour to discuss their day with his sergeant. They had established that Norma Harrington had known of Terry Stevens, but had never made his acquaintance. As both Ed Bellamy and Rick Downton had noticed the glow of a cigarette under the pier, Logan was anxious to learn whether Stevens smoked.

The uniformed sergeant eyes looked at Logan obliquely as he humorously anticipated the detective's reaction to what he was about to say. A slow smile played around his mouth a moment before he spoke. 'Act three, scene two, Randy. Sir Laurence Olivier is waiting in the wings.'

'Jason Fulton,' Logan guessed with a sigh. 'Did he say what he wants?'

Tom moved his grey head in an easy negative. 'No, but he said plenty of other things, Randy. I learned the complete history of the music hall and vaudeville.'

'That's the problem with Fulton,' Logan groaned.

'I reckon he's as bent as a hockey stick.' The old sergeant pulled a face.

Logan shrugged. 'He's got an eye for the women, Tom.'

'Maybe he goes both ways, Randy.'

'I don't care which way he goes,' Logan muttered, 'as long as he goes away from here.'

Shelagh frowned, studying Logan, her teeth white against her full bottom lip as she nibbled at it. She was an excellent partner and a good companion. On odd occasions she held Logan entranced with her brief, vivid stories of policing in London. She listened well too, and laughed well.

'I could see him if you like, guv,' she offered.

'He won't talk to anyone but you, Randy.'

'Give us five minutes, Tom,' Logan instructed, 'then bring him up to my office.'

The salesgirl told Toby Wallace in a quiet voice to go through to the back room of the shop to see Mr Hailston. The jeweller was sitting at a table, a magnifying glass held to his eye by an exaggerated squint. Plucking the glass from his face he placed it beside a glittering necklace that lay on the table in front of him. He was a little grey man, calm and unhurried. He smiled at Wallace meaninglessly, a studied yet unconscious gesture of someone who sells to the public.

The phoney smile went past the detective, who was concentrating on getting a good result to take back to DI Logan. He'd had a good day so far with his wife and little daughter. After going on a modest shopping spree, they had driven out of town to a remote lake. They had hired a new round-bottomed rowing boat bright with varnish and with slat seats. As he rowed steadily, Toby Wallace had realized the immense strain of the life that he lived. He had found peace on the water but he had not known what to do with it. There had been a few other boats on the lake, the people in them waving, and they had waved back.

Afterwards they'd lunched in a cafeteria, and while he was here at the jewellers, Sherri and Cait were enjoying the attractions of an amusement park while waiting for him to complete the police business that had brought them to Twyverne.

'Detective Constable Wallace,' he reintroduced himself. 'Possibly you recall that I visited you recently, Mr Hailston.'

'Of course I remember you, Mr Wallace. How can I help you today?'

Taking the photograph from his pocket, Wallace laid it on the table. 'The man I was enquiring about, your customer who purchased a bracelet, do you see him in this picture?'

Hailston replaced his eyeglass, causing one corner of his mouth to twist up as if he was about to impart something in confidence. Moving both the photograph and his head this way and that, the jeweller took a long time before he gave a grunt of satisfaction. Holding the print down with the forefinger of one hand, he pointed with the finger of his other hand at Terry Stevens.

'That's him, officer.'

'Are you absolutely certain, Mr Hailston?' Toby Wallace earnestly enquired.

'In this business, Constable,' Hailston said, as he yawned and closed his eyes, 'we deal in considerable sums of money, therefore one develops a good memory for faces. That's the man.'

'Thank you, sir, that's good enough for me.'

'I take it that you will be paying me another visit, officer?' the jeweller said as the detective went out of the door.

With a backward wave of his hand, a pleased Wallace replied, 'You can count on it, Mr Hailston.'

He hurried to the fairground, where sunlight dappled the soft turf like gold coins. He spotted his wife and daughter. He was back sooner than Sherri had expected, and she greeted him in delighted surprise. They were surrounded by brightly coloured whirling rides and harshly serenaded by jangling modern music. With his daughter clutching one of his hands in both of hers, Toby kissed his wife lightly on the lips.

'I want to go on something else, Daddy,' Cait squealed, jumping up and down in excitement.

'Just one ride, then we have to head for home,' Toby said. 'What is it to be, my lovely?'

'Up there!'

Cait was pointing at the big wheel, causing her mother to exclaim, 'Oh, no, Toby, she'd be too frightened.'

'You know Cait,' he said, grinning as he surrendered to his little daughter's wish. 'She's got more guts than the pair of us put together.'

They climbed into a gently rocking car. The wheel moved them slowly skywards as other fairgoers boarded. They were raised up into a new and surprising air and into a different world in another time. Reaching the highest point they stared out over a breathtaking panorama. Far off in the west a snow-fall of gulls wheeled against the backdrop of a cloud-free sky of cobalt. Past rolling green hills and a valley dotted with farm-houses, the sea and a few Havensport rooftops were just discernible in the far distance.

'Top of the world, Ma!' Toby made his wife smile with an impression of James Cagney from an old gangster movie they had recently watched on television.

Though high above the fairground, faint sounds of merry-making still reached up to them. At first having found the drop in front of them dizzying, Sherri was now mesmerized by the view, and said, 'I feel like we're the only three people in the world. And that no one down there can touch us.'

'A world of our own, Sherri. How long would it take us to get bored?'

'We never would,' she replied fervently. 'It would suit me fine.'

They fell silent then. Their relationship was so close that they could get tremendous pleasure from sharing periods of quiet. Then their car rocked as the wheel moved. Sitting between them, Cait squealed in delight but reached out to each side to clutch at her parents for security. They held her tight as the wheel gathered momentum.

Logan was waiting back in Havensport for his report, but the usually conscientious Toby wasn't inclined to rush back. In fact, having that day sampled a very different kind of living, he was searching his mind for a means of escape with his family from their present police-pressured existence.

'I could do nothing else but agree to go along with the idea,' Jason Fulton said in a regretful tone. 'Everyone in the show will be on the float with the carnival queen. It will put bums on seats, as they say, but I am not in favour. On the stage one can keep separate from the plebs, maintain an air of mystique, as it were. To mix with the mob is to shed the special kind of majesty that a top performer acquires.'

Fulton had poise, but his fingers betrayed him. With elbows resting on the arms of his chair and his hands together as a steeple pointing at the ceiling, his fingers were tapping against each other.

'Maybe it's a case of being over-sensitive, Jason,' Logan remarked, willing Fulton to come to the point. An electronic clock/radio/calendar/ thermometer on the desk in front of him silently announced that it was 5:45 p.m. on 22 August, and that the temperature in his office was 78 degrees Fahrenheit. Though it was a superb technological instrument, it couldn't tell him what this garrulous old guy was doing there.

'A high degree of sensitivity is a prerequisite in my profession.' Jason Fulton's steeple parted. His hands lay twitching slightly in his lap. 'As a consequence, we are easily hurt. My greatest humiliation was in '43 in the North African desert. We had a wonderful show prepared, but not one soldier was interested. The only way we got an audience was when they marched the troops in at gunpoint.'

Logan consoled him. 'You're just entering a carnival now, Jason, not fighting a war.'

'Be that as it may, Inspector, this is the age of the yob. By riding on a float we will be making ourselves targets for hurled insults.'

Logan said, 'Wasn't it Sigmund Freud who said the first person to hurl an insult instead of a stone was the founder of civilisation?'

'I'd say that depended on how one views civilisation, Mr Logan,' Fulton replied indignantly.

'Whatever, I think you'll find that the carnival here is pretty tame, Jason.'

'No doubt, Inspector, no doubt. But I still prefer to be on stage where the world, with its loud trafficking, retires into the distance. Nevertheless, I shall do my bit for your fair town on its big day,' Jason Fulton said, smiling. Then the smile was gone as he added, 'Which brings me to what had me come here to see you. You probably aren't aware that I compered the carnival queen competition at the theatre.'

Logan made a quick apology. 'We knew about it, but missed it, I'm afraid. Pressure of work.'

Poking an admonishing finger out at Logan, Fulton said, 'You are being patronising, Inspector Logan, and it doesn't work. If the magnificent Marlene Dietrich was by some miracle resurrected and appeared in public with a rendition of that haunting song, "Where Have All The Flowers Gone", a man like yourself wouldn't walk across the street to buy a ticket.'

'Guilty as charged,' Logan confessed.

'Oh well, to each his own, I suppose.' The entertainer gave a resigned sigh.

'You were about to tell us your reason for coming here,' Shelagh tactfully reminded the old man.

'Oh yes, forgive me, I digress. As I said, I compered the contest. The winner comes from Havensport. A lovely young girl, really lovely. Put me in mind of a young Irish actress I starred opposite to in the 1930s. She was Desdemona to my Othello.'

'Your visit to us has something to do with this girl, the carnival queen?' Logan prompted impatiently.

'Good heavens, no,' Jason Fulton exclaimed. 'I was simply remarking on how lovely she is. No, indeed, this concerns Debs. You remember her, Penny Silver's flatmate, so to speak?'

'Of course.'

'Debs sang "Beautiful Dreamer" at the contest. She sang it with real feeling. There wasn't a dry eye in the house, to employ an overworked cliché.' Fulton did a misty-eyed reminiscence. He put his hands tightly against both sides of his head. 'I'm rambling again, aren't I?'

'You are,' Logan answered bluntly.

'Take your time, Mr Fulton,' Shelagh said solicitously, and Logan couldn't be sure whether she was slyly joking.

'Thank you, Sergeant.' Fulton smiled sweetly at her. 'In your presence, more light falls on the dark stage of my being and, thus illuminated, I find my way to an inner peace.'

'Is there any chance of you finding your way to telling us why you came here?' Logan asked harshly.

'My apologies, Inspector,' Fulton said guiltily. 'Well, now, the long and the short of it is that Debs recognized one of the judges at the contest – a councillor, Gerald Reynolds, I believe his name is.'

'So?' Logan said with a dismissive shrug. 'Councillor Reynolds is a well-known local dignitary.'

'Point taken, Inspector, but please allow me to finish. Debs recognized him as a man she had several times seen with Penny.'

Exchanging a meaningful glance with Shelagh, Logan sat upright in his chair, saying, 'Now, Jason, you have my undivided attention.'

'Then I fear that I will disappoint you, Mr Logan.'

With a shake of his head, Logan said, 'I am sure that you won't. In what circumstances did she see them together?'

'Debs was somewhat vague on that.' Jason stared thoughtfully out of the window. 'I gathered it was not out in the open. Penny and this councillor were not … what is the modern term? Ah, yes, they were not an item. The stagedoor-johnny of days gone by was a rascal, a philanderer, but he was honest about it. Today the politician, the judge and the bishop furtively practise their perversions in the shadows.'

'But there was some kind of relationship between this councillor and Penny Silver?' Shelagh asked.

'Plainly, Sergeant. A middle-aged man doesn't trail around behind a pretty young dancer for no reason.'

'Did Reynolds ever visit the room this girl shared with Penny, Jason?' Logan enquired.

'Not while Debs was there, Inspector.'

With a quizzical look at the entertainer, Logan said, 'There's something incomplete about your answer, Jason.'

'Deliberately so, Inspector Logan, because all I can add is an impression that Debs has.'

'Which is?'

'That this man came to the room when Penny knew that Debs wouldn't be there.'

'You did right to come to us with this, Jason, but I can't help wondering why,' Shelagh said. 'There is no longer an enquiry into the murders of Penny Silver and the local girl.'

'Come now, Sergeant, this is real life, not something directed by Alfred Hitchcock.' Jason Fulton wagged his head disapprovingly. 'I pride myself on being a good judge of character. I doubt that you think that poor boy killed those two girls, and I'm certain that Detective Inspector Logan doesn't believe that he did.'

Not taking this up, Logan said, 'We are grateful to you for sparing the time to come here, Jason, and what you've told us will be noted.'

'I'm thankful that I never played poker with you, Inspector Logan,' Fulton said, a faint smile twitching at one side of his mouth. 'I'm damned if I can figure what kind of a hand you're holding.'

Standing to indicate that the interview was ended, Logan folded his arms. 'When and if I put my cards on the table, Jason, you'll be the first to see them. Now, Sergeant Ruby will drive you back to your lodgings.'

'That is most kind of you.' Fulton bent a scrawny arm to consult his wristwatch, then told Shelagh, 'Better take me straight to the theatre, dearie. There's just half an hour to go to curtain-up, the time when I must once again carry the light of my art to the dark corners of our globe.'

It was late when they got there and the Blue Angel was packed. From behind a desk in reception a pretty Asian girl with dimples smiled at them. Julie was proud to be seen on the arm of Matthew Colby. His hard good looks had him stand out in a crowd. Tonight the T-shirt he wore was eggshell-white, with yellow stitching, tailor-made with his initials embroidered over his heart. In a rare moment of immodesty, Julie was confident that, though she was casually dressed, she did him justice as a partner.

They went up a wide stairway to the second floor. This was a part of the club that was whispered about in the town. As they entered a spacious, amber-lit room, they had to gingerly step over a brunette who lay peacefully asleep on the floor. It was a subtly attractive place with oak-lined walls, red carpeting and red velvet draperies. The lighting was pleasantly discreet,

Sitting at small oak-wood tables along the far wall were unaccompanied young women, some of them not so young. Julie assumed that they were the house whores who came to Havensport for the summer.

On a bandstand at the rear of the room, a drummer was warming up his traps while two teenage girls wriggled to his jungle beat and a cluster of gay men swayed to the rhythm with their arms round each others' waists.

'A glimpse of how the other half lives.' Matthew smiled at Julie.

Julie, giving a little shudder, replied, 'I don't think I want to know. Why have we come here, Matt?'

'I just want to see someone. A small matter of business, Julie,'
he explained. 'One drink and we'll be off to wherever you want
to spend the remainder of the evening.'

She looked into his face, and all the longing she would ever
have was in her eyes then. Though dreading the time when he
would leave, she was determined that this wouldn't be a short-
lived holiday romance.

'My dad would go spare if he knew I was here,' Julie said
with a little shiver.

'I won't tell him if you don't.' Matthew winked at her.
'What'll you have to drink?'

'Just a coke.'

'Bacardi and coke,' Matthew said, enlarging on her order.

Though Matthew dominated her, Julie didn't mind. It
seemed right because he was so much cleverer than she was.
Matthew Colby was a man in possession of knowledge that
couldn't be got from books She meekly agreed. 'OK, Matt. I'll
be back in a moment.'

When she came out of the Ladies, Julie saw Matthew at the
bar. With a drink beside him waiting for her, he was with the
club doorman. They stood close together, and Matthew was
talking earnestly, speaking too low for Julie to catch his words.
The unexpected little scene puzzled her.

A spotlight was playing over a black girl singer up on the
stage. She wore a shiny red gown with gold chains and a lot of
bosom exposed. The singer was making more music with her
hips than she was with her voice.

The song, 'You're Still The One', was sending good vibes
through the room, creating a nice atmosphere. But the sight of
Ed Bellamy chilled Julie. The memory of the last time she had
been at the Blue Angel came rushing into her mind, bringing
with it a sharply focused image of Norma. It felt as if an abstract
chasm of time and sound and colours had opened up and Julie
had toppled into it.

By odd coincidence, Matthew had been in the Blue Angel then, although she hadn't been aware of him. Norma and Rick Downton had been talking to Ed Bellamy. A lot of thoughts went through Julie's mind, but most of all she thought of how desperately she missed her closest friend. It was easy to imagine a phantom Norma there now, gazing longingly at the doorman she had fallen so heavily for. Julie broke into a light sweat as Matthew beckoned her to him.

The two men moved further apart. Bellamy was saying to Matthew, 'I owe you a drink, but I don't even know your name.'

'The name is Matthew, but you don't owe me anything, kid.'

'What's all this about?' Julie asked, picking up her glass.

'The last time your boyfriend was in here he saved my hide,' Bellamy answered.

Matthew gave a modest shrug. 'It was nothing.'

'Nothing!' the bouncer exclaimed. 'I reckon you must be a reincarnation of Bruce Lee.'

'If you're going to say nice things about me, then I'd better buy you a drink.' Smiling, Matthew Colby placed a ten-pound note on the bar. 'Drink up, Julie. We'll have one more here then move on.'

'I'd come with you if I wasn't on duty here,' Bellamy told them wistfully.

Slowly scanning the bar, Colby said, 'I don't see anyone here likely to give you trouble.'

'You can never tell, Matthew. The place can be as dead as a graveyard at midnight, but it only takes one word spoken out of place, or a hand furtively placed on the wrong place on the wrong person, and the whole place explodes. It's worse up here than it is downstairs.'

A busty barmaid brought their drinks. Matthew drank in a half-hearted manner that said he wasn't a drinker at all but was simply being sociable.

'No, I didn't really know either of them. That night was the first time I'd spoken to them, and then it was only for a few minutes.'

Julie was puzzled to hear Bellamy say this, then she realized that he was continuing the conversation he'd been having with Matthew when she had come out of the Ladies. Matthew stumbled over an explanation.

'Ed and I were talking about the tragedy of those two kids, and I was telling him that Norma had been your best friend. But at least we've seen justice at work.'

Close to tears as memories of Norma came flooding in, Julie was unable to speak. She heard Bellamy say: 'I wouldn't be sure.'

'That's daft,' Matthew said with a short laugh. 'I know that they didn't exactly get the kid who killed the girls, but he proved his guilt by topping himself.'

'Maybe so, but that woman detective, the real fit one, came round my digs this morning, asking questions.'

'What sort of questions, Ed?' Matthew asked.

Head bowed, Bellamy thought hard. Then he shook his head violently in an effort to clear it. 'Lots of questions. I get confused, forget things real easy.'

'Never mind, don't strain the old grey matter, Ed,' Matthew chuckled as he made a pretence of punching Bellamy in the ribs.

'That's funny,' Julie said, frowning. 'While I was home at lunch today a woman phoned the shop to ask if I'd be working tomorrow morning if she called in. Mandy, that's a girl in the office, told her that I would be. I took it to be someone with something to do with the carnival, but now I'm wondering if it was that detective.'

'That would hardly be likely.' Matthew smiled and cuddled her. 'You worry too much, Julie. You forget that you're a celebrity now, a star. I'd put my money on that being a reporter from the local paper.'

'You're probably right,' Julie outwardly agreed.

Matthew's glass was empty and he seemed edgy, keen to get away. 'Finish your drink, Julie, and we'll go.'

They said goodbye to Bellamy. Matthew placed a hand on Julie's elbow and guided her down the stairs. Outside it was one of those rare nights. Looking up to find a sky dotted with twinkling diamonds, Julie was momentarily in the grip of something instinctive. Though this was her hometown, the low shops and taller ugly buildings around them seemed grotesquely foreign.

Remembering, she said, 'I thought you wanted to see someone in there, Matt.'

'He didn't seem to be there. Anyway, it wasn't important.' He put an arm around Julie's waist and squeezed her.

This was the old Matthew, and Julie was reassured. Feeling secure and contented, she snuggled against him as they walked slowly off into the night.

Gerald Reynolds lived at the top of the Drake Building on the corner of Sea Road. The Drake Building was an expensive house, in which Reynolds' apartment was the most expensive. It was a classic four-storey building of hamstone and decorative ironwork, a memorial to an era of horse-drawn buses, straw boaters, bustles and striped bathing costumes with half legs. The ground floors of fine Victorian buildings in the area around it had been ripped out to accommodate gaudy gift shops and tatty cafés, but the Drake Building still stood, a breakwater against the turbulent seas of change.

Logan apologized. 'I'm sorry about calling on you at this hour, sir.'

Shelagh looked out through a window at the Havensport skyline. The sun was out of sight now, but it had left a memory of gold where it had set. The molten shadow that was night blended through the spectrum to the black silhouette that was the distant horizon. There were a few dark shapes and winking lights that were ships.

'Not at all,' Reynolds assured Logan. 'I am sure it has to be something important that brought you here.' He motioned for Shelagh and Logan to be seated on a settee.

Shelagh sank into the sofa, her legs high. Though a dedicated police officer, she didn't envy Logan the subject he had to broach. Toby Wallace had confirmed that Terry Stevens had bought the bracelet that had been a gift for Penny Silver.

'I live alone, by choice, so it isn't possible to disturb my evening,' Reynolds said, smiling, as he sank into a deep armchair.

Acknowledging this with a nod, Logan said, 'I'm pleased to say that I live alone.'

Logan noticed that Shelagh didn't seem to have the same aversion to Reynolds that had been in evidence when they'd met him at the club he owned. She voiced her opinion. 'I'm in lodgings, but I've really missed my folks since leaving home.'

'We may inhabit families, enjoy friendships, experience moments of love, Sergeant,' Reynolds said, 'but in reality all of us live alone.'

'You make it all sound very depressing,' the girl unhappily remarked.

'On the contrary, acceptance of that fact is an antidote for depression. But you, mercifully, are too young to understand.' Daintily lifting his glass, he drank from it before turning to Logan. 'Now, Inspector, in what way can I help you?'

'Maybe I should have spoken to Terry Stevens first,' Logan began. 'We know about the bracelet that was given as a present to the girl found murdered on the beach.'

'Penny Silver,' Reynolds said in a half whisper. He left his chair to go to the window and look out. He spoke without turning. 'I may not be particularly proud of myself, Inspector, but as a single person I have neither to answer nor to apologize to the police or anyone else.'

'We haven't come for an apology, Mr Reynolds. Sergeant Ruby and myself are simply continuing with our enquiries,' Logan explained.

'I thought that ghastly business was all tied up.'

'It requires the finishing touches, Mr Reynolds,' Logan explained.

'Should we first discuss this with Terry Stevens, sir?' Shelagh enquired.

Giving a jerking shake of his head, Reynolds turned to face them. 'No, you did right in coming straight to me. Stevens was no more than the messenger. As you probably guessed, I purchased the bracelet for the girl.'

'You were having a relationship with Penny Silver, sir?'

Reynolds' face wore a sheepish smile. 'Shall we say an incipient relationship, Sergeant? My intention was to get to know her.'

'Was she not interested?' Logan was genuinely surprised.

'On the contrary, Inspector.'

'But your hoped-for relationship,' Shelagh said. 'Didn't it get off the ground?'

'I'm afraid not.'

'Why?'

'Simply lack of time, Inspector Logan. The poor girl died while my overture was still being played.'

'But you had spent time with her.' Logan made this a statement rather than a question.

'I would be silly to deny it,' Reynolds said calmly. 'Though reluctant to speak ill of the dead, Penny was by no means an innocent little miss. I am not saying this to excuse myself.'

'Then why are you telling us?'

'Because, Sergeant, it could well aid your investigation.'

'You have some specific information about the girl, sir?' Logan asked.

'I suppose one could use the term specific,' Reynolds mused.

'Perhaps you could tell us what you do know, Mr Reynolds,' Logan suggested.

'Simply that though Penny was mercenary and without shame, I found her unexpectedly apprehensive about someone or something on occasion.'

Shelagh asked sharply, 'You thought that she was being threatened?'

'Oh no, nothing of that sort. But I do feel that she was living dangerously.'

'What exactly was your impression of her situation, sir?' Logan enquired.

'Well,' Reynolds deliberated, 'I would say that she was in some kind of lucrative arrangement. Though she was greedily entertained by me, she was nervous of spoiling some arrangement that she had.'

'A sugar daddy?' Shelagh watched Reynolds intently.

'That was how I saw it.'

'Someone local to Havensport, sir?'

'I think not,' Reynolds replied. 'And to save you asking your next question, Inspector Logan, I can account for my movements at all times on the relevant night.'

'I never doubted that for a moment, but I do wonder if Terry Stevens is able to do so.'

'You think that I may have had someone do my dirty work for me?' Reynolds asked with a sad smile.

Logan put him right. 'I did not in any way suggest or imply that, sir. As Stevens is your employee, I enquired whether his movements that night could be accounted for.'

'That, Inspector Logan, is something that you must take up with Mr Stevens.'

twelve

'That is the word that has got back to Malcolm Braithwaite.'

Alex Morton spoke the sentence quietly without turning his head to look at Melanie. Those around them wouldn't know that he had spoken. In his fifties, Morton was tall and lean, face craggy, hair greying. An impressive man. They were at a Moorfield site meeting with Melanie's fellow councillors, and Morton had surreptitiously moved her a little way apart from the others to issue the warning. Feeling weak at the knees, Melanie was starkly aware of the enormity of the implications, the seriousness of the consequences, should there be anything in what the Compat Leisure man had told her. It was rumoured that an as yet unidentified member of the council was said to be wise to the illegal fast-track planning for the leisure centre.

This was an unwelcome new worry for Melanie. She was no longer being followed, and had found the absence of the stalker to be an anti-climax that was every bit as traumatic as being stalked. Now it was plain that someone had been spying on her to gain evidence to prove her conspiracy with Compat Leisure.

'Harvey Reynolds?' Alex Morton suggested.

'Definitely not.'

A fit of pique was probably the cause of the absence of the Reynolds father and son not attending this site meeting. If there was any truth in what Morton had said, then she had no doubt who the source of danger was.

'Most likely it's the son, Gerald Reynolds,' she was saying as the rest of the group moved close to them.

The councillors were squinting through bright sunlight at large and floppily uncontrollable plans that they held. Plans that defied their understanding. Only the young Larry Petersen, dressed in a multi-coloured Hawaiian shirt and a pair of below-the-knee-shorts, admitted his total ignorance of what was going on and distanced himself from it. He was play-acting to a small group of giggling girl fans standing a little way off. The girls began to make cheerleader movements.

Councillor Monica Shelby glanced in disgust at the antics of the young councillor and the girls. Then she tucked in her chin and fixed Morton with a steady glare through her thick spectacles. 'I must say, Mr Morton, that I can picture your planned leisure complex and that I find it quite exhilarating.'

'But …' Larry Petersen warned Morton with a grin before humming a tune and doing a Michael Jackson moonwalk in front of the group.

'Councillor Petersen,' Monica Shelby admonished the gyrating pop singer, 'having your infantile behaviour erode the dignity of the council chamber is most distressing, but now you are making a spectacle of us all here in public.'

Petersen kept a straight face as he excused his behaviour. 'I am doing my best to contain a difficult situation, Councillor. Fan worship can turn ugly if it gets out of control.'

'This is hardly the Beatles at Heathrow,' Monica Shelby observed scathingly.

'Do you have a *but*, Councillor Shelby?' Morton interrupted the exchange

'I still hold the opinion that the cost of draining this site will be phenomenal,' Monica Shelby said, looking out over the vast acreage of land.

Making her wait while he shuffled some papers and fastened them to a clipboard, Morton said, 'Compat's engineers and accountants have together gone into this thoroughly, Councillor Shelby.'

A middle-aged man, Councillor Eric James, who had a thriving unisex hair salon in Sea Road, had been listening. Now he questioned Morton. 'But what if?'

'If? If what, Councillor …?' Morton fiddled with his glasses.

'James, Eric James,' the councillor replied anxiously. 'I was asking, admittedly imprecisely, what happens if the cost of drainage should eventually prove to be prohibitive and Compat Leisure decided to drop the scheme?'

'That's simple,' Larry Petersen smilingly advised. 'Our council pays for the drainage and becomes a partner in the leisure centre.' He pleaded exaggeratedly with Alex Morton. 'Can I be entertainments manager, sir?'

'Really, Councillor Petersen!' an appalled Monica Shelby exclaimed. 'I often wonder what you have inside that head of yours.'

'It's as empty as a church on Sunday, Councillor Shelby,' a grinning Petersen quipped.

Melanie raised her voice. 'May I remind you all that the carnival isn't until Saturday. Right now we have serious council business to deal with. Compat Leisure has already stated that they will bear the full cost of drainage.'

'I can only reiterate that we will bear the full cost,' Morton responded with an eloquent shrug.

'Then, if there are no more questions?' Melanie looked at the other councillors. They remained silent. 'Perhaps we could move to the east side of the site to discuss the location of a new road.'

The others followed listlessly in the wake of Melanie and Alex Morton. Behind the slowly moving platoon of councillors, Larry Petersen's impromptu fan club trailed along like a bunch of mini-skirted camp followers.

There were just the three of them in the closed Ocean club. They occupied a booth, with Shelagh and Logan sitting on one side of a fixed table and a restless, hand-twitching Terry Stevens sitting opposite. Half hearing Shelagh asking questions, Logan realized that he wasn't supporting her as she deserved. He was unable to take an interest after coming to the conclusion that Gerald Reynolds and his club manager were non-runners as far as the murder investigation was concerned. Penny Silver's mystery benefactor was now a priority.

'You say that you left here shortly after Penny Silver, Mr Stevens?'

'That's right. It was my night to finish early. Ginger Bartlett, he's a sort of under-manager, will vouch for me leaving that evening.'

'I'm sure that he will, Mr Stevens.' Logan pushed himself to take part in the mild interrogation. 'But will he be able to tell us where you went or who you were with?'

'Why would that be necessary, Inspector?'

'Do you smoke, Terry?'

Stevens, off balance, stammered his answer. 'I-I used to.'

'How long since you quit?'

'Six or seven years.'

'Tell us where you went and what you did when you left here that night,' Shelagh said.

'I had some work to do for Mr Gerald Reynolds.'

Shelagh made a note in a small book. 'At another of the Reynolds' premises?'

'No, it involved driving.'

'Was anyone with you?' Shelagh looked up, her pen poised.

'No. I was alone.'

'What sort of car do you drive, Mr Stevens?'

'I own a Vauxhall Vectra, but I wasn't driving it that night. I was using one of Mr Gerald's cars. This is all very disturbing.'

'Relax, Terry,' Logan advised. 'What did this driving job entail? Deliveries of some kind?'

'I will answer any questions about myself,' Stevens replied, 'but this is Mr Gerald's business.'

'This is a murder enquiry, Terry, and you are obliged to answer,' Logan said flatly.

A high vehicle passed by, darkening the room momentarily as it shut off light from the window. Terry Stevens was thrown into shadow, and a small vacant compartment in Logan's mind was suddenly filled. Stevens was definitely the intruder who had knocked him unconscious at the Biles' house. Shelagh came in at this point. 'Did the job you did that night take you away from Havensport?'

'No, the furthest I went was the outskirts of town.'

'You are pretty vague about your movements on that particular night,' Logan complained. 'Is that because you weren't working at all, but drove off somewhere to meet a boyfriend?'

Face flushing, Stevens asked haughtily, 'What are you implying, Inspector?'

'Don't waste our time,' Logan snapped. 'While I was in the army I locked enough batty boys in the guardroom to recognize one at three hundred yards on a foggy, dark night.'

The term 'batty boys' wasn't politically correct, but neither were the murders of two girls.

'Being abusive won't benefit you, Inspector Logan. I'm not ashamed of what I am.'

'I was making a point, Terry, not airing my prejudices.'

'I'm prepared to accept that, Inspector,' Stevens said graciously. 'And the answer is no, I was not meeting a friend.'

'Then just tell us what kind of work you were doing, and where,' Shelagh said.

'It was Mr Gerald's private business,' Stevens protested.

Shelagh said, 'We are always discreet, Mr Stevens.'

When Stevens still hesitated, Logan stood and gestured to Shelagh that they were leaving. 'Leave it, Sergeant,' he said, then turned to Stevens. 'We'll be back, Terry.'

'I know.' Stevens nodded glumly.

When they were out of Steven's earshot, Shelagh enquired,

'Are you all right, guv? I detected some hostility towards Stevens.'

'You probably did, Sergeant,' Logan replied. 'I just don't fit into this modern world. There's too much acceptance.'

'Now your prejudices are showing, guv.'

'Your profiling is faulty if that came as a surprise,' Logan remarked with a tight smile.

'Maybe I share your view. I've never really gone into it,' she half agreed with a small nod of support.'

Holding the door for her to go out, Logan said, 'I think I know what he was doing for Reynolds that night, Sergeant.'

'Then I think it fair that you tell me, guv.'

'Right now that would be superfluous information, Shelagh,' he explained, 'and I want you to have a clear head for a trip back to London.'

'London! Whatever for?'

'We need to know more about Penny Silver. Much more,' Logan replied.

The telephone was ringing as Melanie let herself back into the house. It was Alex Morton.

'Are you alone, Councillor Biles?'

'This isn't one of those funny calls, is it?' Melanie giggled, although she didn't feel like laughing. Morton didn't either. 'I'm alone.'

'Then we need to talk. Could Councillor James be the one?'

'Possibly.' Melanie drew the word out wonderingly. 'I don't know a lot about him. He's a bit of an odd fish.'

'You never can tell.' Morton made a noise like he was sucking a morsel of food out of his teeth. 'There has to be something deficient in the sort of prats who put themselves up for election to a council.'

'I am one of those prats, Mr Morton,' Melanie reminded her caller.

There was a long silence as Morton recognized his gaff and

tried to find a verbal antidote. Eventually he said, unconvincingly, 'I'd say that you are the exception, Councillor Biles.'

Dismissing this with a brittle little laugh, Melanie said, 'Whoever it may be, this is serious.'

A lot more serious for her than it would be for Alex Morton, Malcolm Braithwaite and the other Compat Leisure people. Misconduct in public office was treated harshly by the courts.'You are in the most vulnerable position, Councillor Biles,' Morton was telling her as if he cared. 'But you're lucky in that you are married to the chief constable.'

'I wouldn't involve Kenneth in this, whatever may happen,' she retorted.

'Then it's in your best interest to discover who the spy is, Councillor Biles. Just tell us that and we'll take care of it.'

'Take care of it?' she questioned shakily. 'You make your organisation sound like the Mafia, Mr Morton.'

'Nonsense,' he disagreed. 'But believe me, Mrs Biles, Compat Leisure will protect the money it has invested in this project.'

Chilled by this, Melanie protested. 'But ...'

'Find out who it is, Councillor Biles.'

'But ...' she tried once more, but Alex Morton had hung up.

Julie Bolt stood waiting at the corner of the High Street and the promenade, enjoying the attention she was being paid as the carnival queen. Though there were just a few days to go to Saturday, the big day seemed an awfully long way off. This evening she was going to take Matthew home to meet her parents. It would be great if Matthew was standing in the crowd on Saturday beside her mum and dad.

She looked along the High Street, the way that Matthew would come. There was no sign of him. Julie checked her watch. It was close to a quarter to eight, and their date had been for half past seven.

She studied her reflection in the window of a chemist's shop. Her black hair was swept back from her face, but left flowing loose behind. She wore a sleeveless white dress that hugged her figure, and her arms were tanned. Tilting her head on one side, she squinted, pressing her hands against her stomach. It was as flat as ever.

'Been stood up, Julie?'

She hadn't heard William Weight, an undersized teenage shelf-stacker at the supermarket, come up from behind her to ask the question jokingly. He was so close that she could smell his cheap shaving lotion. She took a step backward and felt the glass of the shop window against her back.

'That isn't likely to happen, William,' she replied.

'Ooh, hark at her!' the boy hooted. 'Wins a poxy carnival queen contest and thinks she's Catherine Zeta-Jones. Still, if he doesn't turn up, I'm available.'

'In your dreams, William,' Julie retorted. 'I want a man, not his shirt button.'

'Surprises often come in small packages,' the boy said cheekily as he walked off.

An anxious Julie looked along the High Street again. There were a lot of people strolling along the pavements, but Matthew Colby was not among them. In a bustling seaside resort she suffered a sudden and absurd loneliness.

Logan and Shelagh stood together in the chief constable's large office while Kenneth Biles circled them like a commanding officer inspecting his troops. Head down on his chest in consternation, hands behind his back, he paced endlessly.

'Since you've been here in Devon, DI Logan, I've learned to trust your judgment implicitly,' he said at last, 'and it grieves me to question it now. What have you against the principle of letting sleeping dogs lie?'

'Our dogs aren't asleep, sir,' Logan answered.

'Maybe you are keeping them awake, Inspector.'

Logan said resignedly, 'If that's how you see it, sir.'

Frowning worriedly, Biles mumbled as he kept on pacing.

'No, no. But if that boy wasn't culpable, why did he kill himself?'

'I wouldn't attempt answering that, sir,' Logan replied. 'On reaching a certain age we don't refuse to understand the mentality of youth, but we are generally incapable of understanding it.'

An unhappy Biles nodded curtly. 'The eternal conflict between age and youth, Inspector. So, what are you saying?'

'It's a matter of loose ends, sir.'

'Well, tie them up, Inspector, unobtrusively. You know the drill.'

'It's not that easy, sir.'

Spinning on a heel, the chief constable faced Logan, fear in his eyes for himself and for his position. 'Are you predicting some kind of scandal?'

'Not a scandal, something worse, sir,' Logan coolly replied.

'There's nothing more destructive than a scandal, DI Logan. Scandal blights lives, ruins careers, destroys communities.'

'With respect, sir,' Logan said, 'if this isn't attended to it will not just affect us here in Havensport, but will reflect badly on the force as a whole.'

'Explain yourself, Inspector.'

'At present I can't find a common denominator in the two murders, or even be sure that it exists. But if it does, then it is imperative that we discover it.'

The chief constable's respect for Logan was plain on his face. 'And you believe that the answer lies in London, DI Logan?'

'I'm convinced that is where I'll pick up the trail, sir. It is essential to learn the background of Penny Silver.'

'But where do you start?' Kenneth Biles furrowed his b
'I understand that no friends or relatives from London attended her funeral.'

'Her mother was there, sir,' Shelagh put in. 'Her presence was so low-key that we weren't at first aware that she was there. When we did learn that she was it was too late. She left early.'

'Have you an address in London?'

'Yes, sir,' Logan confirmed. 'Penny's home was in Streatham. Her mother's name is Pursey.'

'You'll be taking DS Ruby with you, Inspector. How long do you think you'll be away?'

'Three days – four at the most, sir.'

'Will you be leaving in the morning?'

'I'd like to go this evening, sir,' Logan said.

'Of course.' Biles sanctioned the idea. He studied Logan for a moment, then turned his head slightly to speak to Shelagh. 'Could you leave us for a moment, please, Sergeant.'

'Of course, sir.'

When the door had closed behind the detective, it was a little while before Biles managed to speak to Logan. 'As the request I'm about to make can't come under a heading of duty, you have every right to refuse.'

'Whatever the circumstances, sir, I will do as you ask,' Logan assured his superior, not as a sycophant but because he was moved by the abject worry that was so evident in Biles.

'It's Mrs Biles, Melanie again, I'm afraid,' the chief constable began hesitantly. 'Something has her really agitated. She assures me that everything is fine, but I know that isn't so. I pray that she is not ill and keeping it to herself so as not to trouble me. I've got this damned CCTV discussion with the Chamber of Commerce this evening, Randy. It's a lot to ask, but could you drive out to the house before you leave for London? Maybe you could give me a ring at the town hall after you've spoken to her. Just to put my mind at rest.'

Logan made his distraught superior a promise. 'I'll call on Biles, sir, and I'll definitely telephone you before I leave for London.'

It was five minutes to nine. The music of sunlight no longer played along the seafront and across the white walls of Mediterranean-like buildings that lined the road on one side.

But Julie Bolt didn't notice. A seemingly endless stream of youths in separate groups numbering from two to six or seven had tried to pick her up. Older men had twice blatantly propositioned her. Matthew had still not turned up.

Having stayed at her post she now had to recognize that it had all been in vain. Maybe he had met with some kind of accident. The alternative was that Matthew had abandoned her. It felt as if her insides were coming loose, being stripped off in small little pieces slowly, very slowly. In the now-darkened shop window her reflection was more like some resentful alter ego than the real her.

It was too early to go home. To do so would be to spend a succession of long, restless, sleepless hours trying to cope with total rejection. On a sudden impulse, she walked away, but not in the direction of her home. Instead, she set off on the fairly long walk to the Blue Angel. Julie knew it was a silly notion, but she somehow thought that the familiarity of the club she had visited with Matthew might hold the answer to his not keeping their appointment.

'Poor Kenneth. I wish that he wouldn't worry so.'

Melanie Biles, always so practical and self-possessed, was in something resembling a state of shock. They walked slowly together through the little wood at the rear of her house. She held her age well. The fullness of her breasts was accentuated by the tight white blouse, and a severely tailored black skirt clung to the curves of her hips and buttocks.

'Does he have good reason to worry, Melanie?'

Her only answer was a shrug that told him nothing. She stopped to look at a nest built precariously on the limb of a fallen tree beside the trail. A hungry chirping made it certain that there were young birds in it. A fat bird circled the nest, cautiously watching Melanie and Logan. Deciding to ignore them, the bird alighted on the edge of the nest, a worm in its beak. Four little beaks rose up out of the nest to battle for the meal. The mother bird made sure that the worm was divided equally, that each had a share.

'If only all life was as fair as that,' Melanie said regretfully.

'It was the mother bird who made certain that it was fair, Melanie.'

'In other words,' she said with a faint smile, 'you're saying each of us is responsible for injustice?'

'It has to be so.'

The path took them close to the edge of a little lake. Under their feet the ground was soft, marsh-like. He asked, 'Are you still being stalked?'

'Not any more,' she said listlessly. Then she regained her customary alertness. 'Am I right in thinking that you know who it was following me?'

'Maybe a suspicion, nothing concrete.'

A few facts lay in Logan's mind, unconnected because they took second place to the murder enquiry. It seemed that Terry Stevens was Melanie's stalker, and as Gerald Reynolds was Stevens' boss, it was likely to be connected with council business.

'But you know why?' she asked.

Mystified by her line of questioning, he answered honestly, 'I don't have the faintest idea, Melanie.'

'How would you rate yourself as a friend, Randolph?' she asked with fake casualness.

'Dependable,' he answered modestly.

'Dependable,' Melanie repeated. 'Dependable come what may?'

'You'll have to break that question down for me, Melanie.'

She looked at him quizzically. 'Does your being a policeman come into it?'

They reached the top of a ridge that was so entangled with brush that he had to hold her hand to steady her. The physical contact was electrifying. Neither of them spoke as they descended a small hill, stones slipping out from under their feet in places. When they reached the bottom she stopped facing him, still holding his hand.

'What I was trying to ask, Randolph, is how far your friendship will stretch. Hypothetically, if I confessed a serious crime to you, even murder, say, would you still stand by me?'

Sensing an immense depth to her question, Logan was cautious. He tried to make a joke of it. 'You're not a murderess, are you?'

Obviously disappointed by his use of an evasive tactic, she tried a smile but it faded away almost at once. 'Of course not. You're making this difficult for me, Randolph.'

'It's difficult for me, Melanie. If you tell me something that divides my loyalty, then I'll have to go with my conscience.'

Releasing his hand, she walked away with her head down. Logan caught up with her. 'There's something troubling you, and you should talk it over with someone, Melanie.'

'But not with you?'

'No,' he answered dully. 'If you did, then as a policeman I might have to let you down.'

Halting again, she looked at him, desperation on her face. 'I need help, Randolph.'

'Then you know who you should confide in.'

With a small, self-conscious smile, she said, 'Kenneth is a policeman, the same as you.'

'But he's also your husband,' Logan said. 'He's terribly worried about you, Melanie.'

'Oh, Randolph,' she sighed. 'I can't speak about this to Kenneth. This is very complicated. You see, I …'

'Don't tell me,' Logan said, more sharply than he had intended.

A bleak look on her face, Melanie started to cry softly. Against his better judgment, Logan took her in his arms. He held her as her body shook and trembled. The sobbing eased and she tilted her head back to look up at him beseechingly. Then, lips slightly parted, she stretched her face up to his. By a tremendous effort of will, Logan released her and stepped back.

Crestfallen, she averted her eyes. Her voice was so quiet. 'I'm being stupid again.'

'Maybe it's me that's foolish,' Logan said, as an offering to make her feel better.

'No, Randolph.' She gave a vehement shake of her head. 'I wish I had your strength of character.'

'Maybe I wouldn't be as strong as you in your circumstances, whatever they are. Talk to your husband about whatever it is, Melanie. I'm sure that you'll find him supportive.'

Useless tears brimmed her eyes. 'It's Kenneth that's the problem, Randolph. If I carry on with what I am involved in it will ruin him.'

'Then the answer is simple – stop doing whatever it is.'

She made a small sound like a wounded animal. 'That's the problem. Even if I stop doing it, Kenneth will still be finished.'

This smacked of blackmail. Logan looked around him help-lessly. Unless he knew more he couldn't help her, yet to ask just one question and have her answer would mean being drawn into an intrigue from which he would probably never be able to extricate himself.

The shadows were lengthening among the trees. It was time for him to go. His work and Sergeant Shelagh Ruby were waiting for him. But he was loath to leave. They returned to the house along a footpath made by a series of steps leading up a grassy rise. A row of untended evergreens screened the building from them. They kept climbing, ducking into the shadows of some pines and going through a trellised arch of rose bushes into the well-tended back garden of the Biles home.

With the journey to London pressing, Logan could spare no more time. Holding her gently by the shoulders, he advised Melanie, 'The only way is to talk this over with your husband, whatever the consequence. Will you do that?'

She nodded, a half-hearted gesture that was far from a

promise. Unconvinced, he could only bid her an awkward farewell and leave. As he walked to his car, Logan felt guilty. There had been something shameful, indecent and perhaps even obscene about his hasty exit.

Ed Bellamy was surprised to see her. Tears stung Julie's eyes as she told him about Matt. Bellamy's sharp concern carried her through the first minutes of the dreaded meeting with him.

'Could be that you're wrong, Julie. Maybe he got held up somehow.'

'No,' she said flatly. 'He's gone, Ed. Without even so much as a goodbye.'

Back home her parents were waiting to meet her new boyfriend, she thought miserably. Her mother would have supper ready and they would both be wondering where she was. Some shouting interrupted her thoughts. Three noisy drunken men came along the pavement, owlishly eyeing Julie as they went to enter the club. Bellamy stopped them by barring their way.

'Not tonight, gentlemen.'

'What are you on about?' the eldest of the three asked belligerently. He was short and stout. His tongue flicked out like a toad's, licking at his lips.

'Come back tomorrow night when you're sober.'

'You barring us?'

'Yes.'

One of them, a younger man, a wannabe hard man, took a step forward. 'You'll be sorry if you try to stop us.'

'Not as sorry as the three of you will be if you try to get past me,' Bellamy countered.

Though she admired Bellamy's cool and manly stance, Julie was on edge. The three men, muttering foul language, stared angrily at Ed. He didn't back down, and to Julie's relief the trio of drunks turned and walked away. She gave a little shudder.

'I don't know how you do this job.'

'It's a living,' Bellamy replied with a wry smile. 'Do you want to go into the club, Julie?'

After a moment's consideration, Julie shook her head. 'No, I won't go in on my own. I don't know what to do. Perhaps it'll be best to go home.'

'Maybe you'll meet your guy along the way.'

'I don't think so,' Julie said despondently. She wanted to tell Bellamy how it was with Matt, the electricity zigzagging between them, but she knew how trite it would sound. 'Did he say anything to you about leaving?'

Frowning, Bellamy replied, 'No. He didn't make a lot of sense, Julie. Do you know what he does for a living?'

'He never told me. Did he tell you?'

'No.' Bellamy pursed his lips as he thought. 'But I wondered if he was some kind of private detective.'

'What on earth made you think that?' Julie heard herself laughing, but it was a wrong kind of laugh. She had suspected that Matthew was a cop when she'd first met him.

Bellamy shrugged his wide shoulders. 'It's just that he asked me a lot of questions. He wanted to know if your friend, the one who died, or that kid who committed suicide, had told me anything about the night that girl was murdered on the beach.'

'And had they?'

'No, not a thing.'

'Strange,' Julie agreed, 'but I know that he felt bad about Norma and the other girl dying like that.'

Julie turned to walk away, but Bellamy put a hand on her arm to delay her. 'I get muddled in my mind sometimes, Julie, real mixed up, but I think he asked me if I knew whether your friend had told you anything on the night she was killed. Why would he ask me when he could have asked you?'

'I couldn't have told him anything, Ed, although Norma did say who she thought it was that Rick saw that night.'

'If she gave you a name, Julie,' Bellamy said worriedly, 'you should have gone to the police.'

'That would be daft.' Julie dismissed what he said. 'She was only guessing from what Rick had told her.'

'It seems important to me.'

'Like you said yourself, Ed, you get mixed up,' Julie said easily as she left the doorman.

But as she walked back into town she had misgivings about Matthew Colby. He had questioned her a lot about Norma. She turned into her road. It felt as if weights had been shackled to her legs and she had to drag them. Rejection lay heavy on her, though, and to salve her ego she ran pell-mell through her memories of being with Matt. He must have left Havensport urgently on business. He would be back. Probably tomorrow, she told herself. Made content by that thought, she slowed her pace as she neared home, making up an excuse to tell her mother and father.

thirteen

In Streatham there were some nice houses and then some worse ones and then some truly horrible ones. The place that Shelagh stopped the car outside most definitely belonged in the latter category. The 'Hotel' on the broken sign outside was a misnomer. It was little more than a dosshouse with rooms let at a high rental to no-hopers who carried all their worldly belongings in Tesco plastic carrier bags.

Switching off the car's ignition, Shelagh sat, waiting. Logan, depressed by the surroundings, delayed speaking. He had been in a low mood since telephoning the chief constable before leaving yesterday evening. There had been no comfort for Kenneth Biles in the message that his wife did have an undefined problem and that, hopefully, she would discuss it with him soon.

'No wonder Penny Silver left home,' Shelagh remarked as she ducked her head to look at the grim building.

'The Evelyn Pursey residence,' Logan said cynically.

'What do you think she is, guv, a boarder or the landlady?'

'Whichever, this isn't going to be pleasant,' Logan warned as he opened the car door.

They learned that Evelyn Pursey was the landlady. A middle-aged, ugly woman, she opened the door and eyed them aggressively. Making the presumption that they were would-be lodgers, she asked, 'What are you, on the Social?'

'Sort of,' Logan laconically replied as he and Shelagh produced their warrant cards. 'Police. Are you Mrs Pursey?'

'I thought you'd know who I was by now,' she answered, then gave an exasperated sigh before asking. 'You lot are here often enough. What's the problem now?'

'We're not from the Met, Mrs Pursey,' Shelagh said. 'We've come up from Devon. It's about your daughter, Penny. May we come in?'

'There's not much point in you doing so.' The woman held the half-open door with both hands, ready to slam it, knuckles showing white. 'I can't tell you nothing. Penny had a bust-up with Ralph, my bloke, when she was barely fourteen, and moved out. I never clapped eyes on her again.'

'Do you know where she went when she left home?' Logan enquired.

'Yeah, she went off to live with the family of a boy she was at school with.'

'Do you know his name, Mrs Pursey?'

'Yeah, Leroy, or was it Winston? It's either one or the other of them names with them, ain't it?'

'Her friend was black?' Shelagh checked.

'Yeah. She didn't move far away, just to Brixton, but that was too far for her to come back to see her mother.'

Evelyn Pursey was closing the door. Logan tried to get a salesman's foot in to stop it shutting, but he wasn't quick enough. He spoke through the narrow gap. 'Do you have the address of where Penny was staying in Brixton, Mrs Pursey?'

Annoyed, the landlady then said, 'Hang on.'

The door slammed shut tight, leaving Shelagh and Logan on the stoop. He excused the woman's rudeness. 'There are times in everyone's life, Sergeant, when a door that shuts is more important than a roof.'

'Very philosophical, guv,' Shelagh said cynically, 'but do you think this particular door is ever going to open again?'

After what seemed like half an hour, the door was eased ajar just far enough so that the filtered voice of Evelyn Pursey reciting an address was audible. Then the door was slammed closed.

Life was suddenly exploding with colour and music and gaiety for Julie Bolt. She learned that she was to be throned on a carnival float shared by the entire cast of the summer show. From the anonymity of supermarket checkout operator to celebrity status was a huge leap for a local girl.

She was in the theatre now in the period between the end of the afternoon and the start of the evening performances. With Jason Fulton as her guide-cum-chaperone, she thrilled while listening to the cast recording a mixture of songs old and new that would be played through amplifiers on the float in the carnival procession.

'Some of the pop numbers mean nothing to me,' Jason confided to Julie as a Kylie Minogue song flooded the darkened theatre, 'but you can't go wrong with the likes of Ella Fitzgerald and Ethel Merman, and, of course, old blue eyes himself, Sinatra. Though Dean Martin was my favourite. When I was in the States in the early seventies I was on the same bill as Dean. He was a perfect gentleman, not at all the alcoholic the media portrayed him as.'

'I wish my life was as exciting as yours, Mr Fulton,' Julie sighed.

'It will be, dear. As carnival queen and with your beauty you are on the threshold of a brand new life. Your boyfriend will be the proudest chap in town right now.'

That remark by the entertainer took some of the gloss off Julie's pleasure. Two days had passed since Matthew had let her down, and she had heard nothing from him.

'I don't have a regular boyfriend at the moment, Mr Fulton.'

'Playing the field, eh?' Jason chuckled and gave her an exaggerated wink. 'Good thinking. A lovely girl like you can afford to pick and choose. Take your time, dearie. Don't go rushing into anything. Getting married the lower side of twenty-eight usually leads to disaster. I was thirty when I got wed. She was an American vocalist on a tour of England. I fell instantly in love when I heard her singing "Stormy Weather". We honeymooned in Iceland, Julie. That was the one and only time that I witnessed the splendour of the setting sun in the Arctic Ocean, but I will never forget the purple cliffs of Iceland and the magnificence of the ice-capped "jokylls" towering above them.'

'Have you had a long and happy marriage?'

'Hardly,' a solemn Jason replied. 'She left me nine months later for a drummer in Ted Heath's Band.'

Spontaneously bursting into laughter, Julie recovered as quickly as she could and apologized. 'I'm sorry, Mr Fulton.'

'Don't be, dear.' He creased his face in a smile. 'By the time she left I couldn't stand the sight of her.'

Still giggling, Julie stopped suddenly and her heart missed a beat. In the shadowy auditorium she could see Matthew Colby walking towards the stage. He had returned to Havensport and had come straight to her to explain his absence and tell her that he was sorry.But then her spirits sagged as he neared and she noticed that there was something indefinably different about him. He came up to the front row of the stalls, and Julie squinted as the lights on the stage illuminated him.

Bemused, she was aware of Jason Fulton beside her. Julie heard the old man call down to Matthew. 'Hello, Mr Stevens, so good of you to come.' The entertainer turned to her. 'Mr Stevens is an expert who's going to fix up the amplifiers and lighting on the float for us.'

It wasn't Matthew Colby but Terry Stevens, manager at the Ocean club, who came up on the stage to shake Fulton by the hand. Julie blamed a combination of wishful thinking, low lighting and Stevens' long hair for her error. She found herself cringing inside at the nearness of Terry Stevens, and she couldn't think why. Maybe it was connected to something Norma had told her on the night that she died.

*

'My old stamping ground, guv,' Shelagh announced nostalgically.

'More crime in one night than you'll get in five years at Havensport.' Logan grimaced as they drove into Brixton.

'I was in the West End, guv, not here. Even so, in close to three years I don't recall ever having investigated two murders in quick succession,' Shelagh said pointedly.

'You've got me.' Logan, acknowledging the killing of two girls in Havensport, held up both hands in surrender.

The address Evelyn Pursey had given them was on a well-ordered street at the rear of the public library. It was a two-storey house made sprightly by a fresh coat of pale blue paint and new windows. A pretty black girl, who looked to be in her late teens, was weeding a flower patch in the small front garden. Straightening up, she gave them a nice smile.

'Hi.'

They returned her greeting and Shelagh asked if Penny Silver had once lived in the house.

The girl's face grew overcast. 'She did, but if she's in more trouble, then we are not responsible for her. What are you two, debt collectors or something?'

Shaking his head, Logan said that they were police officers. He asked if either of her parents were at home. But the girl was cagey now. 'No, my Dad's at work and Mum's gone to the shops.'

Shelagh told the girl that they would like to speak to a boy named either Leroy or Winston about Penny Silver.

'Winston's my brother, but he finished with Penny just before she moved out. That was ... oh, in early spring, I suppose.'

Logan asked if Winston was around, stressing that it was simply a matter of getting some information from him about Penny. But the girl wasn't entirely reassured. 'He's not here, and I can't tell you where he is. Come back in an hour and you can talk to my mum.'

They thanked her and left through a small gateway, moving to the Mercedes car they had parked by the kerb, when they were stopped by the girl's call:

'Mister!'

They turned. The girl hurried to them. 'Winston started work a couple of months ago with an estate agent in Kennington. I can't remember what firm it is. It has three names, I think, and the first one could begin with W. There's a baker's shop on the corner of the street, and Winston's place is next to it.'

They thanked her again.

Logan and Ruby discovered that the black boy pinning up photographs of properties on a display board inside the estate agent's window was Winston. Smartly dressed in a grey suit, he had a personality that was every bit as pleasant as that of his sister.

'I'd guess that you are police officers,' he said, saving them an introduction, 'and that this is about Penny. What has she been up to now?'

Shelagh enquired, 'What makes you think that Penny has been up to something?'

'I don't remember a time when she wasn't involved in some escapade or other, Officer. She didn't get on with her stepfather, and when she left home I felt sorry for her and asked Mum if she could stay with us. That was a mistake. Big time.'

'You looked upon her as your girlfriend?' Shelagh asked.

Winston answered, 'At first, maybe. But Penny Silver is trouble.'

'Not any more she isn't,' Logan told the boy bluntly.

'Have you arrested her?'

With a negative shake of his head, Logan said, 'We've come up from the West Country. Penny was down there, appearing in a summer show.'

'*Was*?' Winston, quick on the uptake, frowned.

'She's dead,' Logan said flatly.

'Dead?' the black boy croaked.

'She was murdered a few nights ago.'

'Murdered?' A badly shaken Winston looked wide-eyed at Shelagh. 'Good God! She must have been up to the same thing down there as she was up here.'

'Which was?' Logan asked quickly.

'She was on the game.'

Shelagh couldn't hide her surprise. 'She was on the streets, Winston?'

'Nothing like that,' the boy replied. 'She only had one client, so far as I know. He was some toff who rented a room that he and Penny used a couple of times a week.'

'Do you know where this room was?' Logan enquired.

'Yes. It's in Paddington. I followed Penny there one afternoon,' Winston said, made dismal by remembering the occasion.

Shelagh, who had been idly looking at the details of a property, asked, 'Did you happen to get the address, Winston?'

'Of course, Officer. I'll jot it down for you.'

When Winston passed the address to Logan, Shelagh, looking over his shoulder, said, 'I know that gaff, guv. Up to a dozen toms rent rooms there. We turned the place over a couple of times, but the girls work independently, and there was no hope of lifting anyone for living on immoral earnings.'

'The gods are smiling on us, Sergeant,' a pleased Logan remarked before asking the black boy, 'What's the chances of there being a photograph of Penny Silver at your home, Winston?'

'There's no need for you to go back there,' an abashed Winston said as he took a cheap plastic wallet from the inside pocket of his jacket. Opening the wallet, he took out a photograph and passed it to Logan. 'I don't know why I kept this.'

Logan and Shelagh found themselves looking at a studio

shot of a smiling, blonde girl that they had known only as a corpse. Thanking the black boy, Logan said, 'We'll let you have the picture back in a day or so.'

'Keep it, sir,' Winston told him. 'Carrying it around with me was silly, but now that she's dead it would be creepy.'

When they were outside, Shelagh asked, 'I suppose we'll have to liaise with the local boys if we're going to make enquiries at this place, guv?'

'That's the correct way, Shelagh,' Logan agreed, ' but I don't want the Met in on this. We'll make it unofficial, but to do that I'll need to call at this brothel, or whatever, alone. Can you spend a couple of hours shopping, or something like that?'

'I have a sister living in Kensal Green,' Shelagh replied enthusiastically. 'Would you mind dropping me off there, guv?'

One of her hands rested on the roof of their car, and a butterfly alighted on it. Moving its wings slowly, dusty gold and black in the afternoon sunshine, this symbol of the countryside here in the big city held both of them in confused enthralment for a moment.

Logan said, 'The perfect solution, Sergeant,'

'Do you know who they are?' Toby Wallace wrapped a handkerchief around the bruised and bleeding knuckles of his right hand as he asked Ed Bellamy the question.

Two uniformed officers were ushering four battered, dishevelled troublemakers out of the Blue Angel. Bellamy was using the back of his hand in an attempt at stopping a flow of blood from his nose. There had been a short but ferocious punch-up in which Wallace had been in his element.

Now that the fracas had ended, it was business as usual in the club behind them. Music blared, loud even by Blue Angel standards, threatening to drown out all other sounds. A few girls stood watching at the top of the stairs. They had caught the scent of violence and it had aroused them.

Wallace and Bellamy went down the curving steps. The

doors to the club were wide open; the night outside was very black.

'I don't know their names, but I think that they came back for revenge tonight. They were in a while back, and I had to throw them out.'

'All four of them?' Wallace was sceptical. 'You handle yourself well, buster, but it took four of us tonight.'

'I had help from a customer the other time,' Bellamy explained.

Face still registering a respectful disbelief, Toby Wallace remarked, 'Just one customer? He must have been pretty good.'

'He was. He was a guy named Matt.'

The detective grinned. 'I'd like to meet him.'

'There's not much chance of that. He was here on holiday. Him and the carnival queen were an item, but I hear that he's gone home now,' Bellamy said.

With a shrug, Wallace said, 'Never mind. I'll need a statement from you in the morning.'

'Don't make it too early,' Bellamy warned.

The large terraced house was squeezed between two other decaying tenements. Time had washed over the ancient building, leaving the scars of fading paint and crumbling brickwork. It was an environment of cramped hopelessness. When Logan turned the handle, the unlocked door opened inwards. He stepped into a hallway. There was a smell of decay. The light was poor, with a venetian blind blacking out the one window in the hall. He gave an experimental call:

'Hello?'

Though he thought he caught a faint sound of movement somewhere deeper in the house, silence prevailed. Then a woman slipped out of a room at the far end of the hall, closing the door behind her. Nudging fifty, she was of medium height and wearing pink pyjamas. With a towel draped over her shoulders and her long hair wet, she was grotesque.

She peered over silver-rimmed glasses, imprisoning Logan with an invisible peripheral glance. 'You haven't rung, have you? It's OK to come at any time in the evenings, but those who turn up early knows that they got to ring in advance.'

'I wanted to ask about a girl.'

'I gathered that much.' The woman blew out her thin lips with a little fluttering sound. 'But, like I said, you gotta ring beforehand. There ain't no one here at this time of day. I might be able to get Bella to come here for you, if you don't mind waiting for twenty minutes or so.'

Walking to the window, she tried to open the blinds. On her third unsuccessful tug the pull cord tangled on a slat. Cursing under her breath, she yanked hard on the cord and the slats clattered and tilted at a crazy angle. She abandoned the task.

'You rented a room to a man who entertained a young girl here once or twice a week,' Logan said.

'Did I? Darned if I remember,' the woman replied.

'Tuesday and Thursday afternoons,' Logan pressured her.

'Then she wouldn't be one of the regulars. I'm only the care-taker here, nothing to do with any of the girls. Anyway, what you are talking of would be a private arrangement, dear, and something I can't help you with.'

'I believe that you can,' Logan disagreed, taking Penny Silver's photograph from his pocket and holding it out to her.

The woman shrank back, not taking the photograph. 'Here, are you the Old Bill?'

'Do I look like the Old Bill?' Logan enquired with pretend disgust.

Her smile was a mite fidgety. 'No, you don't.'

'Take a look at that. You must have seen her here.'

'Nope. Is she some kin of yours?'

'Take a better look. You'll remember her.'

'That's the problem,' she said. 'My memory's going. All I seem to be able to recall is that in my younger days men paid me for my services.'

Taking the hint, Logan passed her a £20 note and she nodded her old witch's head. 'I remember the kid. Room twenty-two, Tuesdays and Thursdays.'

'I want to know who she used to meet here.'

Pushing her lips out to indicate that Logan had asked an unanswerable question, the woman said nothing. Logan gave her another £20 note. 'Give me a name.'

Taking off her glasses she managed a little smile. 'Certainly, sir. The chap she came to see was Bill Sykes.'

Irritated by her greed, but not prepared to pay good money for the name of a Dickens character, Logan's professionalism warned him to be careful. There was danger for a policeman operating outside of the law. He spoke tersely. 'A proper name.'

She said a single obscene word then argued, 'That is a proper name. All of the johns here have nom de plumes?'

'I'd expect to get a real name for my forty quid!'

'Forty smackers don't even begin to stir my memory,' she complained, then quickly added, 'I tell a lie. I do seem to remember that it was a very expensive name.'

Logan passed her a £50 note. Taking it, the woman looked unhappily at the banknote. 'The name I have in mind is worth more than that. That girl was underage, and if you're going to shake him down, then you'll get a bloody sight more than ninety measly smackers.'

'That's the last,' Logan warned as he handed over another £50 note. 'Come up with his name now or I'll give you real bother.'

The woman's body convulsed just once, violently, and a long sigh came from her slack mouth. Folding the notes and sliding them into the breast pocket of her pyjamas, she mumbled, 'He's a lawyer by the name of Malcolm Braithwaite.'

Drawing in a deep breath of satisfaction, Logan spun on his heel and headed for the door.

'What are you trying to do to me, Len?'

The custody sergeant added a silent curse to his question as he looked from PC Leonard Cobbie to where the homeless wino sat slumped on a bench. He was a wreck. Alcohol had rotted his nerve ends raw. He had been sick, polluting the air with the stench of his foul-smelling vomit. Probably a lot younger than the straggly hair and beard made him look, he sat head down, eyes closed, arms wrapped round his shaking body.

'It's Ronnie Peters, Sarge,' PC Cobbie replied.

'I know who it is, Constable. Why didn't you just move him on from wherever you found him?'

'He stole a packet of cigarettes from Quentin the newsagent on the Esplanade, Sarge.'

'A packet of cigarettes?' The custody sergeant pretended to be shocked at the enormity of the crime.

'I know what I'm doing, Sarge,' Cobbie said, too pleased with himself to let the sergeant's attitude rattle him, 'and I think DI Logan will want a word with Ronnie. I found that he's been bedding down under the pier for the past few weeks.'

The sergeant was still derisive. 'For a start, Mr Logan isn't here. He's in London. Anyway, he wouldn't want to be within twenty feet of Ronnie.'

'Ronnie is lucid enough when he's sober, Sarge,' Cobbie defended his arrest. 'I'll ask Toby Wallace to speak to him in the morning.'

Peters moved suddenly and screamed. It trailed off in an eerie sound that sent icy shivers up Cobbie's back. He saw the Catholic sergeant go white-faced and cross himself. Cobbie saw Peters start to run, and there was something so wild in his movements that to try to stop him would have been like trying to catch the wind.

But the sergeant shouted at an immobile Cobbie, who sprang after the fleeing Peters, capturing him at the door. There was a brief but violent struggle. Both of them fell to the floor. Vomit erupted noisily from Peters as Cobbie scrambled to his feet.

There was silence for a moment, then, with an expression of

disgust on his face, the sergeant said, 'Get him into a cell, Constable, and I'll have the FME take a look at him.'

'I still want Toby to see him in the morning, Sarge.'

'Let the morning take care of itself,' the custody sergeant said gruffly. 'Right now, Len, you need to clean up that bloody mess.'

As Logan drove them south-west out of London, Shelagh was unable to share his elation. 'The name Malcolm Braithwaite means nothing to me, guv.'

'It wouldn't. I was forgetting you are new to the area,' he answered apologetically. 'In Havensport there are one or two names that everyone knows, and Braithwaite is one of them. He lives at Radley Chase, just outside of Havensport, Sergeant. He's a right-wing political power broker in London and locally. He was once the county's under-sheriff, with more unquestioning loyalty from the establishment than Robin Hood ever got from his merry men. The sea of politics may be turbulent, but Malcolm Braithwaite can walk on water.'

'That's an awful lot to risk for whatever pleasure there is in an underage girl, guv.'

'Braithwaite wouldn't see it as a risk, Shelagh,' Logan said with a shrug. 'He can buy himself out of anything.'

'But we end up with his little girlfriend dead on the beach.' Shelagh, a trifle bewildered, was reaching into the glove compartment for a bag of sweets.

'There's far too much here to be coincidence,' Logan agreed. 'Penny Silver lived in London. Malcolm Braithwaite's office is in London. Braithwaite has an arrangement with Penny in London. Braithwaite's home is in Havensport. Penny comes to Havensport with the summer show.'

'You think that he moved the girl down here, guv?'

Logan took a sweet that she had unwrapped for him, and replied, 'No. You know the old adage about keeping your own doorstep clean, Sergeant. Braithwaite spends most of every week in London, so he had no need to move Penny down close to his wife and his home.'

'Which means that the girl moved to Havensport of her own accord.' Shelagh gasped as realisation hit her. 'She must have been putting the bite on him, guv.'

'I don't doubt it. Attempting to blackmail someone like Braithwaite is inadvisable, to put it mildly, Sergeant,' Logan said grimly.

'So he killed her to keep her quiet,' Shelagh half whispered.

'No,' Logan disagreed. 'Braithwaite is one of society's generals, Shelagh. A general never joins his troops in a trench; neither does he risk his arse in the front line. He'd have some psychopathic hitman do the killing for him.'

'Who, guv?'

Logan had no answer for his sergeant. 'Whoever it was, Shelagh, Braithwaite will have set up an alibi for him.'

'What if the girl was doing the same thing to Gerald Reynolds, guv?'

'It wouldn't work,' Logan said. 'She'd be of age when Reynolds met her, and as a bachelor he wouldn't care if his relationship with the girl became public knowledge.'

They were nearing the resort of Havensport and took their place in the traffic-stream with urban obedience. They slowly topped a rise and down below the buildings of the town were pink and misshapen and unfledged, like young birds in a crowded nest.

Logan spoke speculatively. 'If I'm able to persuade the chief, Sergeant, you'll probably be taking the first train back to London.'

'What for, guv?'

'All solicitors use detective agencies in their work,' Logan replied. 'Braithwaite's firm will not be an exception, and I want you to find out who they hire.'

'I think I'm with you, guv,' Shelagh said with a small smile of self-congratulation. 'Braithwaite probably paid a private detective to silence Penny Silver.'

Logan gave a nod of agreement. 'More likely some heavy the detective agency provided.'

Toby Wallace waited as a sound like the hissing of steam came from Ronnie Peters. It sounded as if there was a leaky valve somewhere deep in the bundle of filthy, raggedy clothing. Peters laughed and then coughed and wheezed. The lung-rattling coughing went on for a time, and then he raised a dirt-stained hand and patted his mouth delicately, like a vicar at tea with the WI.

'I'll try not to make you laugh again, Ronnie,' Wallace said. 'I didn't realize that I said something funny.'

Peters looked at the detective, the whites of his eyes blood-red, but he was sober now that it was morning. 'You wouldn't know, Mr Wallace. You and me look at life from different view-points, a fact that makes it impossible for us to share a sense of humour.'

When sober, Ronnie Peters spoke well. Wallace never ceased to be fascinated, as well as disturbed to an uncomfortable degree, by the winos he met who must have once been cultured men, and the foul-mouthed prostitutes who had hearts of gold.

'Constable Cobbie tells me that you may have been under the pier on the night that girl was murdered.'

'That's a distinct possibility, Mr Wallace, considering that I am under the pier every night. I'm not complaining. A man likes to have at least the illusion that he chooses for himself.'

Unable to accept that a man like Peters chose the life that he presently lived, Wallace made no comment. He asked, 'Did you see anything unusual that night, Ronnie?'

'What's in it for me if I tell you?'

'What do you want?'

'Your men kept back, a car brought to the door for me, and one hundred thousand pounds in used notes with non-consecutive numbers,' a serious-faced Peters replied, then went on, 'No, that's the wrong scenario, isn't it? If I tell you about that night I want to be signed up as an informant, be paid regularly and have twenty-four-hour-a-day police protection.'

It was a situation in which Peters could have made Wallace feel extremely ridiculous, but he chose instead to make him laugh. And Peters laughed too.

Wallace said, 'I think you're wrong about our sense of humour, Ronnie.'

'As long as that's all we have in common, Mr Wallace. You seem a decent enough bloke, but you're a policeman.'

'If you know something, tell me, Ronnie,' Wallace urged. 'I'll see that you get a hot meal, a new outfit so's you can burn those rags, and I'll put fifty greenbacks in your pocket.'

Nodding, Peters said, 'You've got yourself a deal. I'd just bedded down that night when this chap came creeping under the pier. I was on my guard, thinking he could be one of those sadists who enjoy giving people like me a kicking. But he stood with his back to me and lit a cigarette. I could tell that he was watching and waiting.

'Then this other bloke comes down onto the beach. He goes over and is sitting on a rock, smoking, when a girl walks down towards the water and strips naked.'

'Do you think she was aware of the presence of the two men, Ronnie?'

'I wouldn't say so, Mr Wallace. When she's naked, this bloke gets up from the rock and looks like he's going to go up to her. But I reckon he must have been smoking a reefer, because he was out of it. He did this crazy dance like a whirling dervish, spinning round, like, then fell flat on his face and stayed there. This other chap then flicks his cigarette away, and runs towards the girl. I heard her give a kind of small scream, but I wasn't going to get involved in whatever was happening.'

'You had a duty to report it to us the next day, Ronnie,' Wallace reminded him sternly.

'Report it to the police!' Peters scoffed. 'How far do you think I'd get inside your station before getting thrown out on my ear, Mr Wallace?'

Having to concede that what Peters said was true, Wallace enquired, 'Did you get a good look at the man under the pier, Ronnie? Is there anything distinctive about him that you remember?'

'Long hair, which is unusual nowadays, Mr Wallace, when most young blokes shave their heads.'

'If you get cleaned up and we drive you around town,' Wallace suggested, 'do you think that you'd recognize him?'

Smiling at him, Peters answered, 'No need to go to all that bother, Mr Wallace. I know who he is.'

'You do?' an astonished Toby Wallace managed to say.

'Yes, and I don't really want to cause him trouble because he's a kind man who often slips me a free bottle. He's the manager at that club the kids go to. The Ocean, isn't it?'

fourteen

'Have you noticed, Randolph, how ships appear on the horizon and seem to stay there?' the chief constable asked idly.

He and Logan were leaning over the railings of the pier like passengers on a liner looking down at a passing blue ocean. It had puzzled Logan on his return to learn that Toby Wallace was holding Terry Stevens at the police station. But he hadn't the time to look into that, as finding Kenneth Biles had been his priority. Eventually locating the chief constable on the pier, Logan had given his report on Malcolm Braithwaite, receiving the evasive response he had anticipated.

They had moved away from the carnival fund-raising festivities, distancing themselves from the crowd that was cheering whatever it was that was happening on a makeshift stage. Melanie Biles and other councillors were up there, drawing tickets from a revolving drum and calling out numbers. Each time, an arm was raised in the crowd and a shout of 'Here!' rose above the sugary piped-in music that was coming through loudspeakers. On stage, a lovely girl wearing a silver crown would then hand over a prize, embarrassed as she permitted a stranger to kiss her on the cheek.

His chief's detached remark about ships and the horizon didn't fool Logan. Hearing of Braithwaite's probable involvement had unnerved Kenneth Biles, who was playing for time.

The chief constable picked absently at the rusty rail. His face had the bland look that comes with wearing sunglasses. His brilliant-white shirt was sweat-stained. Being obese, he could sweat with the best of them. 'A short while ago, Inspector, this case was dead and buried, in more ways than one. We didn't even face the gamble of a trial. I must say that I don't care for the present turn of events. I believe DC Wallace to be in error, and I was relying on you to release this Stevens fellow.'

'I haven't spoken to Wallace yet, sir,' Logan said. 'Your advice on how to proceed with a Braithwaite investigation seemed to be of the utmost importance.'

The chief constable gave him a quick look. 'My considered opinion on that, Inspector Logan, is that we wait a while.'

'Wait for what, sir?'

'Perhaps …' The chief constable was conscious of every movement he made in the company of Logan, who was always busy interpreting. '… delay would be a better word. Hold off at least until after Saturday, the day of the carnival procession.'

Logan said, 'A couple of days won't make a lot of difference,' Malcolm Braithwaite will be there when we go for him. But, with respect, sir, I don't see a connection between our investigation and the carnival.'

'Ah.' Biles drew in a deep breath. 'I used the day of the carnival procession merely as a marker. The following morning, Randolph, Walden Griffiths will be back from his honeymoon. After all, Walden is my deputy, and ethics demand that we discuss this with him before making any kind of a move. We simply cannot afford a blunder of any kind. You mentioned sending DS Ruby back to London to make further enquiries. Delay that until we have a meeting with Walden. If he should agree, then she can leave for London first thing on Monday morning.'

'It's too late for that, sir,' Logan said calmly. 'I put DS Ruby on the six o'clock train this evening.'

Anger had reddened Biles' fleshy cheeks as he yanked off his sunglasses to glare at Logan. 'You should not have done that without my permission, Inspector!'

'I considered it to be a matter of urgency, Sir, and I didn't make the decision until all attempts to find you had failed. It was only a little time ago that I learned that you were at this event.'

'Well …' the chief constable said lamely, wiping his forehead with a khaki handkerchief.

Logan saw the flick of Melanie's skirt and her legs. She was heading for them, smiling. She was beautiful and intelligent, but it wasn't just that or the subtle combination of a hundred facets known as personality. Melanie was special. There was a depth to her that was beyond the senses. As she approached, her stare seemed to penetrate him. He had the impression that she was studying his mind, and it made him feel oddly insecure.

'Hello, Inspector Logan, welcome back.' Her eyes were as lively as a flamenco. She kissed her husband on the cheek. 'I'm all finished here, darling. Where are we having dinner? At the Sailor's Return? I'm simply famished.'

She looked at Logan enquiringly, as if expecting something from him. He said nothing. Melanie glanced at him again, covertly, her eyes reflecting uncertainty. He couldn't decide whether she was looking strong or vulnerable.

Slipping an arm round her slender waist, Biles used his free hand to make a little farewell gesture at Logan. He smiled. It was not an unpleasant smile but it was a little strained. 'I'll leave you to call in at the station and clear up that business of Wallace, Randolph.'

Fingertips drumming a cadence on the steering wheel of his car, a nervous Wenzell Carmen watched the shabby blue Peugeot 406 climb the hill to where he was parked. He turned to look through the windscreen at the curving downland, its long slopes cropped to a lawn-like smoothness by slowly mean-dering sheep. There had to be ground here on which no man had ever set foot. The downs had no water for the thirsty, so no one had ever erected an ugly building or even pitched a tent. The Roman legions may have marched here, and the armies of the civil war probably passed by, but no one ever stayed to love or hate or set up house or gossip with the neighbours. These downs were free of human emotion.

But Carmen was too fear-filled to appreciate the magical solitude of the place. He was here under duress as the result of a telephone call. The voice had been muffled, unrecognisable, but the message had been terrifyingly clear: 'Be there at seven-thirty this evening – and be alone.'

The suffix 'or else' had remained unspoken but implied. It was enough to frighten him sufficiently to keep the rendezvous.

Carmen's body was shaking from head to toe as the car drew nearer. Maybe he had been selected at random as the next victim of a maniacal serial killer. There was something familiar about the blue car, but Carmen's mind was whirling in panic and he couldn't place the vehicle. He stayed facing front as it pulled in beside him, some twelve feet distant. Hearing the clicking of the handbrake ratchet and then the opening and slamming shut of the driver's door made him flinch. There was the crunch of footsteps on gravel.

Unable to stand the suspense, Wenzell Carmen, not prepared for violence but resigned to it out of terror, turned to look with wide-staring eyes. Then relief flooded through him. It was a hoax! A cruel joke played on him by the silliest fool ever to be elected to a local council. With fear ebbing away in him, anger became a replacement as a grinning Larry Petersen came towards his car.

The local pop idol's head swung from side to side and his right hand beat time as he walked. Carmen was further irritated when the young councillor did a flamboyant musical 'Ali shuffle' before reaching to open the car door and dump himself unceremoniously into the passenger seat beside Carmen.

'Wenzell the high-rise hustler,' he said in greeting.

'This isn't on, Councillor Petersen. I shall lodge a complaint in the strongest terms, involving the police if necessary,' Carmen warned tersely. 'This isn't funny.'

'I agree with you there, Wenzell.' Petersen took a hardcover notebook from his pocket and tapped it twice with a finger. To Carmen's ears the sounds were like shots from a rifle. 'This is my little joke book. I've been through it again and again, but I haven't laughed once. Go on, take a look.'

'What's this all about, Petersen?'

Having automatically reached out for the book, Carmen had second thoughts and withdrew his hand. Petersen forced the book on him. 'Go on. Take it, Wenzell. It's a duplicate, so you can keep it if you wish.'

'I think you had better explain, Councillor Petersen,' an ashen-faced Carmen said, holding the small book but making no attempt to open it.

'You're spoiling my fun,' Petersen complained. With the ease of a contortionist he doubled up his legs and rested both feet on the dashboard.

'Please take your feet down,' Carmen said as he reached into a door pocket for a duster, ready to clean the dashboard when Petersen had removed his feet.

But the councillor bluntly refused. 'No! I'm sitting comfortably, so I will begin. Sounds like *Watch with Mother*, doesn't it, Wenzell? But this isn't a fairy story. In that little book of mine are dates and details that link Malcolm Braithwaite down through Councillor Melanie Biles to you and then on to Compat Leisure.'

Wenzell Carmen tried to say something, but nothing came out.

'I'm not an expert in these matters, Wenzell,' Petersen said conversationally, 'but I'd say you could be looking at twenty-five years inside, max.'

Staying silent while Petersen beat a tattoo on his knees with both hands and sang a few bars from a pop song, Carmen tossed the book back to him and managed to ask, 'What do you want, Petersen?'

Taking his feet down, marking the dashboard as he did so, Larry Petersen grinned. 'I thought you'd never ask, Wenzell.'

Toby Wallace came out of an interview room as Logan came along the corridor. Closing the door behind him, the frowning detective said, 'Am I glad to see you, guv!'

'Problems, Toby?'

Explaining how Peters was willing to testify that he had seen Terry Stevens lurking under the pier and then going after the girl who had been murdered, Wallace added, 'But I've spent hours interviewing Stevens, and it just won't come together. Gerald Reynolds has been telephoning, threatening to send a solicitor down to represent Stevens.'

From the corner of his eye Logan could see Jason Fulton coming towards them. Whatever the old guy wanted, Logan knew that he would have to give him the bum's rush. He asked, 'Is there some kind of angle that you can't get around, Toby?'

'Several, guv. One of them is that Peters saw Stevens smoke a cigarette, but Stevens claims that he hasn't smoked for years, and there is not a trace of a nicotine stain on his fingers.'

Fulton was beside them now, standing silently, politely waiting.

'I checked Stevens out as a smoker, and got the same result as you, Toby,' Logan said, then turned to ask Fulton, 'What is it, Jason? This isn't the best of times.'

'It was the best of times and the worst of times. The opening of *A Tale of Two Cities*, as easy to remember as the date 1066,' Fulton said with an inward smile. 'I digress. This is just a simple enquiry, Mr Logan. We are putting the finishing touches to our carnival float, and I've heard a whisper that you have Mr Stevens here, the man who will be wiring up our sound system.'

'Terry Stevens is helping us with our enquiries,' Logan confirmed.

'Oh dear, that could mean a considerable delay,' Jason sighed. 'Inspector, this is something of an intrusion, I accept that, but I couldn't help overhearing the conversation that you were having with your colleague as I walked up. In matters such as this an observation from someone not close to the subject matter can often prove useful.'

'Are you about to tell me that you were in an episode of television's Inspector Morse, Jason?' Logan sarcastically enquired.

'No. But I did once play Dr Watson when on tour with a small repertory company. To the best of my memory it was Derek Farr who was Holmes ... but I could be wrong. In what year did Denis Price die? You wouldn't know, of course. When returning to what I term my middle years my memory tends to play tricks. There were so many brilliant actors in those days.'

'Jason!' Logan spoke the name sharply. 'Please come back in an hour or two.'

Face falling, Fulton said in mitigation, 'I am quite an observant and perceptive person, Mr Logan, and I could make a very real contribution if you would permit me.'

'Against my better judgment.' Logan sounded grudging, but a familiar inner voice had urged him to heed what the entertainer had to say. 'I'll give you two minutes.'

'Brevity isn't a strong point with me, Inspector, but this will take only seconds. I think your having Mr Stevens here could be a case of mistaken identity.'

'What makes you say that, Jason?'

Pointing a finger at Logan, Fulton warned, 'This could take a little longer. I was on stage with this year's carnival queen when Mr Stevens came into the theatre to see me. I noticed that his appearance had quite a traumatic effect on Julie, and I gently questioned her about it afterwards. I learned that in the half-light she had mistaken Mr Stevens for a boyfriend of whom she was very fond, but who had apparently abandoned her recently.'

'Did she give you a name, Jason?'

'No, Mr Logan, and at the time I didn't consider it important enough to ask.'

Motioning for Logan to step to one side, Toby Wallace asked, 'Can I have a word, guv?'

They took a few steps to ensure that Fulton couldn't hear their conversation, and Logan asked, 'Does what old Jason said ring a bell?'

'It certainly does, guv. This guy's first name is Matt. Ed Bellamy, the bouncer up at the Blue Angel, mentioned him to me. He helped Ed out when there was trouble in the club one night. According to Ed the guy's a martial arts expert.'

Logan felt his stomach knot. He could hear Simon Betts' voice in his head, echoing as it had in the mortuary: 'The neck was broken, as I said previously, but in a way that suggests either a lucky blow from the killer's point of view, or the work of someone skilled in the martial arts.'

'Well done, Toby,' he congratulated the young detective. 'See what you can find out about this Matt.'

'He left town unexpectedly,' Wallace reported. 'I think Julie, his girlfriend, is my best bet, sir.'

'Talk to her, Toby, but do it subtly. If her family panics and throws a wobbly over their daughter being in danger, then Matt isn't likely to come back.'

'I'll play it down, guv,' the young detective promised.

'I know that you'll do it right, Toby,' Logan said before going back to Jason Fulton to pat him on his thin, narrow back. 'Your help has been invaluable, Jason. I'll see that you get a reward, perhaps a gold-plated pooper-scoop for when you next go on tour with *The Hound of the Baskervilles*.'

Smiling, enjoying Logan's sense of humour, Fulton replied. 'Just having Mr Stevens released to do our float will be reward enough, Inspector.'

'You can take him with you now,' Logan offered expansively.

One o'clock in the morning. It was mayhem in the London police station. Though she would not have noticed a few weeks back, the room seemed full of noise and movement to Shelagh Ruby. Nothing seemed orderly. A redhead was struggling with a uniformed policeman. Another woman, who unexpectedly looked like a schoolteacher, was hysterical. Shelagh looked from them to the big white face of the clock on the wall. She idly watched the second hand pass jerkily around the white circle, past all the numbers, past the heavy black hands that pointed to the time. It was going to be a long night. Waiting for DS Chiro, who was in charge of the brothel bust that had just been made, Shelagh was resigned to getting no sleep.

It was astonishing what a change of environment did to a person. With the arrested women milling around, shouting, cursing, occasionally laughing shrilly, what was once a normal scene for Shelagh was now close to unbearable.

Denny Chiro stood nonchalantly, hands in pockets, one shoulder resting against the wall, watching his men do their work. A sergeant with drooping Richard Nixon jowls sat behind a long counter-like desk, asking names and filling in forms:

'Name?'

Standing there, swaying, a wish to die on her white face, the teacher-type's voice rose hysterically. 'I won't tell you. Do what you like, but I'll never tell you my name.'

'Address?' the desk sergeant asked in a monotonous drone.

'I've no address! No home! Only the hotel where you found me. I won't tell you anything!' she shouted. A uniformed officer caught hold of her arm. She jumped in fright and whirled round, eyes dilated. 'Let me go! Let me go!'

Breaking away from the officer, she dashed crazily towards the wide door. She wasn't given a chance to get away. Three policemen caught her and dragged her back. They did it as gently as they could. They were not rough, but considerate. They only manhandled her because they had to, because she refused to walk.

'She isn't doing herself any good,' Chiro commented as he came to Shelagh's side.

'She looks terrified, Denny,' a sympathetic Shelagh said.

As handsome as ever, his thick black hair tumbling over his forehead, Chiro said, 'Probably a respectable little wife, Shelagh, earning money to get herself out of debt before her old man finds out how much she owes.'

'He's about to find out something worse.'

'Poor sod,' Chiro said. 'All human life is here, Shelagh.' He looked around at what to the man in the street would seem to be a bad dream. 'Which brings me to the 64,000 dollar question – what are you doing back? Shouldn't you be sitting on a seafront licking a strawberry ice cream?'

'I passed on that just to come back to see you, Denny,' Shelagh said, tongue in cheek. 'We've been friends a long time.'

'Long enough for me to know that you're after something, Shelagh.'

'I'm after some information,' Shelagh confessed.

'That's better, I prefer you when you're being honest,' Chiro said, smiling at her. 'Don't tell me that some of the London gangs have moved out into the sticks.'

Shaking her head, Shelagh said, 'No, this is white-collar stuff.' She told Chiro about Malcolm Braithwaite and her need to find out what detective agency his firm might use.

Lighting up a cigarette, Chiro took a deep drag on it. His mind was working hard and this was reflected in his expression. A minute passed before he spoke. 'I know of Braithwaite, but if he is mixed up in anything, then it's in the higher echelons and out of our reach. But I can find out if he uses any heavies, and, if so, who they are. But I've got to clear this lot up first. Have you got somewhere to kip down tonight, Shelagh?'

'No. Can you fix me up with a cell and a clean blanket?'

Pulling a face at her, Chiro said, 'In this dump? By morning you'd have every known STD and a few more besides.' Taking a key from his pocket, he passed it to her. 'Go to my place and make yourself at home.'

'Won't Rachel be there, Denny?'

He gave her a cheeky grin. 'Time goes by, Shelagh. Rachel is now an ex three times removed. I'm back to being a bachelor, coming to work from a different direction every morning. You'll have the place to yourself.'

'I'm really grateful, Denny.'

'Then show it by having breakfast ready when I get home at eight,' he suggested cheekily. 'With luck I'll have the information you want by then.'

The four of them sat in the front room of the Bolt home. The room was as shiny and bright as a temple of faith, with icons that were ornaments and heirlooms and pictures lovingly displayed. But it wasn't a happy get-together. Megan Bolt sat stern-faced and upright, knitting furiously, click, click, click. Toby Wallace guessed that she was almost as worried about the neighbours as she was about her daughter. There's nothing alarms a suburbanite more than a neighbour in real trouble.

An ice-cream van passing slowly outside played a jolly tune that clashed with the tense atmosphere of the room. Reg Bolt looked anxiously at Julie who sat on the settee beside Toby Wallace. The worried father asked the detective a question:

'Has Julie got herself mixed up with a bad 'un, Constable?'

'I'm afraid that I am unable to answer that, sir,' Wallace replied. 'All we are doing at the moment is making enquiries. We know absolutely nothing about the man, apart from him being called Matt.'

Blushing, Julie spoke very quietly. 'Matthew. Matthew Colby. That's his name.'

'What can you tell me about him, Julie?'

'Not very much. I am not even sure where he came from.'

Julie, looking very young and schoolgirlish, stared unblinkingly at Wallace, and he stared back. Her eyes were dark lashed and terribly innocent, but they were also terribly wise with a dawning wisdom that threatened to change the innocence to cynical knowledge. Wallace found himself illogically wishing that his little daughter would forever remain an infant.

'He didn't tell you what line of work he was in?'

Shaking her head, Julie kept her face averted from her parents. 'No. I sort of asked him, but he made a joke of it.'

'Can you describe him?' Wallace enquired. Remembering what Jason Fulton had said, he made a surreptitious suggestion. 'Did he put you in mind of any local boys that you know?'

'Matt wasn't a boy. He was a man.'

'At a guess, Julie, what age would you say he was?'

'Between thirty and thirty-five.'

'Far too old for you, my girl,' Reg Bolt said angrily.

Wallace silently agreed with the girl's father that Colby had been too old for her. For all her Hollywood looks there was something very simple about Julie Bolt, he thought. The girl-child evoked the protective instinct in him.

'I couldn't bring him home because he'd gone.' Julie stared at her father with the hurt, wondering eyes of a thrashed spaniel. To Wallace she said, 'I mistook someone else for Matt the other day.'

'Someone who lives here in Havensport, Julie?'

'Yes, that man who works at the Ocean club.'

'Terry Stevens?'

'Yes, I think that's his name.'

'Stevens has long hair, Julie,' Wallace said. 'So plainly Matt also wore his hair long.'

'He did … does have long hair, but he is much better looking than that other man.'

'Did he ever speak of the murder of your friend Norma and that other girl, Julie?' Wallace enquired.

The question, innocuous and posed in calm tones, appeared to cause something of a sensation. Megan Bolt's knitting needles fell silent and Reg Bolt's anger changed to dread. 'Is that what this is about, Officer? You are saying that Julie's boyfriend, for want of a better word, is a killer?'

'I didn't either say or imply that, sir,' Wallace corrected the older man.

Julie pleaded, 'Please, Dad,' before telling Wallace, 'I remember him saying how terrible it was. He did ask me a lot of questions about Norma.'

'What sort of questions, Julie?'

Hesitating, Julie then replied, 'I shouldn't have said a lot of questions. What I really meant was that he asked me the same question lots of times.'

'What was the question?'

Giving a kind of shrug in reverse, her shoulders slumping, Julie answered, 'It's difficult to put it into words because Matt was sort of vague when he asked it. He seemed to think that Norma might have told me something before she died.'

'But he didn't say what that something was?' Wallace queried.

'No, he didn't.'

Julie was wiping her eyes with her fist, crying like a kid. Embarrassed, Toby Wallace stood, saying, 'Thank you, Julie, you've been very helpful. I am sorry to have intruded on your evening, Mr and Mrs Bolt.'

'Not at all,' Megan Bolt assured him with a smile, racing ahead with a two plain and one purl clash of needles.

'Is that it?' her husband asked Wallace. 'It would seem to me that our daughter could be in danger from this man.'

'At the very worst she might be, Mr Bolt, but only if she was a danger to him,' Wallace replied. 'The fact that he established that Norma had said nothing to Julie means that he wouldn't consider Julie to be any kind of a threat.' He passed Julie a business card. 'However, should he come back to Havensport, keep out of his way, Julie. Both the station and my mobile telephone numbers are on this card. If you see any sign of him, let me know. You can get me at any time of the day or night.'

'I envy you your uncomplicated bachelor life, Randy.'

Melanie Biles spoke wistfully from where she stood looking out of the drawing-room window of Logan's house. She had her back to him as he poured drinks. Waiting for her to continue, Logan conversely hoped that she wouldn't. Fifteen minutes ago she had telephoned to say that she desperately needed to speak to him, almost begging to be allowed to come to his house. Logan had reiterated his stance as a policeman, but Melanie had assured him that if he would let her talk to him she wouldn't expect what she said to be treated as confidential.

She was speaking again now, making small-talk as a prelude. Looking out to where some of the glow of a lowering sun had seeped into the sides of the cliffs and hills, creating an illusion of masses of colourful flowers, she said:

'You have a splendid view from here, Randolph, away from the hoi polloi but close enough to appreciate the beauty of the coastline. I went out in the garden before I left home, and it seemed to smile at me. It was formal and polite, but warm. I realized that my garden makes no differences: it accepts me as I am, and I had nothing to fear.'

Turning to walk to him, she accepted the glass he held out and sat in an armchair without being invited.

'But in reality you do have something to fear,' he observed.

With a little nod, she said earnestly, 'I want you to accept that when I leave here I am going home to tell Kenneth exactly what I'm about to tell you.'

'I wouldn't doubt your word, Melanie, but I don't understand why you want to tell me first.'

'Maybe I want your advice, and I'm hoping against hope that I might by some miracle persuade you to help me.'

'I'll hear what you have to say, Melanie, but I can make you no promises.'

With her elbows on her knees, she leaned towards Logan, her eyes level with his, swallowed hard, then cautioned: 'This is one really rotten story, Randolph.'

Sitting without interrupting, without even making a comment, Logan listened. Melanie began with the night of the accident that made her husband and herself beholden to Malcolm Braithwaite, right through to her abuse of her position as a councillor and the recruitment of Wenzell Carmen.

When she had finished, Logan commented. 'I take it that you have two sets of plans relating to the drainage of the site. One set for now, and another to spring on the council when everything is too advanced for the council to pull out.'

'Yes, like those tax-evading firms that keep two separate accounts, one for themselves and the other for the authorities. Shocking, isn't it?' Melanie said. 'The second set will be revised plans submitted to the council after an imaginary snag has been encountered.'

'And this will cost local ratepayers a lot of money?'

'Thousands upon thousands of pounds,' Melanie concurred, misery on her face.

'But now you've got cold feet and want out?' Logan guessed.

'No!' Distressed now, Melanie half shouted the one word. 'Though I despise myself, I'd carry on, Randolph, for I have no choice. But something has happened. Wenzell Carmen telephoned me last night to say that one of the councillors knows everything. Carmen has been approached and put under pressure.'

'Gerald Reynolds?'

'He's the logical choice, isn't he,' Melanie said with a pained smile.

Logan nodded. 'He is for me. I don't believe you were being followed by a stalker, Melanie, but by Terry Stevens under orders from the young Reynolds.'

'That makes sense. I know that Gerald had his suspicions, but someone else beat him to it.'

'Did Carmen tell you who this other councillor is?'

'Yes. It's Larry Petersen.'

'Petersen?' Logan exclaimed. 'Petersen is nothing but a prize prat.'

Close to tears, Melanie said, 'I couldn't agree more, but he's a clever and dangerous prat.'

'How could he have got wind of your illegal activity, Melanie?'

'I've tried to fathom that out,' she said, frowning. 'However he did it, he's got Carmen in an awful state.'

'Has Wenzell Carmen told Braithwaite about this?'

Melanie bit her lip, looking down. 'I wouldn't say so. He's had no contact with Malcolm Braithwaite all along. I'm the go-between.'

'What did you advise Carmen to do, Melanie?'

'Advise him?' Her eyes grew opaque. 'I don't even know what to do myself. Anyway, Wenzell was in too much of a state to listen if I had a plan of any kind.'

'So he'll go along with Petersen?'

'I suppose so.'

'What's Petersen after?'

'I'm not sure, Randolph. He wants Carmen to meet him after the carnival procession tomorrow night. Wenzell has to hand over all of the paperwork, including the two sets of plans. I've been keeping them, but Carmen has insisted that I pass them over to him.'

'I don't think there's any doubt that Petersen is going to ask you for a lot of money,' Logan opined. 'Where does Carmen have to meet him?'

'We don't know. Petersen's going to ring to tell him half an hour before.' Melanie began to cry softly. 'Oh, Randolph, it's all such a terrible mess. I've gone past caring about myself, but this will finish Kenneth. Can you help me, help us?'

Delaying his answer, all of the complications and possible, most likely probable, consequences running through his mind, Logan couldn't think of anything constructive to say. Though he was drawn to Melanie by a powerful magnetic force, he detested the upper echelon of local society in which she and her husband and friends moved. Their world was an unreal one of egotism, pretence and snobbery.

At last, he pointed out a truth to her. 'None of this would have happened if the chief constable hadn't been involved in a drink-drive episode. The law is impartial, Melanie.'

'You know better than that, Randolph. For one reason or another, each and every day the rules are bent or broken.'

'Not by me,' he told her flatly.

'I thought that what is between you and me would make a difference just this one time, Randolph.'

'There is nothing between you and me, Melanie.' Logan stood as if to give his words emphasis.

As a distraction, Melanie reached to take a rose from the vase Logan's daily help had placed on the table. She brought the flower up to her nose, eyes closed as she inhaled its delicate fragrance. She let out a sighing breath. 'I didn't mean that in a material sense, Randolph. I am not so stupid as to imagine us each leaving a note as we run away to live in a bed and break-fast until we decide what our future together will be. But I do believe that somewhere, perhaps in some unseen world that a mystic might understand, you and me are probably soul mates.'

It sounded romantic nonsense, but Logan found that his feel-ings for her would not permit him either to deny or dismiss it. Neither did he intend to go further along this perilous route. Though devoid of illusion, seeing her distressed had Logan, with misgivings, prepared to lower the standards of a lifetime to help her.

'I'll do what I can, Melanie,' he assured her. 'You tell your husband everything that you've told me. Then, if it is what you both want, we can try to find a solution together.'

'Oh, thank you, thank you, Randolph,' she said, tears of relief filling her eyes.

'Have you been up to something that I don't know about, Stevens?' a suspicious Gerald Reynolds asked.

Terry Stevens was close to trembling. He had been summoned to his employer's apartment immediately upon being released from the police station. He'd had to abandon Jason Fulton, who was now waiting for him in the car park that was the marshalling area for the carnival procession. Sitting on the edge of a chair, poised for a flight that he knew Gerald Reynolds wouldn't permit, he looked out under his eyes as Reynolds noiselessly paced the deep-pile carpet.

'N-no, honestly, Mr Gerald,' he stammered. 'I don't know why the police wanted to talk to me. I've done nothing that you don't know about.'

'Did they ask anything about me?'

'No, your name never came up once, Mr Gerald. This policeman, detective, kept asking me about my being under the pier on the night that Penny Silver was killed.'

'You sure that you weren't there, Stevens?' a disbelieving Gerald Reynolds quizzed him. 'You weren't dallying down there in the dark with one of your boyfriends?'

Forgetting his fear of Reynolds for a moment, he raised his voice. 'I don't have boyfriends, plural. I am not a promiscuous person. That is a coarse, horrid thing to say, Mr Gerald.'

'OK, OK.' Reynolds raised both hands placatingly.

'I'm still prepared to do that job for you tomorrow night, Mr Gerald.'

Shaking his head, Reynolds said, 'You won't be doing it. The police have taken an interest in you, so you're hardly the ideal choice to burgle the chief constable's house.'

'Have you got someone else to do it?' Stevens enquired. He sat, head down like a tired horse.

'No, I've had no option but to cancel those plans of mine.

Now, you get off down to the club, and I'll talk to you again tomorrow.'

Watching Stevens leave, Reynolds was both worried and suspicious. Something wasn't right with Terry Stevens, and it wasn't just his being picked up by the police. Gerald Reynolds had been growing increasingly uneasy about his club manager long before that had happened.

Logan pulled in behind a car that was at the kerb, its blue light flashing. Further along were two smashed cars locked together by mangled metal. Two uniformed constables were talking to two well-dressed civilians. A kid of about nineteen sat on the edge of the pavement, holding a folded handkerchief in a vain attempt at stemming blood flowing from a scalp wound.

As Logan approached on foot, one of the civilians was saying, 'We were doing no more than about twenty-five. It wasn't possible to go any faster because of the traffic. Then he came straight at us out of a side turning, going like crazy. There was nothing I could do. He went straight into the side of us. Are you OK now, Geoffrey?'

'Still a bit shook up,' his friend said.

A siren wailed in the distance as an elderly uniformed sergeant came round the police car to greet Logan. 'Randy! Since when did a detective inspector start attending RTAs?'

The wail of a siren became louder. Then two sirens were wailing.

An ambulance arrived with another police car. A paramedic carrying a bag hurried to the boy with the bleeding head. Two more police constables got out of the second police car, putting on their caps as they walked to join their colleagues.

'I'm seeking some information, Tom,' Logan said.

'Computerized information I can do back at the station, Randy,' the sergeant explained. 'Out here it would be just off the top of my white-haired head.'

'The head bit will do me,' Logan said. A constable was sitting on his heels breathalysing the kid who was having his head bandaged by a kneeling paramedic. 'Larry Petersen, Tom?'

'The singing councillor. What about him?' a laughing Tom invited Logan to go on.

'Has he got form?'

The reply was a negative shake of a silver-haired head. 'Sorry to disappoint you, Randy, but he hasn't a record. But if you want dirt, I can help you.'

'I'd welcome anything you can tell me,' a keenly interested Logan said. 'What's he into? Porn?'

'No, our Larry's a doer not a watcher. But don't risk dropping the soap in the shower when he's around.'

'He's gay?' Logan was astonished. 'Is this just gossip, Tom?'

'You know me, Randy. I can always back up what I say. Ralph Miller shone his torch into Petersen's car up at Priory Head one night and caught him at it. His partner, so to speak, was of age, so Ralph could only caution them about it being a public place. I was duty sergeant that night, and it was all logged.'

Out of mild curiosity, Logan asked, 'Do you recall who he was with?

'A non-entity. No one that would interest you, Randy,' the sergeant said as he started to move away to issue orders to the constables. 'That long-haired bloke that runs the Ocean club.'

'Terry Stevens?'

'That's probably the name, but I can't say for sure,' Tom answered. 'Catch me at the station and I'll check it out for you, Randy.'

A satisfied Logan said, 'There's no need, Tom. It'll be Terry Stevens.'

fifteen

Havenport's carnival day had arrived with a bright dawn that kept its promise of a fine summer day. There was a full day's programme of events leading up to the evening procession of floats. From early morning the streets had been filled with sun and fun. The town was packed with the season's largest influx of visitors.

But the carnival spirit was absent in the lounge of the home of Kenneth and Melanie Biles. Facing a scandal that neither he nor his wife were likely to survive, the chief constable had revealed principles and a rigid moral stance that Logan had not for one moment previously given him credit for. Having earlier made a tearful confession to her husband, Melanie had suggested a spot of blackmail in reverse by threatening the young and egotistical Councillor Larry Petersen with exposure as a homosexual.

Though this idea had initially occurred to Logan, he had dismissed it as unworkable in an age when being outed as a gay brought acclaim rather than the disgust of a decade ago. Kenneth Biles had rejected the scheme immediately, just as he had Logan's outline of a plan to allow Petersen to continue with his pursuit of Wenzell Carmen, but to anonymously inform Malcolm Braithwaite. That way, Braithwaite would have Petersen taken care of and there would be no repercussions.

The chief constable had reacted with a vehement shake of his head. 'No. I fully recognize that Melanie became involved solely to help me, but I have lived under a dreadful dark cloud since the night of my drunken lapse. I would be unable to cope with further chicanery.'

Logan had suggested what at the very least was a mitigating strategy. His plan was for Melanie to see the council's chief executive that morning. Without implicating herself or naming names, she should put on record that she suspected Compat Leisure was duping the council, who would eventually have to bear the financial burden for draining the holiday complex site.

'That's good thinking, Randolph,' Kenneth Biles said with a nod. He looked weary. 'But Malcolm Braithwaite will see this as a betrayal. Consequently it would solve nothing.'

Logan confidently dismissed this possibility. 'Forget Braithwaite, sir. DS Ruby has come back from London and confirms that Matt Colby is a heavy who works for a firm of detectives that Braithwaite employs. It is only a matter of us picking up Matt Colby, then Malcolm Braithwaite will be arrested in connection with the murders of Penny Silver and Norma Harrington.'

'Good God!' The chief constable's eyes went inward as he thought for a few seconds. 'It is fortunate that I only have a few more years' service to go, Randolph. I'm past being able to handle this sort of thing.'

'Nonsense, sir,' Logan lied to be kind.

'We'll do as you suggest, Randolph. It's a sound scheme,' Biles said. 'What is your priority today? Guarding our carnival queen in case the killer should return?'

'I don't think that is necessary, sir. Matt Colby kills for money not for fun, and he has no reason to harm Julie Bolt. I will be concentrating on Larry Petersen and Wenzell Carmen.'

When Logan had drained his coffee cup and stood to leave, Biles shook him by the hand. 'You are an excellent police officer and a valued friend. Thank you for your help, Randolph.'

Melanie expressed her gratitude by way of a quick and

surreptitious squeeze of Logan's hand as she showed him out of the door. The grip of her slim, cool fingers was firm. When her eyes met his for a brief moment they were invasive rather than hypnotic. Her smile came easily as she bade him a silent but very special farewell.

They stood on the edge of the pavement waiting for the carnival procession. Toby Wallace's daughter sat on his shoulders so as to have a grandstand view, and he held both of her little legs. His wife looked happily at him. 'I hope Randy Logan gets promoted to chief superintendent for letting you have the day off.'

'He's one of the good guys, Sherri,' Toby agreed.

'You'll be every bit as good when you make detective inspector, Toby.'

'I don't kid myself that I could ever be like Logan,' Toby admitted. 'He's a one-off, Sherri.'

'Daddy,' Cait called down, 'when are we going to the circus?'

'When we've seen all the floats go past. There will be lots to see, Cait.'

'But I want to go to the circus.'

'Be patient, darling,' a smiling Sherri advised. 'See all the pretty floats and hear the music first. The circus hasn't opened yet.'

'Let's go and find out,' the child said, bored with the long wait for the procession.

'Now I wish Logan had made me work,' Toby complained.

'You fibber,' Sherri laughed, hugging him.

Logan stood at the traffic roundabout at the end of the seafront where the procession would first make an appearance. Music blared through loudspeakers that had been bolted to lampposts along the carnival route. The song 'There's No Business Like Show Business' was blasting out a few feet away from Logan. Reaching into the top pocket of his shirt for his mobile phone when it buzzed, he doubted that he would be able to hear Shelagh, who had been tailing Wenzell Carmen. Someone dressed as Disney's Goofy jostled him, almost knocking the mobile from his hand.

Not apologising, the cartoon figure went prancing off, swinging a collection tin and doing a sing-along with the piped tune: '...*a clown, with his pants falling down* ...'

The lead float was coming colourfully into view as Logan pressed the little instrument tight against his ear so that he was able to make out what Shelagh was saying.

'Chummy's left his office, guv, but he's not heading for home. I'm not familiar with this area, but he's taken a narrow road. It doesn't seem to have a number. The signpost just says "Ashcroft".'

'That road's unclassified, Sergeant,' Logan said. 'It's a dead end, leading only to the old Ashcroft Rope Works. The factory is derelict now. That must be where Petersen has arranged the meet.'

'Shall I follow him, guv?'

About to answer yes and say that he would be right behind her, a movement among the stationary carnival spectators caught Logan's eye. Then he recognized Matt Colby. The long-haired man was watching the advancing floats as he moved slowly through the crowd. The sight of a man he believed to have killed two young girls alerted Logan. Danger was a companion he had lived with for years, every minute, every day. Right now it was worse because he was expecting something but didn't know what.

'No, Sergeant, it could turn nasty,' Logan shouted to ensure that she would hear him over the loud background music. 'I can't leave here because I've just spotted Colby, who seems to be looking for the carnival queen float. We could be wrong about there being no threat to Julie Bolt. I'll have to call Toby in to go after Petersen and Carmen with you. Wait where you are and Toby will pick you up.'

'Understood, guv.'

Switching off his mobile, Logan moved off in the direction Matt Colby had taken. He asked a uniformed police officer who was holding the crowd back off the road, 'Have you seen Toby Wallace, Constable?'

'Yes, sir. He's with his wife and kiddie, about fifty yards along.'

Thanking the constable, Logan walked along the road in front of the crowd at a pace that kept him just ahead of the lead carnival float. Dreading ordering a young family man to work on such a festive occasion, his reluctance was eased by the realisation that the expression on his face warned Toby Wallace what to expect as he approached.

'Mr Logan!' Cait shouted excitedly as he joined the little family. 'We're going to the circus.'

'That's nice, Cait,' Logan said guiltily under Sherri's knowing gaze.

'I've a horrible feeling that only Cait and I will be going to the circus,' she said.

Forcing himself to face her, Logan said, 'I'm sorry, Sherri.'

'What's happening, guv?' Toby Wallace asked as he lifted his daughter down off his shoulders.

'There are complications, Toby,' Logan replied.

'And complications don't come anywhere as complicated as they do in the police,' Sherri said unhappily.

'I agree with you, Sherri,' Logan said before going on to explain that he wanted Toby to collect Shelagh from outside the council offices and check on Petersen and Carmen out at the old Ashcroft factory. 'Did you bring your car into town, Toby?'

'Yes, it's in the Sea Road car park, next to yours, guv.'

'Good,' Logan said, relieved that there would be no delay in Toby and Shelagh getting to the factory. He added, 'Neither Larry Petersen nor Carmen is dangerous, Toby, but I wouldn't want DS Ruby to go out there alone.'

'Of course not, guv.'

chapter fifteen

'Bring them both in and we'll sort things out at the station, Toby,' Logan said, then apologized once more to the detective's wife. 'I'm really sorry about this, Sherri.'

Sherri Wallace responded only with a curt nod, and the sad look on her daughter's face was more than Logan could bear. Turning quickly away, he saw that the float slowly passing him was decorated with a glittering gold material. A smiling Julie Bolt sat on a high throne, holding a sceptre and with a crown on her head.

Keeping level with the float, Logan scanned the crowd for a sight of Colby. The long-haired man was nowhere to be seen, and that puzzled him. Making his way with difficulty among collectors dressed as various characters holding out tins to the crowd, Logan dodged the prancing Goofy of earlier, only to violently collide with Donald Duck. The duck called him a name that was both crude and very unDisney-like.

There was still no sign of Matt Colby. What had begun as a niggling fear in Logan grew rapidly into a massive worry. It dawned on him that he had got it all wrong in thinking it was Julie Bolt that had brought Colby back to the town. Leaving the road, Logan was bombarded with complaints as he forced his way through the crowd. In a quieter spot behind the line-up of spectators, he tapped in the Biles' telephone number. Melanie answered.

'It's Randolph, Melanie. Is there any way that Braithwaite could have heard of the Larry Petersen thing with Carmen?'

There was a long pause at the other end. Then Melanie spoke hesitantly. 'Not from me, Randy. But I have been thinking about Wenzell, and I'm worried. He's not the stuff that heroes are made of. I don't think that he'd be able to stand the strain.'

'Could he have contacted Braithwaite, Melanie?'

'I feel pretty sure that he will have done so.'

Logan knew instantly that his hunch had been right. Matt Colby had returned on Braithwaite's orders to stop Petersen from getting his hands on the Compat Leisure plans. Toby and

Shelagh would be heading for Ashcroft believing that they were dealing with nothing more than a homosexual councillor and a weak-kneed architect. Instead they would come face to face with Matt Colby, a cold-blooded killer.

Ignoring Melanie's frantic cry of 'Randy?' he switched off, then on again. He had started to call Shelagh's number before remembering that it was impossible to get a signal at the lower end of town where the council offices were located.

Pocketing his phone, Logan forced his way through the crowd and out into the street. Running beside the procession, dodging the collectors, he made it to the car park. There was a space beside his car where Toby Wallace's Ford Escort must have been parked. Now desperately worried, Logan got into his own car and drove it fast out of the car park, tyres shrieking in protest.

'Bingo,' Shelagh Ruby said as they topped a rise to see a dilapidated factory up ahead with two cars parked outside.

Slowing his car, Toby Wallace said, 'We'll make a quiet approach so as not to panic them.' Then he muttered a curse at the sight of a third car that was half hidden in bushes just up ahead. 'Looks like complications. What do we do, Sarge?'

'Pull in here, Toby, out of sight, until we see what is happening.'

Wallace switched off the ignition and they sat in a new quiet that was filled with tension. They could now see that there was no one in the car parked in the bushes. Then they spotted a man moving away from a clump of trees and heading in a bent-over run towards the factory, his long hair streaming out behind him.

'Terry Stevens!' Toby Wallace exclaimed. 'What's he doing here, Sarge?'

'That's not Stevens, Toby. It's a guy named Matthew Colby.'

'The man DI Logan has in the frame for the murder of the two girls. Is he mixed up in this business with Petersen and Carmen, Sarge?'

'He's not a part of it, not in the way you mean, Toby, ' Shelagh said with a shake of her head. 'We need back-up, but by the time they got here it would be too late to save Petersen and Carmen.'

'So, Sarge?' Wallace asked calmly.

'We'll have to move in on foot, Toby. But take great care. Colby is really dangerous.'

Leaving the car, they made their way to the old factory, using what cover was available along the way. Reaching the front wall, they moved carefully along to raise their heads just high enough to peer in a broken window. Colby was in the main, debris-strewn part of the factory, angrily hammering on the door of a side room with his fist. The two detectives quickly sized up the situation. Having seen Matt Colby arrive, Petersen and Carmen had wisely barricaded themselves in. As they watched, Colby looked around him. Then he effortlessly picked up a heavy balk of timber and laid it lengthways on an old four-wheeled trolley. Standing back to admire his improvised battering ram for a moment, Colby bent over and pushed the squeaky-wheeled trolley to line up the end of the timber with the door.

'He'll shatter that door,' Wallace whispered to Shelagh. 'I'll have to go in and stop him, Sarge.'

'Be careful, Toby. Matt Colby can handle himself.'

'So can I, Sarge,' the tough detective replied confidently as he moved away from her.

'Toby,' Shelagh hissed. 'Have you got your baton with you?'

'No, Sarge. I came straight from the carnival to pick you up.'

'Here, take mine.'

'No.' Wallace turned his head to whisper, 'You might need it if I have a problem with Colby, Sarge.'

Jumping into the factory through the doorless opening, Toby Wallace shouted, 'Police! Hold it right there, Colby.'

Casually turning to face the detective, Matt Colby spread his arms wide and made a come-and-get-it gesture with both hands.

Unhesitatingly moving towards the long-haired man, Wallace feinted with his left hand and threw a powerful right hand. Had it landed it would have snapped Colby's jawbone like a carrot. But Colby was too old a campaigner, too experienced a rough-and-tumble fighter to be caught by so simple a trick. Totally ignoring Wallace's phoney left-hand punch, Colby blocked the detective's right-hand swing with his left forearm. His finely tuned reflexes working perfectly, Colby then cut the detective across the bridge of the nose with the hard edge of his right hand. With the bone between his eyes smashed, Toby Wallace still came forward on the attack. But he was no match for Colby, who turned away from Wallace and back-heeled him in the groin. Groaning in agony, Wallace doubled over. Moving in fast, Colby felled him with a vicious rabbit punch. Wallace lay quivering on the dirty floor of the factory.

'Colby!'

Fighting to control her shaking legs, Shelagh Ruby came into the factory holding a steel truncheon in a practised stance, ready to defend or attack.

Surprised at first, Matt Colby then laughed a cold, sniggering laugh at the sight of her.

Logan heard that laugh as he slammed on the brakes of his car outside the factory and jumped out. With no time to appraise the situation, he leapt in through the door. First glancing at Toby Wallace, who now lay crumpled and still, he snapped an order at Shelagh. 'Lower your baton and stand back, Sergeant.'

'Be careful, sir,' she cautioned, starkly aware of how swiftly and effectively Colby had dealt with Wallace.

Taking his mobile phone from the pocket of his shirt, Logan tossed it to Shelagh, who caught it deftly. He said, 'Ring in for back-up, Sergeant.'

Before she could tap in the first digit, Logan moved in on Colby. Making confusing passes in front of Logan with both hands, the long-haired man suddenly snaked out his right foot.

Moving fluidly, Logan caught the ankle with one hand. Swinging his right leg over Colby's, trapping his knee under his own knee. With his back to him, Logan grasped Colby's ankle with both hands and pulled up sharply. Rewarded by the sound of the ligaments tearing, Logan dropped the leg and stepped away from his opponent.

Colby was tough. Though standing in a way that favoured his injured leg, he made no sound and his face was expression-less. He even managed a derisive smile as Logan came at him once more.

Raising both hands as if intending to fire left- and right-hand punches, Logan took advantage of what he had already gained. Lashing out with a kick aimed at Colby's damaged knee, he found he had underestimated the other man's reflexes. Moving just enough to have the kick miss his knee, Colby caught Logan a stunning blow to the head with the side of his hand. Staggering back, Logan was too shaken to defend himself as Colby caught him in the throat with his elbow. Coughing and spluttering, Logan closed with Colby, trapping his arms against his sides to protect himself while he waited for his brain to stop spinning.

Colby struggled vainly to get free, and Logan took heart at discovering that he was stronger than his opponent. Though it was going to be a hard fight, he was sure now that he would triumph eventually.

Reaching up, he shoved the heel of his right hand under Colby's nose, fingers gouging at his eyes. Confident that he was gaining the upper hand, Logan was planning his next move when Shelagh Ruby came up, swinging her baton.

Seeing her coming, Colby swung the arm that Logan had freed. He caught Shelagh a hard backhander in the mouth. Steel baton clattering to the floor, the detective sergeant was dumped on her behind.

Worry had Logan glance down at her. That was a mistake. Shaking his head to dislodge Logan's gouging fingers, Colby twisted away from him. With both arms free he clasped his hands behind Logan's neck and pulled his head down. Logan saw the knee coming up but was powerless to avoid it.

Knocked backwards by the impact of Colby's knee, feeling the warm flow of blood from his nose and mouth, Logan didn't go down. But Colby was following up fast. Despite the fact that pain caused him to grimace, he kicked out at Logan with his damaged right leg. This time Logan caught the foot with both hands, and with a supreme effort threw Colby upwards and backwards, head over heels. Even as his opponent hit the ground, Logan was there standing over him. Drawing back his right foot he delivered a terrific kick to the side of Colby's head.

Slumping back, Colby proved what a hard man he was by coming up on to his hands and knees. As he looked up at Logan, he was a grotesque sight. Logan's kick had dislodged the bottom half of Colby's face so that it was right out to one side, out of line with the top part of his head. Yet he was still game and would probably have got to his feet had not a battered and exhausted Logan kicked him hard under his already dislodged chin.

Colby fell on to his back as Shelagh climbed unsteadily to her feet to throw a pair of handcuffs to Logan. Catching them, Logan bent to roll Colby on to his face and cuff his hands behind his back.

Straightening up, Logan put one arm round Shelagh's shoulder and took out a handkerchief to gently dab at the blood round her mouth.

'You're bleeding worse than I am, guv,' she protested. Then, suddenly remembering, she gasped, 'Toby.'

'No, Shelagh,' Logan said, holding her so that she couldn't go to check on the young detective. On first coming in the door, Logan could tell that Toby Wallace's neck had been broken.

'Is he ...?' she enquired fearfully.

Nodding, Logan said, 'Come on, we'd better get Petersen and Carmen out of their hiding place.'

*

It was hot and crowded in the circus, but Sherri hardly noticed. Aware of how much her little daughter was enjoying the show, she enjoyed it through her. She watched Cait now, who with a hand over a mouth wide open in awe, she watched a trick rider leaping on and off a horse as it galloped round the ring.

'Attention, please,' a voice said over the tannoy system. 'Will Mrs Sherri Wallace report to the pay desk. Mrs Sherri Wallace to the pay desk, please.'

Fumbling excitedly in her bag for the raffle tickets she had bought earlier, she said, 'We've won it, Cait. We've won Gus.'

The prize was a lovely stuffed toy, a huge gorilla that Cait had christened Gus when the circus girl selling the tickets had showed it to her.

Mother and child, one just as excited as the other, made their way out of their seats and along the grass-carpeted aisle towards the pay desk. They were just yards away from it when Sherri realized that she hadn't been asked for her name when buying the tickets. The raffle winner would be decided solely by the drawing of numbers out of a hat.

That was when she caught sight of Shelagh Ruby. The detective sergeant's mouth was puffy. Then Sherri saw Logan. The two police officers were standing with a circus woman. Logan's face was bruised and swollen, but the expression on it confirmed Sherri's worst fears.

'It's Toby, isn't it?' she asked, surprised at how controlled her voice sounded.

'Yes, Sherri,' Logan said flatly. Music and cries of delight were coming from inside the Big Top, and the detective inspector sat on his heels and caught hold of the little girl's hands. 'You don't want to miss the show, Cait. Shelagh will take you back in.'

Puzzled, Cait Wallace looked at her mother, then made up her mind and went skipping off into the circus tent, holding Shelagh Ruby's hand.

'I thought we had won the raffle prize,' Sherri said with a self-deprecating little laugh.

Then she burst into tears. Both Logan and the circus woman held her as massive sobs wracked her body.

'Do you think we should stay with her for a while?'

Shelagh asked Logan the question as she paused at the cemetery gates to look back at Sherri Wallace. Her relatives were supporting the new widow as she moved shakily away from a graveside that was hidden by a mass of floral tributes.

'Her parents have come down to stay with her, so we'd probably be intruding,' Logan heard himself say. He wondered if he was lying to his sergeant and himself. Was he just making an excuse to avoid being with the young widow? He had long ago recognized that he was a coward where the grief of others was concerned.

They walked slowly. Toby Wallace had been buried with full honours, and the smart, uniformed police party was boarding a minibus further down the road. Chief Constable Kenneth Biles had delivered a moving eulogy at the graveside. Malcolm Braithwaite had been arrested and would be standing trial with Matthew Colby. Even if he wanted to cause the chief constable trouble, no one would now believe the disgraced Braithwaite. Larry Petersen had learned his lesson and was not in any way a threat to Melanie. Kenneth Biles had won Wenzell Carmen over by offering to help him with clearing his debts. The old adage that all's well that ends well would apply had it not been for the Toby Wallace tragedy.

The cemetery was high on a hill. Far below in the bay the afternoon sun on the blue sea and the sails of some small boats were still. Though muted, the joyful cries of holidaymakers were audible on the flower-scented air. In a reflective mood, Logan envied the strangers down on the beach who were bursting with joy while up here on the hill everyone was full of sorrow. The holidaymakers hadn't ever known, and they never would know, a great guy named Toby Wallace.

Yet logic told Logan that they had their own worries, ambi

tions, dreams and tragedies that he would never know about. In life the vast majority of men and women moved through your range of vision without touching you or you touching them. The problem lay in the chaotic random factor that selected those who became your friends or your lovers.

Shelagh broke in on his brooding thoughts, her voice subdued as if they were still in the church or at the graveside. She looked anxiously at Logan. 'Tell me if I'm overstepping the mark, guv, but it would help me decide my immediate future if I had some idea how Toby's death might affect you.'

He knew that Shelagh, being familiar with his innate restlessness, was wondering if what had happened to a likeable colleague would be the tipping-point for Logan. That was a very real possibility that had been niggling at him. Though aware that there was no escape from bad memories, Havensport held too many problems for Logan. Heading the list was the charismatic Melanie Biles.

Too mixed up to give a straight answer, he turned the sergeant's question back on her. 'You did a pretty good psychological profile when you first came here, Shelagh. You tell me.'

Biting her bottom lip, she said, 'That was a long time ago, guv, and things have changed. You have changed.'

'Have I? In what way?'

'Let's just say that the Detective Inspector Logan that I knew then would right now be preparing to move on,' she replied carefully.

'So, why isn't today's Detective Inspector Logan getting ready to leave, Sergeant?'

'Because he has sacrificed the thing that he held most dear.'

Fascinated, Logan asked, 'What is that, Shelagh?'

'His freedom, guv,' she answered nervously.

She knew! Somehow, his clever detective sergeant had deduced that he was under the spell of their chief constable's gorgeous wife. In mock reprimand, he told her, 'You are a witch, DS Ruby. A beautiful witch, but a witch nevertheless.'

She had no chance to respond because a few feet in front of them the chief constable's driver was holding open the door of the car for Kenneth and Melanie Biles. Catching sight of Logan, the chief constable stepped back from the car. He and his wife stood waiting on the pavement for Logan and Shelagh to walk up to them. Melanie's eyes danced a little solo as she looked at Logan.

In spite of the solemnity of the occasion, Logan felt a need stirring deep within him as he saw her. It was the very familiar, yet ever-new birth of desire. As he drew closer to her, he was puzzled by the feeling rapidly fading until it was no more than a faint tendril of sensation.

'A bad business this, Randolph,' Biles said. 'It doesn't end with the funeral, does it? Not for Mrs Wallace nor any of us.'

'I don't think the reality of it begins to register until after the funeral, sir,' Logan agreed.

By exchanging only small-talk, the four of them got through the next few minutes without any embarrassing silences. But the chief constable suspected that Logan was avoiding what he regarded as a pressing issue.

Lowering his voice, Kenneth Biles spoke worriedly. 'I'm half expecting, nay, I'm dreading, your application for a transfer after what has happened here. I want you to know that, though it would be with immense regret, I will fully support such an application.'

Noticing that Melanie was watching him apprehensively as she awaited his answer, Logan was shaken to the core by a sudden realisation. It had to be a mental aberration. He felt nothing whatsoever for Melanie Biles. His feelings had changed in an instant. Now the woman who had come to mean more to him as each day passed held not the slightest interest for him. This had to be the way that marriages fell apart, when one partner suddenly couldn't stand the mannerisms or bear to be in the presence of the other.

He guessed that the reason in his case was a combination of

lies and deceit that had caused the deaths of two young girls and an admirable young policeman. The same corruption had indirectly caused the suicide of a lad. If his relationship with Melanie developed, then he would soon be caught up in the kind of web of half-truths and outright lies that he despised.

'Well, DI Logan?' Biles prompted him impatiently.

'It is not an easy decision to make, sir. I will let you know very soon.'

'I understand.' Biles shook a glum head as they said stilted goodbyes and he ushered his wife into the car.

Melanie turned her head to look at Logan, and he could see in her eyes that she knew. Though he felt sorry for her, that emotion was suffocated by an overpowering sensation of relief. When the driver closed the door of the car, Logan said to Shelagh, 'Congratulations are in order. You are looking at a man who has just regained his freedom.'

'I hope that's what you want, guv.'

'Does any one of us know what we want, Sergeant?' he asked.

'Right now I'd settle for knowing whether or not I want to stay here in Havensport,' she said dismally.

'Perhaps ...' Logan began, falling quiet as Sherri Wallace came up to them.

This was a meeting that disturbed Logan. At times like this it was a mistake to have rehearsed what you were going to say. You were left floundering around when nothing went according to your invisible script.

Eyes red and swollen from crying, Sherri was accompanied by an elderly couple. She introduced them as her parents. The father shook Logan by the hand and thanked him. 'We are most grateful to you for taking care of our daughter and grandchild.'

'There's nothing to thank me for,' Logan said humbly. 'Whatever we do or say seems woefully inadequate in these circumstances. How is Cait?'

'She's with a neighbour. Cait's bearing up quite well but she is too young to really understand, of course,' Sherri's mother said.

'I'd like to come and see her when it's convenient, Sherri.'

'Any time. As soon as you like, Mr Logan,' Sherri offered eagerly.

Placing a comforting hand on her shoulder he said, 'Why so formal? It's Randy. I am still and always will be your friend.'

'I know that,' a sad Sherri said. 'It is something I wanted to ask you about, Randy. I heard some of the chaps saying that you would be putting in for a transfer. I have no right to say this, but I pray that it isn't true. I'd feel better knowing that you were around for Cait and me. I wouldn't make any demands on you, of course.'

'I know that, Sherri,' Logan assured her. 'Don't worry, I'm not going anywhere. I'll be here whenever you need me.'

When they had left Sherri and her parents, Shelagh said, 'You made your mind up pretty quickly, guv.'

'Why don't you do the same, Shelagh.'

'Would you want me to stay, guv?'

'Of course I would.' Logan placed a hand on her shoulder. 'We make a good team. That's what we'll be, remember, colleagues.'

'What else, guv?' Shelagh's lips struggled with an incipient smile. Then the smile took hold and moved up to include her eyes. 'I won't be asking you to surrender your recently regained freedom.'